Only A Good Man Will Do

Dee S. Knight

ISBN 978-1-912768-21-9

Published 2018

Published by Black Velvet Seductions Publishing at Smashwords

Chapter One

"Look! It's Mr. Goodman." The young boy stage-whispered but didn't bother to hide his incredulity. "I wonder why he's sitting out here? He looks like he's sleeping."

The man on the bench knew his long legs stretched almost to the middle of the sidewalk, and he judged the kid stood practically on the toes of his boots, exposed below worn and faded jeans. His bristled chin rested on his flannel-encased arms, folded high on his chest. "*NASCAR: Then, Now, Forever*" emblazoned the cap pulled low on his face, and his hair brushed the back of his neck and tickled his ears. He figured he didn't look too bad for someone who'd been up all night traveling to New Hampshire from South Carolina, but he wasn't what these rich kids were used to.

"No, it's not, dufus. Mr. Goodman wouldn't be caught dead looking like that in public, and this guy looks too old. Besides, the first form boys haven't been let out yet, so Mr. Goodman's still in class."

Firm, commanding. This kid sounded older—at least nine or ten.

Damn. Mr. Goodman wouldn't be caught dead *looking like him?* Had no one ever arrived on the campus of Westover Academy dressed in jeans and flannel? Maybe he was blazing a trail.

And old? Hell, as one of triplets, he and Daniel were the same thirty-six years of age. *The kid obviously needed glasses.*

Meanwhile, the man fought the urge to smile as he listened to his two examiners.

One of the boys advanced to bend over and peek under the brim of the cap. His breath smelled like butterscotch.

"It is too Mr. Goodman. He's my dormitory master, so I guess I know what he looks like," the less fervent voice intoned with more confidence.

"Is not! Why would Mr. Goodman be sleeping outdoors on a bench like a bum? Headmaster wouldn't allow it and Mr. Goodman has too much pride to look so … so … shabby."

Why, the little shit! He'd like to bend the twerp over his knee and—

"Quite right, Mr. Wainwright. I certainly would not be sleeping on a bench dressed thusly."

The man heard at least one gasp and the rapid shuffling of feet.

"Ha! I told you, Torrington, that this wasn't Mr.—"

"And *you* were quite right, Mr. Torrington, when you insisted this poor example of a gentleman is Mr. Goodman. It's not your fault you have the wrong Mr. Goodman."

There, Wainwright! Take that, you big bully. Jonah Goodman thumbed the brim of his cap up high on his head to gaze at the boys and the tall man—his mirror image as far as facial features were concerned—standing behind them.

The boys shifted their stares between Jonah and his brother, Daniel, who was dressed in a way that surely pleased even young Mr. Wainwright. Trim, short hair gleamed in the sun. Although the afternoon wore on, there was no five o'clock shadow marring the sharp angles of *his* jaw. A black, wool, three-piece suit covered a pristine shirt, with a blood red and gray striped tie knotted under the chin. A flowing dark blue silk gown, opened in the front, topped all of that. Three orange velvet chevrons piped in dark blue satin striped the gown's sleeves. Last but not least, if the sun shone just right, they could all be blinded by the reflection from Daniel's shoes. And the hell of it was, Jonah suspected Daniel dressed like this every day.

What a way to live!

***

"Gentlemen," Daniel said, addressing the boys. "May I present my brother?"

"Hello, sir." The taller boy bowed slightly. Wainwright tended to push the propriety envelope, but Daniel had always felt the boy's heart was in the right place. Lucky for him he wasn't as much of a bully as his father, though he had all the tendencies.

The smaller boy practically bounced with unconcealed excitement.

"Is your hat about the racing cars, sir?"

Daniel hid his smile. He loved Torrington. The boy's enthusiasm for life and adventure always reminded him of Jonah, in fact. But, in all things, Westover Academy demanded proper behavior. He lightly touched the boy's shoulder and pursed his lips when Torrington looked up. Having been reminded he'd once again stepped out of bounds,

Torrington heaved a sigh before turning back to face Jonah , this time more sedately.

The object of Torrington's curiosity stretched his arms over his head, then scraped his hand over his roughened chin and leaned forward, elbows on his knees. Even sitting, Jonah and the boy didn't meet gazes. Torrington was a long way from his growth spurt and his small size often earned him scorn even from those the same age. Another reason why Daniel had a soft spot for the boy.

"Hello, sir. Pleased to meet you." Like Wainwright, Torrington dropped a quick bow before staring longingly at Jonah's cap.

"Hello, men," Jonah said in his deep, clear voice. The voice that sounded exactly like Daniel's, but without the cultured tone and sophisticated verbiage. He addressed Torrington. "What's your name, son?"

For a moment, the boy looked puzzled. "Torrington, sir."

Jonah smiled. "No, I mean your real name. Whaduz your mama call you?"

Torrington's face brightened and he opened his mouth to speak.

"Sweetie pie," Wainwright interrupted in a taunting tone.

"Mr. Wainwright, please go to the dining hall and inform Miss Nilson that I will be absent for the evening meal." There was no sharpness to Daniel's tone, but the dismissal was unambiguous.

Wainwright looked unhappy that he would miss the remainder of the conversation, but he said, "Yes, sir," turned on his heel and marched off.

"Now, Mr. Torrington, I believe you were asked your name." Daniel touched his shoulder again, this time as a sign of support and permission.

"Yes, sir." Torrington looked first to Daniel with respect in his eyes, then to Jonah with open interest. "It's Jeffrey, sir."

"Well, Jeff," Jonah replied, removing his hat and handing it to Torrington to study up close. "You were right about this hat. It is about the racing cars and stuff. Do you like racing?"

"Oh, yes, sir." His eyes glowed and he touched the satin-stitched, embroidered words with reverence. "I've only been to a race once. My Uncle Neil took me when we visited family down in South Carolina."

"Why, Jeff, I believe you were at the racetrack near where I live, in Darlington. Did you like the race?"

"It was ... wonderful! So loud, and fast. And my uncle bought me hot dogs and candy and even let me sip his beer—"

He jerked around and stared at Daniel in wide-eyed shock.

"I wasn't supposed to tell anyone that."

Daniel nodded sagely. "I can see why; it wasn't a very good idea. But I don't believe we need to say anything, do we Jonah?"

"Absolutely not." Jonah winked at Torrington. "It's a secret between us men."

Torrington's shoulders relaxed, and a grin crossed his face.

"Mr. Torrington, my brother is an ace mechanic. He works on those race cars. In fact, teams fight for him, he's so good. So, when you visited Darlington, Mr. Goodman was most likely in the pits for one of the famous drivers."

"Wow!" Torrington regarded Jonah with something close to hero worship. "Gosh, wow!"

Jonah chuckled. "I don't do that work anymore, but I'd sure be happy to introduce you to a few of the drivers."

He didn't do that work any longer? Had Jonah left yet another position? The man had no staying power. Sighing inwardly, Daniel clucked his tongue.

"Yes, well. I suppose you'd better go along now. It's almost time for lacrosse practice and you still must change."

At the boy's obvious reluctance to leave, Jonah added, "Hey, Jeff, you know how important sports are to us guys. Lacrosse is fun—you don't want to be late."

"No, sir—I mean yes, sir."

He slowly handed back the cap and began to turn when he cast a quick glance at Daniel. Standing straight with hands folded in front, he looked at Jonah and politely said, "I enjoyed meeting you, Mr. Goodman."

Jonah held out his hand, and, with another grin, Torrington took it for a manly shake.

"It was a pleasure, Jeff. You know, if I had another cap with me, I'd leave you this one. But I promise to send one up to you. And if your uncle ever brings you back to Darlington, let Daniel—uh, Mr. Goodman—know, and I'll find some time to show you around."

"Oh! Oh, *sir.*" In a rush, Torrington threw his arms around Jonah's neck then dashed off before the surprised man could hug him back.

Jonah stood to face his brother squarely at last. He held out his hand again, and Daniel took it then pulled him up for a quick pat on the shoulders.

"What a kid," Jonah said, watching Torrington flee across the grass fronting the administration building.

"His parents are deceased. His uncle has custody but he lives out in Oklahoma and the boy doesn't see him often." Daniel sighed and shook his head. "He shouldn't be running, and he especially shouldn't be running on the grass. And if he was going to run on the grass, he shouldn't be doing so in front of the administration building. He's a good boy, but I see extra duties in Mr. Torrington's future."

"You won't turn him in!"

"Lord, no! But there are eyes everywhere, and there are standards. At Westover Academy, as in life, there is a proper way to behave. Parents send their sons here for consistency, to have those standards of behavior applied and instilled, as well as to receive a first-class education."

"Sounds boring as hell," Jonah muttered.

"Yes, well..." Daniel turned away from the retreating figure of Torrington and led Jonah toward the dormitory where he had a kitchenette, a small sitting room, a bedroom, and bath in a building with thirty lower form boys.

Jonah jammed his hands in his pockets as he strolled beside Daniel. "What's lacrosse, by the way?"

"A game with a net at the end of a stick. The ball moves down the field by being tossed from net to net. It can be pretty fast and sometimes kind of violent."

Jonah's face creased into a frown. "Jeff looked too young to be involved in something like that."

"He's not very good at it," Daniel admitted, "but then none of the boys in his age group are, so they're all equally safe. Mostly they miss the ball and spend their time simply running from one end of the field to the other."

Jonah's frown disappeared. Nothing bothered him for long. "That's okay, then. You know, it's pretty up here in the fall."

"Yes, isn't it? You came at the perfect time, too. Good thing you can stay with me. During foliage, when the leaves are turning, you can't get a hotel room from here to Connecticut."

"Oh, I can't stay, Daniel. In fact, right after dinner I have to make the train to Boston so I can catch the six a.m. flight back to Charleston."

Daniel stopped and spun toward his brother in amazement.

"What? Jonah, your note didn't say you'd only be here a couple of hours. I would have made arrangements for someone to take my classes. We could have had more time. Jesus, it's been two or three years since we've seen each other."

With a concerted effort, he refrained from raking his hand through his hair, a nervous habit from childhood it had taken him years to break. His near relapse must be due to the emotion he felt seeing Jonah again. If it was true that a special bond existed between twins, then an even stronger tie bound the set of rare, identical triplets. And while he, Mark, and Jonah had gone their separate ways since high school—almost twenty years ago—he always felt incomplete when they weren't in contact, as though a small piece of him was missing. Being with Jonah now made him realize how alone he was. Not for companionship, but for someone who understood the soul of him, without words or judgments or questions. No one did that but his brothers.

Jonah laid his hand on Daniel's arm. "I know. I feel the same." Their telepathic communication always surprised, and in some cases frightened, friends and relatives. But Jonah and Daniel took it as a matter of course.

They began walking again.

"What do you hear from Mark?" Daniel asked.

"Nothing much." Jonah frowned. "Why don't we stay in better touch?"

"Because we're guys? I don't know."

"Well, as far as I know, Mark is still in Richmond, being a nerd." Jonah flicked a leaf that had drifted into his hair to the ground.

"Still with that same finance company?"

"Hell, you probably know as much as I do. But gossiping about Mark is not why I came up. I came up to deliver a message. It's something I didn't think you should hear over the phone. It's about Mom and Dad ."

Daniel stopped again and grabbed Jonah's arm to halt his progress. "Oh, my God! They're not—"

"No, sorry, no. Nothing like that."

Daniel blew a breath of relief. "Then what could be so important you'd fly all the way to New Hampshire to tell me?"

Jonah grinned. "Well, Daniel, it's like this."

He pulled himself to his impressive full six feet two inches, clasped his hands in prayer and recited, "Friends, we are gathered here in the presence of God and this company, to witness—"

"*What!?*"

"Yeah! Isn't it great? This November we can give thanks that our parents are finally getting married."

Jonah, the idiot, grinned even wider, like a puppy who'd just been tossed a big old steak bone. Obviously, he didn't understand the gravity of the situation.

"And they're not keeping it quiet, either. Nope, they're doing it up right. Turns out, one of the men who knew Mom from her days in show business—"

Daniel closed his eyes. "She was a stripper, Jonah, not a movie star."

Jonah flapped his hand. "Whatever. Anyway, he's arranged for them to use the country club. And you know Dad's old friends at the bank never held his troubles against him—"

"His *troubles*? He stole money, Jonah. It was only because the bank president liked Dad and the money was returned that he didn't spend hard time in federal prison."

Jonah put a hand on his shoulder, thinking to calm him, no doubt. Too late for that.

"I know. But the fact remains, Dad's well-liked, so they've got a big bachelor party planned."

The groan he heard had to have come from him. His brother was having too much fun to make a sound filled with such angst.

"They've scheduled the whole shebang for over the Thanksgiving holidays. I don't have to work and you won't have school, so we can both be there. The local paper's already featured them in the society section. *Couple Finally Ties Knot After Thirty-Seven Years Together. Sons Serve As Witnesses.* You should see them, Daniel. They're like kids."

Yes, he could just imagine. The stripper and the embezzler. Sounded like a farce from a burlesque show. Daniel frowned. How was it Jonah didn't see the ridiculousness of the situation? Daniel loved his parents dearly, but really, what was the point in getting married *now*? Why hadn't they committed to each other when it could have served some purpose? Like *before* their sons were born.

Life had always been like this for him. Calling his parents free spirits would meet no contradiction. His mother had "danced" in the top clubs all over the country, and even in Paris. His dad had met her in New York where he was attending a finance conference. They always told him and his brothers that they'd fallen in love immediately. Their mom had followed their dad back to Lucky Strike, North Carolina where he handled business accounts in a regional bank, and a few months later, Daniel, Mark, and Jonah had entered the world.

Unfortunately, a few years after that, a bank audit had revealed their dad had been regularly skimming from two or three accounts. Not much, only enough to tide them over now and then. "Takes a lot a money to raise three strong 'good men'," their dad had declared at the trial, and their mom had smiled at his pun, telling the boys later that their father *was* a "good man" and so were they, and they should never forget it.

Their dad waved and made funny faces through the window of the bus taking him to Cabarrus Correctional Center in Mt. Pleasant. ("Doesn't that sound like Daddy is going to have a wonderful time?" their mother cooed in their four-year-old ears. "Who wouldn't want to go to a place called Mt. Pleasant?")

In the meantime, their mom put Captain Crunch on the table by going back to New York, where she was hailed and declared to be "the greatest exotic dancer in three decades."

As children, they thought their mama danced in Broadway plays with loud music and lots of men in the audience, and their dad was teaching arithmetic to bad men in prison and having fun in a happy place called Mt. Pleasant. Not until years later, when teased by kids at school, did they ever see a different view of their life. By then, they'd moved back to Lucky Strike, where their dad joined them in a pretty little double-wide next to an apple orchard. The boys were spoiled on hugs and kisses and lots of apple cobbler.

When kids taunted them about having a criminal father and stripper mother, and that their parents weren't even married, the boys sat down and discussed what they knew to be true. Their dad, a smiling, hardworking man, managed the orchard next to them and three others besides, but still found time to toss a football and tell corny old jokes during dinner. Their beautiful, graceful mother made them laugh instead of cry when they had scrapes and bruises, and always sang when she cooked, using fancy little dance steps when she moved from the sink to the stove. They didn't know for sure if their parents were married, but there was no question but that they loved each other, and Daniel, Mark, and Jonah.

Jonah settled the taunts with his fists or by brushing off the insults. Daniel blotted out the jeers by reciting a poem or the multiplication tables to himself and then withdrawing into books. Mark, genius as he was, might not even have understood the snide comments. The effect was that he looked down his nose at the bullies and blithely showed them up in every classroom subject.

As he withdrew from the taunts and jeers at school, Daniel withdrew from his family, too. Years later, he realized how different from his parents and brothers he'd become. Serious and more sensitive than he cared to admit, he found himself the lonely outsider in a family of carefree extroverts. Even Mark was more easygoing. By the time Daniel wanted to be more like them he didn't know how, so he moved into a world where he felt more comfortable.

The strange thing was that, despite their past, his parents were well-liked—his dad respected and his mom embraced by the town. They were happy and still in love. Nothing had changed. So why did they feel the need to marry, something sure to draw gossip again? He knew no one would understand how he felt—what else was new?—but he couldn't help wondering why *now,* when their actions would cause irreparable damage to his career, just as he was reaching the pinnacle of his dreams?

Daniel was so engrossed in his internal analysis that he almost missed the bombshell.

"The reporter said the story had enough appeal to attract international attention. Mom and Dad are both kind of famous, after all," Jonah chuckled. "Won't they get a kick out of that? Having their story on cable news?"

"No!"

Daniel hoped no one saw him, looking as though he'd had the worst shock of his life. Which, of course, he had.

The blood drained from his face, his eyes popped open wide, and so did his mouth. He'd probably laugh if he could see himself. Or maybe not. This was horrible.

His parents were getting married on international TV.

Chapter Two

Daniel drove Jonah to a restaurant in the village, not far from Westover Academy, and parked his Volvo in the cobblestone lot's only vacant space. Judging from the building's exterior, Freddie's Tavern had once been a roomy clapboard home. The entrance led downstairs to a dark, paneled room. The after-work crowd gathered for drinks; some unwinding, others networking. A muted, wall-mounted TV aired a news program with stock market results ticker-taping the bottom of the screen.

Daniel led him past the bar to the hostess.

"Two for dinner, please."

Jonah removed his NASCAR cap.

"Guess I'm underdressed, bro."

"No, this is a casual place."

Jonah knew better. In the south, flannel shirts and blue jeans worked in most restaurants. He'd even gone to church dressed this way, although only to the contemporary service. But this was New Hampshire, the heart of New England, home to bluebloods, not rednecks. He smiled, thinking of the picture he and Daniel presented. Daniel was the polished, finished version of Jonah, right down to the perfect eyebrows and flawless hair. Jonah had a scar over one eye from a childhood daredevil stunt, a mechanic's rough hands, and nails severely trimmed to prevent them from collecting grease.

"Your waitress will be right with you." The hostess stopped beside a small table draped in white linen and handed them tall menus. "The special this evening is veal *scaloppini.*"

"Thank you," Daniel answered.

Jonah claimed the chair opposite him. "Veal *scaloppini*, eh? Sounds great."

Daniel reached for the wine list with his perfectly manicured hand. "How about a nice—"

"Samuel Adams. I'm dying for a longneck."

Clearing his throat, Daniel abandoned the wine menu. "They have it on draught."

Jonah took the hint. God forbid Daniel be seen with his brother guzzling beer from a bottle.

"Great."

The perky waitress, a college student he'd guess, arrived with a pitcher of iced water, and filled their goblets.

"You guys care for a drink before dinner?"

Daniel answered. "Two Sam Adams. I think we're ready to order, too."

They each ordered the special. The red-haired waitress collected their menus and disappeared.

"You ready to tell me why you were apoplectic earlier about our parents getting hitched?" Jonah asked.

Daniel's eyes widened and he glanced around the room.

"Lower your voice, please."

Jonah choked back laughter at the stricken look on his brother's face. "Why?"

"Discretion is important at a place like Westover. What would the parents say, or the board of directors, if they—"

"If they what? See your parents married on television? It has nothing to do with you or your proper conduct. You're just attending the wedding—"

"I can't. You don't understand the situation, Jonah."

Daniel exhaled a long, weary sigh.

Jonah almost sympathized with his brother's distress. Almost.

"You're right, I don't understand. The three of us are their only children. They love us unconditionally. How can you even consider skipping out on something so important to them?"

"And I love *them* unconditionally. My not attending the wedding of the century isn't going to change that, and they know it. Besides, it's assumed that my parents *are* married. That *is* the proper order of things in a civilized society."

He stared off into space for a moment, then looked back.

"Furthermore, I found out last month that I'm being considered for the position of headmaster of the school. Headmaster! Do you have any idea how hard I've worked—"

"To become a class A prig? Christ, Daniel, listen to yourself."

"No, you listen. I love Mom and Dad, and I know they're good people. But the perception of them is the issue. Dad may be the most lovable man in the world, but is that going to be the focus of the TV reports? No, it'll be that, no matter what spin you put on it, he's still an ex-con embezzler."

"He paid his debt to society—"

"And while I'd vote for Mom to be Mother of the Year, she was a stripper, and a famous one. You can't expect that's going to be overlooked."

"Exotic dancer. She also gave birth to us—"

"Without benefit of a marriage license, which makes the three of us illegitimate. And there we'll be, smiling in the background like Tweedledum, Tweedledee, and Tweedlenerd. Their backgrounds and our legitimacy are now going to be blasted internationally."

Was this guy for real? Is this what happened when they stayed apart too long? Jonah needed to spend quality time with his anal-retentive brother, loosen him up a bit.

"Bastards, huh? Well, it makes us *lucky* bastards, if you ask me. Who could ask for more loving, devoted parents?"

"I don't argue that. But why the spectacle? Why, after almost thirty-seven years, do they have to *publicly* flaunt their indiscretion and embarrass—" Daniel stopped, as if sensing he'd said too much.

"Are you saying you're ashamed of our parents?"

"I'm not! Not exactly." Daniel sighed and rubbed his temple. "It's complicated. There are things you don't—"

The waitress saved Daniel from answering further by delivering their drinks. She placed two pilsner glasses at each place setting—Happy Hour.

Jonah needed both beers. One to quench his thirst and one to wash down the load of crap Daniel had just fed him. What had happened to the fun-loving brother who'd shared so many adventures with him? They'd never been well-off financially as kids, but they had a wealth of good memories. Was it too late to recapture that camaraderie? He had to try. No way he'd disappoint Mom and Dad with a no-show brother.

Changing his approach, Jonah said, "She sort of looks like Kelly Shepherd, doesn't she?"

"Who, the waitress?"

"Yeah. Picture her with lighter, longer hair, and eyeglasses."

"Kelly Shepherd. You mean our senior class president, back in high school? Jesus, I hardly remember anyone from high school."

No surprise there. Daniel seemed to have abandoned everything from his past. He hadn't been home to Lucky Strike, North Carolina, since two years ago last Christmas.

Jonah, on the other hand, remembered Kelly too well. She'd never forgiven him, not that he blamed her. Or had she? Jonah had been home for graduation, but she'd disappeared soon thereafter. He hadn't had contact with her since. For all he knew, she was probably dumpy and dowdy now.

Daniel snapped his fingers.

"I've got it! Kelly Shepherd! Strawberry blond hair, big green eyes, and a nice set of—"

"Yeah. Don't forget the freckles and skinny legs."

Daniel grinned.

"You didn't complain about her skinny legs when you two were going together. You took her to the homecoming game, right? And the dance after?"

So, he did remember.

"We double-dated."

Daniel sipped his beer.

"We had just the one car, if you could classify that heap as a car."

"Heap? It was a one-of-a-kind classic. Nobody else had an AMC Pacer with a 327 Corvette engine. Manual fuel injection, too. That baby would run!"

"When it ran at all."

Jonah chuckled.

"Okay, maybe it was temperamental, but we had a lot of good times in that Pacer."

"We had a lot of fun building it, too," Daniel said. "We were the star pupils in shop class."

"The three of us are a good team."

Or were. He hoped the trip down memory lane would rekindle Daniel's nostalgia for family and home.

"Now that I think about it, you had all the fun that particular night. Left me stranded with Marilyn Taylor at the homecoming dance. Wasn't that the night you ... you know."

"Lost my cherry?"

Jonah hid a grin behind his pilsner glass at Daniel's grimace.

"That's one way of putting it. With Kelly Shepherd. Right, it's coming back to me now. Later, I begged you for details and you claimed there wasn't much to it."

That was the problem. There hadn't been much to it. Thanks to his inexperience and hormones, Jonah managed to score but only after fumbling. He'd been too embarrassed to face Kelly afterward. She'd called him a dickhead, which shocked the hell out of him since she never spoke crudely, further proof of how much he'd upset her. Or disappointed her. He'd never been clear on her exact feelings since he'd dropped out of school shortly after the fiasco and moved down to South Carolina to live with his uncle.

He'd all but forgotten her until he'd seen the resemblance in the tavern waitress. Who was he kidding? He could never forget Kelly Shepherd. Even after all these years and a number of women. Although his sexual prowess had improved, his women had not. None held a candle to the intelligent, pretty Kelly. Adding insult to injury, he'd not only lost a high school sweetheart but a good friend, too.

"Whatever happened to you two, anyway? At one point you were inseparable—until after homecoming."

Jonah took his time, drinking a long swallow of his Sam Adams.

"I think we were just too immature for sex. Of course, I didn't believe so at the time. So what about Marilyn Taylor? You took her to the prom, too, right?"

"We were friends. I was comfortable around her because we weren't trying to impress each other. Less pressure. And who did Mark take?"

"No one. Mark wasn't into things like school dances. By then he was concerned with theoretical mathematics and unconcerned with girls."

"That's right." Daniel rotated his pilsner, drawing a line in the condensation. "You know I was jealous as hell of you."

"No, I didn't know. Why?"

"You got laid first." His grin broadened. "You and I may be identical, but I never had your smooth charm with the ladies."

Jonah ignored the charm reference. "You have anyone special up here?"

"No. It's not easy. I don't exactly see a lot of women at a boys' academy."

"You get lonely?"

Daniel held his gaze. "Do you?"

"Yeah, I do. That's why I'm asking. Over the years it seems we go through various stages in life at about the same time." Jonah paused to give his brother a minute to tune in. "You are lonely without a woman. Admit it."

"I'll admit it. The living quarters at the school are great, don't get me wrong. But how do you entertain a lady friend in a dormitory full of boys?"

"*Major Payne* did it."

"Who?"

Jonah sighed. He doubted Daniel knew Damon Wayans or any of his films.

"It's a movie. Never mind. I have my own place but can't seem to find the right woman."

"Really, Jonah. I've watched NASCAR. You have nearly as much celebrity as the drivers. Women throw their motel keys at you."

An exaggeration, but Jonah wasn't going to debate the issue. He didn't want his brother's envy. He wanted him to come home for Thanksgiving and the wedding, to be part of the family again. Besides, he'd outgrown the NASCAR groupies scene.

"*Threw* their keys. I must be getting pickier in my old age."

"Speak for yourself," Daniel said. "I'm not admitting to middle age yet, and certainly not to old age."

But Daniel already seemed far too old.

"Not middle age? You drive a Volvo station wagon, for Chrissakes."

What pushed Daniel to be staid and proper? True, he'd been the more serious brother growing up, but never Volvo-driving-serious. At least he could've bought a Jaguar or something a tad younger and sportier.

Daniel shook his head. "I see you're still doing it."

"Doing what?"

"Judging people by their vehicles. Not everyone follows your automotive mentality."

"They don't?" Jonah deadpanned.

Daniel shook his head. "And why have you given up NASCAR? I thought you loved it."

"Been there, done that. Ready to try something new."

"One of these days you'll have to commit to something, brother."

"Maybe, but not today."

Their dinner arrived, derailing further conversation about women, family, cars, or old girlfriends. Surreptitiously checking his watch, Jonah renewed his determination to lure Daniel to their parents' wedding. He'd have to be careful, though. Daniel could be a stubborn ass sometimes. Just like his brothers.

***

With a disquiet feeling, Daniel dropped Jonah off at the station just minutes before the train for Boston arrived.

"Take care," he said. "Let's not go so long without talking."

Jonah took him in a hug and slapped his back.

"Let's not go so long without *seeing* each other. Like next month at home at Thanksgiving."

Daniel frowned. "Don't count on it, Jonah. But don't worry. I'll call Mom and Dad and let them know I won't be there. You came up to do the asking. I won't make you the bearer of bad news."

"Daniel, I'm not above bribery to get you there. Or guilting you."

Daniel snorted a laugh. "You can try but I daresay it won't work."

Jonah stared at his brother for long seconds and then shrugged. "Well, can't blame a man for trying."

"Nope, can't blame you. I hope eventually you can understand my side of things."

The look on his brother's face was all the evidence he needed to know that, true to form, Jonah would never understand. Fuck it. He could only be who he could be.

The train pulled into the station, initiating a spurt of people rushing toward the doors.

"Better get on and get a good seat. Hope you make all your connections for your flight home."

Now that he knew where he stood in Jonah's estimation, Daniel was ready for his brother to hurry back to his part of the country and leave Daniel in his. Obviously they were worlds apart, and never the twain shall meet.

***

"Mr. Goodman?"

Daniel looked up from his desk where he sat grading papers.

"Mr. Torrington, you should be asleep. Do you feel unwell?"

He rose and went to the open doorway where Jeffrey Torrington stood, looking a mess. His slippers were on the wrong feet and his bathrobe hung half open, showing that his pajama top was buttoned incorrectly. Daniel sighed. Some housemasters would give him demerits for sloppiness, even around the dorm, and maybe for the older boys— those the age of his students—it would be warranted. But not for Jeffrey. He was just a second grader, for God's sake. To his way of thinking, the kids his age shouldn't even be in a residential school. They should still be home with their mothers.

Torrington shook his head. "I'm just worried, sir."

"What are you worried about, Mr. Torrington?"

Daniel opened the boy's robe and rebuttoned his pajama top. Then he retied the robe and led Torrington in to sit on the sofa where he reversed his slippers.

"Do you think Mr. Goodman will forget to send the NASCAR cap, sir?"

That was what worried the kid?

"I don't think so, Mr. Torrington. He won't be home for a day or two but he's good about fulfilling his promises. Don't you worry. He'll send the cap."

The boy heaved a sigh and twisted his hands in his lap.

"Thank you, sir!"

Daniel fought a smile.

"Think you can sleep now?"

Jeffrey nodded so hard he nearly knocked himself off the edge of the sofa.

"Yes, sir. I'll go and do it right now!"

"Good man! I'll see you at breakfast then."

The boy tore off up the hallway.

"No running," Daniel murmured, knowing it did no good. The boy was just a ... *boy*, after all.

Settling at the desk again, he continued on with his paperwork.

Chapter Three

Daniel walked into the parlor of the headmaster's house on Saturday afternoon, seeking first the food table and second his friend, Stan Baxter. He spotted them both near the front window.

"You're late," Stan said.

"Lots of people wanted to chat."

Parents' Weekend, when teachers sat in their classrooms to meet their students' mothers and fathers, meant mandatory tea afterwards for all professionals at the academy. Board members and parents attended at their own discretion, and the boys—the reason that the school existed and that they were all there—mostly stayed out of sight and hearing.

"Fortunately for me, a good many parents have now grabbed their progeny and left campus, so I have access to the snacks unimpeded," Daniel said, examining the finger food on display before making his selections. The challenge was always how to load his plate while appearing to take a socially acceptable portion.

"Did I miss anything?"

"Only an angel." Stan turned toward the window. "Holy Mother! Look at that," he muttered.

"What?" Daniel asked, fitting a cucumber sandwich beside the smoked salmon-topped cracker on his dessert plate. "Am I missing a table of fare? I swear, every year the offerings at these teas are more meager than the last."

Stan chuckled and answered in the same low voice, "Is your stomach all you think about? I was talking about another kind of dish. One you can have fun eating in bed, if you catch my drift. And she just slipped out onto the lawn."

"Is your libido all *you* think about?"

Daniel bit a carrot stick in two and sighed. Only three more hours and he could order a pizza. With all of his charges gone from the dormitory for Parents' Weekend, he had a rare, private, two-day holiday ahead of him. With the tiny plate full, he joined Stan at the large windows.

"Where is this goddess?"

"There. In the red dress and hat."

Daniel saw nothing but the shapely form of a woman walking away. Slender ankles topped three-inch heels. A dress of some kind of lustrous material hit her mid-calf. The style was soft and feminine, and berry red. Not many women showed up at Westover in a color sure to make them the focus of attention. Not that most of them didn't expect to *be* the focus—didn't demand it, in fact—but they usually weren't so obvious. The breeze at her back molded the material to the curves of her hips and ass and fluttered the dress's full sleeves. A wide-brimmed hat hid her hair, but, based on what was visible, Daniel easily imagined a long column of neck designed for kissing.

"If the rest of her matches the back view, you've got reason to be drooling down the front of your gown."

Frowning, Stan glanced down as though to make sure the drool comment was only facetious.

"Can't afford to drool on this. I had to use my tax refund to pay for the thing and show off my master's chevrons. I don't know how you afforded to pay for your Ph.D. paraphernalia."

"The new degree looks sharp on you. Now, why are you mooning over a woman you see at the headmaster's tea when you know she's some student's mother and off limits?"

"She looks young enough to be a sister, so it's not a given she's out of bounds."

At that moment, a young boy wearing the school uniform and a big grin ran up to the woman. She bent to catch him in her arms. When she straightened, she ruffled the boy's hair. His expression and wagging finger showed that he chastised her, but then he laughed and finger-combed the mussed hair back into place. She took his hand and they walked toward the circle where most of the parents parked. Looking up at the woman, the boy's lips moved the whole while, carrying on a steady monologue.

Something in her actions captured Daniel's attention. They were artless, performed naturally and with unabashed love. The child fairly skipped beside her and the frequent turns of her head showed she looked at him as though hanging on every word he spoke.

"How wonderful," Daniel murmured, impressed with her total attention to the boy. "Did you see that?"

"Oh, yeah. I didn't think her hips would ever stop swaying, and it's a crime they make hemlines so long."

Daniel laughed. "You're such a hedonist."

"And proud of it. But you were right. Looks like she's a student's mother after all. Damn the luck."

For once, Daniel agreed with his friend. But not just because of the woman's obvious good figure. More because she seemed to love her son and didn't care who knew it. He normally kept his distance from flashy women, as this one appeared to be based on her dress color, but her easy manner with the boy would be enough to make him ignore his own inclination toward the conservative. *If* she weren't also a patron of the school. Assuming the gods smiled on him and he became headmaster, he and the woman would be on business terms, and nothing good ever came from mixing business with pleasure. *Pleasure* is what every male instinct in him screamed she would be.

When the woman disappeared among other families making their way down the drive, Stan turned away from the window to survey the Victorian parlor. He sent a warning under his breath.

"Danger, two o'clock. Sydney Thomas heading your way."

Casually, Daniel eased right to make a getaway, and found himself a bare twenty feet from the very woman he was trying to avoid.

Stan elbowed him.

"Not my two o'clock, you idiot. *Your* two o'clock."

"Thanks for telling me now," Daniel shot back before pasting a smile on his face. "Hello, Sydney. Enjoying the tea?"

"I am now," she said, returning his smile. "I do find these crushes get more unbearable every year. Thank goodness you're here to keep me from dying."

Yes, thank goodness. He gave a mental shrug.

Daniel sensed Stan moving away—the coward—so he was stuck with the senior board member's daughter. Both Sydney and her father carried a great deal of influence with the other board members. If he was appointed headmaster, cultivating good will among the board members came with the job.

And Sydney wasn't really such a chore. Today her golden hair formed a chignon on her neck above the collar of a stylish sage green suit. Her heels and purse matched, as always. Some light shade of pink touched both her lips and cheeks. She never looked as though she wore any makeup, but Daniel knew, from growing up with his mother, no woman's eyes stood out in her face as Sydney's did without help from cosmetics.

Most men found her beautiful, he was sure, and why he couldn't manage a spark of healthy male interest in her was a mystery. The answer probably lay in the fact that he enjoyed the role of pursuer over that of being pursued. Or *hunted*, as he sometimes felt with Sydney.

"I suppose you met our newest patron?" She plucked the salmon-topped cracker off Daniel's plate and bit into it.

Great. One less morsel to eat.

"Unless the new boy and his parents are in my upper form English classes, I haven't met them. There were lots of talkers today, and I only just arrived here."

"Not parents, a single parent. A widow, actually. You're the only man in the room whose tongue hasn't been hanging out, and now I find out it's because you didn't see her."

She took one of the cucumber sandwiches off his plate and ate it while glancing around the room.

Daniel bit back a sarcastic comment and inched the plate away from her.

"The sandwiches are good, aren't they? I'm starved, having missed breakfast and lunch. Can I get you a plate of something, Sydney?"

She finished off *his* sandwich and waved his offer aside.

"Oh, no thanks. I couldn't eat a thing." Winking at him, she added, "Got to watch my figure you know, and especially after seeing that woman. Her red dress was like waving a flag in front of a room of bulls. I use the word *bull* intentionally. I think every man in the room was primed to rut. It was a disgusting display."

Reaching for the last cracker on Daniel's plate earned her a glare from him, but she didn't seem to notice, concentrating as she was on the snack.

Resigned to starving until he ordered dinner, Daniel gave thought to what Sydney had said about the mystery woman. He couldn't imagine more than one woman coming to the tea in red, so she must be referring to the lady with the luscious ass. So … she wasn't married but she was still off limits. Too bad for Stan. *Hell, too bad for me.*

"Was her husband an alumnus?"

He tried to sound nonchalant, but in case his expression showed the interest he felt, he turned away to find a place for the empty plate.

"No, the boy was recommended by some people in Europe—one of them was a *count*. Can you imagine?" Her eyes scanned the room again. "By the way, don't worry that Daddy is spending so much time talking to Andy Worth. I promise, you're the definite frontrunner for the headmaster position."

Thinking first of his stomach and then of the Lady in Red's posterior, Daniel hadn't noticed Creighton Thomas's attention being focused on his competitor for the high post at the academy. Now, though, his lips thinned at Sydney's revelation.

"Oh, I'm not worried. Your dad usually talks with all of us at one of these social events. I was late, so if he misses saying hello to me, I won't take offense."

He smiled, covering his twinge of worry. Anything could sway the board's decision, but with due modesty, Daniel thought he had the best chance to be appointed headmaster. Or he thought he had, until he found out his parents would be sharing their wedded bliss with viewers around the world.

Hell. He'd been so busy since Jonah left that he'd managed to put his parents from his mind. Now, forcing its way past the growls of his stomach and the sudden worry over Andy Worth and Creighton Thomas spending so much time together, a low-level anxiety filled him. He'd worked very hard for this position and he deserved it, damn it.

"What? I'm sorry, Sydney, I was thinking of something else. What did you say?"

"I'll make sure your name stays in front of Daddy, don't worry. Why don't we have dinner tonight and you can tell me of your plans?"

The last time Daniel had dined with Sydney, her sexual innuendo became more pointed as the evening progressed and her wine intake increased. Tonight, all he wanted was to prop up his feet, have a slice or three of hot pizza and a soda, and watch the playoff baseball game on TV in a quiet, empty dorm. He weighed his evening plans against a chance to keep himself foremost in Sydney's mind and therefore in her father's.

"I might even get Dad to join us," she said in a husky, low voice meant to enslave the listener.

At that moment, providence intervened in the form of Jeffrey Torrington carrying a small tray of wine glasses filled with lemonade.

Students being disciplined were often pressed into light serving duties, and, as predicted, Torrington had been seen running across the lawn earlier in the week.

"I do hope that when *you* host these teas you'll at least provide wine," Sydney muttered, picking up a glass Torrington offered.

Daniel also took a glass.

"Are you looking forward to being away for the weekend, Mr. Torrington?"

A sheen of tears sparkled in the boy's eyes.

"My uncle was going to come and get me, but I can't go now. The headmaster said this morning that I've been caught too many times running on the grass and he needed to"—his forehead scrunched as though trying to pull words from his memory—"impress me in such a way I'd remember not to do it again."

Torrington's words sounded like a direct quote from the prick in the front office. The boy was a *boy*, damn it all. Daniel was all for discipline and teaching good habits and behavior, but kids were going to act like kids. Torrington hadn't been spray painting the fine arts building, for Christ's sake, he'd been hurrying to a game.

Daniel hunkered down. "Well, Jeffrey, it's you and me in the dorm tonight."

Jeffrey hiccoughed he inhaled so quickly. "I'm going to be the only one in the dorm?" Panic filled his eyes.

Hell, poor kid. "Hey, didn't you hear me say it's you and *me*? Do you like baseball?"

The boy's eyes widened. The tray began a slow tilt which Daniel stopped with his index finger. "Because the playoffs are on TV. I thought maybe we men could call for a pizza, have a Coke or two and watch the game. Then you can sleep on my couch. It'd be like a sleepover. What do you say?"

"Oh, Mr. Goodman. That would be so ... so *wonderful!*"

"Okay, then. You go and spread the lemonade cheer and come by my apartment when the headmaster releases you from duty."

"Yes, sir!" He turned away.

"And Mr. Torrington." The boy looked back. "There's no need to tell anyone else about this, okay? We don't want the others to be jealous that they had to go home."

The little boy nodded, his face serious but his eyes twinkling.

Daniel stood and finished the lemonade. "I'm sorry, Sydney. I thought I'd have a free evening, but I can't leave now."

She sighed. "So I heard. Well, Daddy will certainly hear about how dedicated you are. I mean, you still *could* send the kid to another dormitory and we'd have our evening. I'd happily get comfy on your sofa, you know."

Her guileless expression was a counterpoint to her tone. Daniel might have lost his free evening, but relief flooded him.

"If he was staying by his own choice I would have found another dorm for him, but you saw how upset he was. I'll take a rain check for the next time you and your father come for a meeting." He squeezed her arm. "Thanks, Sydney."

She quirked her brows, leaned up to peck his cheek and then swung around to speak to a couple on her other side. Daniel eased away. He smiled hello to several people, then left the building.

***

Well, damn! The unthinkable had happened. The Red Sox had lost their playoff game to some Midwest team that before now hadn't won much of anything. There'd be no World Series in New England this year. Daniel stretched and yawned, trying not to disturb Torrington who slept soundly at the other end of the sofa.

After the tea, Daniel had stopped by the kitchen to pick up a couple of ice cream sandwiches. He'd arrived at his apartment and changed into jeans and a sweater before Torrington knocked politely on the door. Daniel had told him to change into his sweats and he'd raced off to do so. When he'd returned, an energetic bundle of questions, Daniel had smiled to himself. They'd played a board game, then ordered their pizza. The open box between them, they'd eaten off paper plates and drunk their Cokes directly from the can. Propping their feet on the coffee table while watching the baseball game, they'd struck a pose of contentment recognized by men everywhere.

During a commercial, Daniel had accompanied Torrington to retrieve pajamas, slippers, and toothbrush. An hour later, snuggled under a blanket, the boy had drifted into an untroubled sleep. Watching him now, a surprising sense of peace fell over Daniel, too. He'd wanted time to himself, but the evening had been better with Torrington there. Since Jonah's visit, a strange feeling of emptiness had plagued Daniel. Maybe if Jonah had stayed a few days, or if they'd parted with a better understanding between them, Daniel wouldn't be experiencing such a strong urge to connect with family. Tonight, filling a need for young Jeffrey had, unexpectedly, done the same for him.

He took the soda cans and the rest of the pizza into the tiny kitchen. Flipping on the light over the sink so Torrington could see where he was if he woke during the night, Daniel checked that the room was tidy. Only then did he slip into his bedroom. He emptied his pockets and then pulled off his sweater.

Before he could do much more, the phone rang. He grabbed it quickly, hoping it hadn't woken the boy.

"Hello?"

"Is this Mr. Goodman at Westover Academy?"

A woman's hesitant voice came across the line. With the receiver hard against his head, it was as though she stood beside him, lips pressed to his ear, intimately speaking just to him. His groin tightened.

Get a grip. And *find a time and place to get laid if just hearing a strange woman's voice does this to you.*

He kept his voice low.

"Yes. How may I help you?"

"It isn't me you can help, but a student of yours, Michael Haynes. Do you know him?"

Chills ran down Daniel's back. Michael was in his sophomore class, a bright boy but very quiet. What the hell was going on?

"Yes, I know him. State your business, please."

"He's sick, Mr. Goodman, and he asked me to call you. Said you were the only one there he could trust."

Forgetting to lower his voice for Torrington, Daniel spoke loudly but calmly, his worry coming through in volume rather than shakiness.

"What's wrong with him? Where is he? Let me talk to him, right now."

"He's okay. Well, sort of." Daniel heard retching in the background and the woman sighed. "Look, can you come and get him?"

Daniel was already restuffing his pockets with wallet and keys.

"Where?"

"The Bare Moose. Do you know where that is?"

Good God! Michael had gone home for the weekend, and The Bare Moose was a good twenty miles from his town. How in hell had Haynes gotten there?

"I know it."

"Good," the woman said. "Come around to the back. There's a covered stoop at the door. I'll have the light on. Just knock."

"It'll take me fifteen, twenty minutes."

"We'll be here."

She hung up and Daniel wasted no time doing the same.

Pulling his sweater back over his head, he hit the lights and only then remembered Jeffrey Torrington. "Shit!" He couldn't leave the boy here alone, but he hesitated to take him into an unknown situation. This late, there was no other dorm where Daniel could leave him. Nor could he think how to explain where he was going to another dorm master.

He shook the boy's shoulder. "Mr. Torrington? Jeffrey, wake up."

"Hmm?" Torrington rolled onto his back and slowly opened his eyes. "Is it morning?"

"No, not yet. But I need you to get up. We're going on an adventure. Are you game?"

Yawning, he nodded his assent.

"Sure." He pulled off the blanket and stood, rubbing his knuckles into his eyes.

"Just slip back into your sweats, okay?"

Torrington nodded again and took his clothes into the bathroom.

Remarkably, within minutes, Jeffrey returned to the living room fully dressed and ready.

"Good job!" Daniel exclaimed, guiding the boy outside and toward the parking lot.

Daniel told Torrington what little he knew about their mission, while maneuvering along the narrow, windy roads.

When he pulled up behind The Bare Moose, he'd no sooner turned off the engine when the inside door opened, revealing a woman standing behind a screen door.

"I don't want to leave you out here alone, Mr. Torrington," Daniel said, "but I'm not sure exactly what to expect inside. So our adventure is really beginning now. Stay very close to me."

"Yes, sir."

Daniel could tell the boy was both excited and a little fearful, but he looked up with such trust that emotion welled up in Daniel. He cupped Torrington's nape.

"We'll watch out for each other. Okay?"

"Yes, sir!"

They exited the car and walked to the back door.

"I'm Daniel Goodman." Until he was certain of what was going on, he wouldn't reveal Jeffrey's identity.

The woman nodded. "Michael is upstairs."

She pushed open the screen door and held it for them, giving Daniel his first clear view of her.

He knew right away that one look wouldn't be nearly enough. She was gorgeous. Her casual stance, and even more casual Levi's and long-sleeved tee shirt, showed she wasn't working to impress. Below the faded jeans, white sneakers covered her feet.

At least five feet ten inches tall, she was also slender. Chestnut colored hair wildly cascaded over her shoulders, and her eyes were the shade of melted chocolate. He'd been so wrong earlier. If *this* woman had one bit of makeup on, he'd gnaw on Jeffrey's lacrosse stick. And yet, her eyes stood out like beacons in her face. He didn't dare let his gaze linger on her breasts or hips for fear of forgetting why he was there. There was nothing more appealing in a woman than natural good looks, or less appealing in a man than ogling.

"You should be in bed," she said to Jeffrey, then cast a glare at Daniel as though he was negligent for bringing the child out into the night. Which, of course, he was.

He'd noticed her voice on the phone, and now the low warmth of it washed over him again. Good God. If he closed his eyes and listened to this woman talk he'd have a hard-on in no time.

Better not close his eyes.

"He *was* in bed until I received a call from you. I want to see Michael."

"Follow me."

She let them enter the vestibule, then closed the door and locked it. Another closed door faced them, and stairs rose to their right. That's where she led Daniel and Torrington.

It was then, even with Jeffrey on the steps between them, that Daniel noticed the curve of her ass and the sway of her hips with each step.

Well, damn! Daniel was following the Lady in Red!

Chapter Four

Good thing Torrington's ahead of me, or I might have to explain why a man's gaze homes in on a woman's ass like a compass points north, or a teenaged boy heads right to the only red sports car on the lot. Why bees zoom in on a field of clover. Why my dick aims for her—

Get a grip.

"We didn't mind, did we, Mr. Goodman?"

Shit! What the hell is Torrington talking about?

"What was that, Mr. Torrington?"

Okay, we're at the top of the stairs. Focus on something else, Fool.

"The lady said she hated to drag us out in the middle of the night, and I told her we didn't mind. We didn't, did we? Especially if Mike is sick. Is he bad sick, Miss?"

"Is he *very* sick, Mr. Torrington," Daniel said automatically. The question and correction were answered without the woman saying a word. Moans emanated from a room at the end of the hallway to their left.

"Good God!" Daniel grasped Torrington's shoulder to stop him. "Stay here, Jeffrey. Right here against the wall."

He waited to see the boy nod and then brushed by the woman to rush toward the noise.

Michael Haynes sat on the bathroom floor, his back against the tub and his head resting on his knees which were drawn up and lassoed by his arms.

"Mr. Haynes?"

Daniel dropped to one knee. He sensed the female enter behind him, although she stayed near the door.

"What in hell happened?"

The boy panted and moaned again, so she answered. "I believe it's called being drunk."

"What?" Daniel snapped his head around. "He's only fifteen. Where did he get alcohol?"

Then it struck him how wrong this whole scene was. Like an idiot, he'd spent the last few minutes concentrating more on the apartment's occupant than the fact that she lived over a tavern. Or that young Michael Haynes was in her private quarters after midnight. What all that implied brought on a wave of nausea, followed closely by rage.

"I'll make sure the academy's attorneys know about this. The tavern will be sued, you'll be sued, and you can be sure you won't find—"

"Mr. Goodman, please." Michael's voice barely registered, it was so weak.

Daniel looked down into the boy's pale face and bloodshot, watery brown eyes. His light brown hair stuck to his forehead in untidy clumps. Daniel brushed the hair off Michael's face, noting his clammy skin and trembling shoulders.

"Not her fault, sir. All mine. She saved me."

"*Saved* you!" Daniel sputtered. But further talk was halted when Michael twisted away to kneel beside the toilet and tried to void an already empty stomach. Daniel leaned forward to steady the boy's head until, once more, Michael sank to the floor.

Eve handed Daniel a wet washcloth and a Dixie cup of water.

"See if he can rinse out his mouth. I'll bring him some Saltines. I haven't wanted to leave him alone, but since you're here..."

Before Daniel could say anything, the woman turned and disappeared down the hall, speaking in a soft, low voice to Torrington before the sounds of her footsteps faded.

"Is Mike going to be okay, Mr. Goodman?"

His steady voice belied the fear in Torrington's face when Daniel glanced over his shoulder.

"I think he's going to be fine, Jeffrey. If the lady's diagnosis is correct...?"

He looked to Michael for confirmation and received it in the barest of nods. Daniel blew out a breath and shook his head.

"He'll feel miserable for a day or two, though." Daniel lowered his voice and bent nearer Michael. "And he'll deserve it."

Again, Michael tipped his head a fraction of an inch, grimacing with the effort.

"Here we are," the woman stated. "Michael, try one or two of these crackers and see if they stay down."

She handed him two squares. "Just nibble slowly." Watching, she added, "That's right, don't rush it."

Daniel stood to make room for her to crouch beside the teen. Whether due to her closeness or his feeling better, a spot of color returned to Michael's cheeks.

When he kept down a few more crackers and sipped the full cup of water, Daniel thought it was time to get him to his feet. As though in slow motion, Michael made it down the hall and to the sofa in the living room.

"How do you feel?" she asked him. "Are you dizzy?"

"No, I'm okay."

That he didn't move his head when talking and that he had a death grip on the arm of the sofa, told Daniel the boy was far from "okay".

Jeffrey settled beside Michael and looked up at him, puzzled. "You were *drinking*, Mike? I'll bet you were with those Whitney bro—"

"Shh!" Michael turned his head sharply, wincing with the movement. Then he shifted his glance to Daniel.

"Might as well spill it now, Mr. Haynes, because I intend to find out the whole sordid story before you get any rest tonight."

"I made some coffee after I called you. Would you like a cup?" Compared to the men, the woman sounded normal, almost cheerful.

"Please. Black." Daniel sat in a chair opposite Michael.

The apartment was quiet with the tavern closed. He let his gaze roam the room. The furniture was undistinguished in shape or covering. The walls were half paneling, half plaster. Cream-colored paint on the plaster lightened the room and provided a backdrop for several oil paintings that helped hide cracks that extended both below and above the frames. A Formica-topped table with two chairs sat outside the kitchen. A vase of roses that lent a heady fragrance to the room was centered on the table. Atop a small wooden table beside the sofa, a piece of needlework lay unfinished.

Silently, Daniel accepted a cup of steaming dark liquid from the woman. He nodded his thanks and waited while she pulled a straight-backed chair from the table to sit beside him before he addressed Michael. On the sofa, Jeffrey's eyes drifted shut before he jerked them open. Finally, sleep won out.

"All right," Daniel began in a low voice, "tell me about tonight."

Eyes cast down, Michael took a deep breath then sipped water from the cup Eve had filled.

"I caught a ride home this afternoon. My parents and I were supposed to go into Boston for the weekend. Dad had tickets to the Patriots game. But when I got to the house, I found out they'd gotten a better offer."

Daniel cringed at the bitterness in Michael's voice. He knew the boy lived within the twenty-five-mile radius that would have allowed him to attend the academy as a day student, but his parents insisted he board. Over the years, Daniel had seen the loneliness in the boy's face, and this year he'd read it between the lines of Michael's creative writing exercises.

"I'm sorry, Michael. I heard you talking about going to the game earlier in the week and I know you were excited."

Michael shrugged, then made a face.

"After dinner I went down to the high school to shoot some hoops and these guys were there."

"The Whitneys that Mr. Torrington referred to?"

"Yes, sir. I've seen them for years around the basketball court, so we kind of know each other."

He inhaled, then let out the deep breath.

"We shot the ball for an hour or so and then I said I had to go home. They started ragging on me. You know, 'The preppie's mommy is calling him,' and 'It's already dark, Preppie. Can you find the way all by yourself?' Stuff like that."

"Teasing you. You were already mad at your parents and that just made you madder."

Michael looked at Daniel with new respect.

"Exactly. And I got to thinking, what did I have to go home for, anyway? I wished I'd stayed at school, but it was too late for that, so I decided to stay at the basketball court. A little while later, a paper bag appeared with a bottle in it, and when they dared me to drink—well, what could I do?"

Daniel remembered the times he and Jonah and Mark had found themselves in the same situation. Well, not exactly the same. Usually Daniel was the one coerced into staying, Mark used good sense in going home, and Jonah was the one who miraculously produced the bottle. They'd both ended up suffering for it, just as Haynes was now.

He used his teacher voice. "You should have gone home, Mr. Haynes, and not cared what those guys thought."

The woman snorted in a derisive way. Daniel chose to ignore her.

"From there you could have called me, and we would have worked something out."

Michael's eyes sparked. The idea of calling Daniel at nine o'clock obviously hadn't occurred to the boy, whereas calling him at twelve-thirty had.

"I ... I didn't think, I guess. By the time I took a few gulps, suddenly everything looked okay, and I guess I thought I was having fun."

"How did you end up here, so far from your house? You know this bar is off-limits to students. You could be dismissed if anyone found out you were here."

The woman made another sound, this time one of distress. When Daniel glanced her way, she was staring into her cup of coffee. How did she explain working here—living here—and bringing her son to a place he wasn't allowed to be?

Also, in his concern for Haynes, he hadn't fully thought through his own situation. If anyone found out he'd been here tonight, brought Torrington with him and helped conceal Haynes' underage drinking, he'd be tossed out of the academy before he had time to pack. He'd be kissing the headmaster position away, not only here but at any reputable school. They were all taking their chances in this mess.

Michael looked at the woman.

"I guess I told them I knew you, Miss Star. That you and I were friends."

For the first time since starting his tale, Michael looked miserable, and Daniel knew the boy's gloom didn't stem from how he felt physically but from what he was saying.

"They drove me out here, so I could buy more alcohol. The tavern door was locked, though, and when we pounded and no one came, the guys laughed and drove off. I think ... I think I passed out in the parking lot."

He looked at the woman, a question in his eyes.

"That's where I found you."

"And *are* you friends with this lady?"

God help him, Daniel hadn't intended his tone to be censorious, but if the two were "friends" and that information became known, the repercussions could bury them and drag him down, too. Why the hell had he stayed home tonight? If he'd taken Torrington to another dorm and had dinner with Sydney Thomas, he would have had to dodge thinly-veiled suggestions of sex, but he would have been safely out of this damn mess.

"Yes, sir. We've known each other since last summer." The look he threw the woman's way was pure adulation.

"This is just great," Daniel groused, turning to face her. "Do you know what you've done? And who the hell are you, anyway, *Miss Star?*"

She ignored him, focusing instead on Michael. "Do you remember what you told those boys about us?"

About us? Is she admitting *to a damn relationship with the boy?*

"I think I said that, uh, you're a real good cook and that you were teaching me about art."

Hopeful, he turned to Daniel. "These paintings are all Miss Star's. Aren't they good? And she's talented in other ways, too, sir. She's a dancer and has been on stage all over Europe."

Taking a sip of coffee, Daniel deliberately raised his eyes to one of the paintings. A country scene, with trees, fields and a stream, held the signature of Eve Star in the lower right corner. He fervently wished he were there, wherever it was, instead of caught up in this problem that could spell the end of his career.

"Can you close your eyes without getting dizzy, Mr. Haynes?"

The boy tried it. "Yes, sir."

"Just rest for a few minutes. Then you and Mr. Torrington and I will go back to the school. I'll call your house and let them know you're safe, and you'll spend the rest of the weekend with us, okay? We'll discuss penance for tonight's activities when you're feeling a little better."

Haynes blinked at the watery sparkle in his eyes. "Thank you. Thank you both for saving me."

He leaned his head against the back of the sofa and began snoring almost immediately.

Daniel stood. "Shall we talk in the kitchen?" The woman sighed but led the way.

"I feel so awful for that boy," she started, lifting the coffee pot and raising her brows at Daniel.

"No, thanks."

Daniel leaned against the counter and stared at the woman. With only the light over the stove casting a glow, her hair shone like an auburn halo. Her head bowed to blow on the hot liquid in her cup. Full, round breasts rose and fell with each breath, tempting him to touch. Her narrow waist and curvy hips were pure sin and there wasn't anything he wanted to do more than press her against him and explore every curve. He'd never get the chance, considering how tangled she was with Michael Haynes and The Bare Moose.

"Feeling awful. Is that how you happened to put both him and yourself at risk by becoming involved with him?"

Her head snapped up, and eyes he'd fantasized being glazed with lust a brief moment ago now flared with fire.

"We're not involved. He said it, we're friends. My—" she stopped, looked away, took a breath, looked back, "—my son, Timmy, and I were in the park by the river one Sunday last June. I was painting. Michael stopped to talk. We saw him several times in the park after that. I didn't see any harm."

"Didn't see any harm? The boy's infatuated with you, couldn't you tell? Besides, The Bare Moose is a long way from the river." *Fifteen miles from the park, light years from Westover Academy.*

She lifted one shoulder and let it drop. "One Sunday we took a picnic and Michael joined us. He always seemed so alone. When he asked if I knew how to cook pot roast and I said of course, he looked ... I don't know, wistful. So, I asked if his parents would mind if he came to my house for supper the following week, and he assured me they wouldn't. I didn't think it was all that wrong. Until the school year started, I didn't know he attended Westover and he hasn't visited here since then. He's never been inside the tavern, and I certainly *don't* give him alcohol." Her eyes flashed again. "I promise you, we don't engage in anything racier than passing the mashed potatoes or cutting hair."

Daniel frowned. "Cutting hair?"

"Yes. I thought he looked a little shaggy one day, so I cut his hair. Look, he plays with Timmy and tells me jokes and stories. I teach him art. We're company for each other. There's nothing more to it."

Daniel hadn't gotten past Eve's cutting Michael's hair. He could feel her fingers raking through his own hair, skimming his scalp, skating the tips of his ears. His cock rose, hard and throbbing, not caring that he and Eve were strangers and that impressionable children were mere feet away.

"So, you were a dancer?"

She blushed, and the certainty of what caused the blush made his dick ache even more. He'd bet the tassels on his mom's old pasties that he knew exactly what kind of "dancer" Eve Star was.

Evening Star. He could picture what her costume looked like. Battery-powered star headdress to illuminate her path to the center pole, silver lamé cape sailing behind like the tail of a comet, shimmering bra, panties, and high, high heels that showed off her sexy-as-hell legs. He'd bet she made every man in the room salivate and want to become an astronomer, so they could examine her heavenly body up close. Just like Daniel wanted to do right then. The kitchen counter was just the right height to...

He shook his head to clear the image of fucking her senseless on her spotless kitchen counter.

"Dancing's behind me. I run the tavern now."

At least she can do that with her clothes on. Before he commented further, they heard a sound from down the hall. Eve dashed off. Daniel followed more slowly.

Daniel stopped at an open doorway and watched Eve cuddle a snuffling child on her lap.

"It's okay, my darling, I'm here."

Quickly, the child stopped stirring and Eve placed him back in bed.

"Mama loves her baby," she said in a low voice.

Daniel stepped uninvited into the room and walked to the dresser. A framed photo of a smiling dark-haired man caught his eye. "Your husband?" He studied the photo.

"Timmy's father." She brushed the boy's hair from his forehead and came to stand beside Daniel.

She fidgeted, shifting her weight from foot to foot. "Let's go. He's asleep now."

Something about the photo wasn't right. The man looked familiar, maybe an actor or— In a flash of disbelief, he removed the backing from the frame.

"Wait—"

She reached out, but too late to keep Daniel from seeing the printing at the bottom of the folded page indicating the frame was sized four by six and cost nine-ninety-five. *God damn.* She had kept the picture that came with the frame to show Timothy his "father." What kind of woman was this?

There was no sign a man lived there, but Sydney had said she was a widow. She was definitely raising her boy alone. But why not display a real photo of Timmy's father, her husband? For some reason, maybe because he couldn't imagine a guy stupid enough to let Eve Star go, he'd bet she'd never been married. First, she stripped, and now this. She was hiding something. Maybe a great deal, and none of it good.

Hell! The woman who'd most likely be starring in his wet dreams for the foreseeable future, was a girl just like the girl who'd soon marry dear old dad.

***

Eve sighed. Timmy was safe once more from the monsters who chased him in his sleep. If only her own monsters could be dealt with as easily.

She walked past Daniel and back to the kitchen. He came in, hesitated, then poured more coffee for himself.

"Well?" she finally asked, nervous with his silence, and just as nervous wondering what he might say. *Not a lecture, Lord. Please, not a lecture.* If he dared preach what an awful mother she was, she'd have to throw him out. And Daniel Goodman was the first man in ages she definitely didn't want to send away. That Daniel was the person Michael wanted when he was scared and sick spoke to the man's compassion. Dare she hope he'd show her some of the same?

He took a sip, then sighed and stared at her. "I don't know where to begin."

So much for understanding. She'd heard that same opening line from her father more times than she could count, just before he explained how disappointed he was in her.

"If I went to the front office at the academy and looked up Eve Star's address, what would I find?"

Eve blinked. This wasn't the question she expected.

"You wouldn't find Eve Star in your files. But Lauren Knowles resides on a very respectable street in Manchester."

"And Timothy's father?"

She took a deep breath.

"As far as the school is concerned, he died when Timmy was a baby. That's all anyone needs to know." Moisture filled her eyes. She fought back the tears, raising her chin in defiance instead. "He's mine alone. My life and my heart."

"I know you love him very much." He spoke so softly she strained to hear.

Then he cleared his throat and put down his cup. Crossing his arms, he regarded her without the gentleness he'd just displayed. "How long do you think you can get by with a false address? Timothy's bound to spill the beans himself, eventually, that he lives over a bar. He's what? Six? Seven? At that age, they don't know the meaning of the word 'secret'."

"He's six, in first grade. And that's why it's best for him to board at the academy. We don't see each other that often, although I try to take him to dinner once a week or so. When he leaves school for a weekend, it's when I have time off. We go into Boston or somewhere else. We're only here this weekend because an emergency came up. I try to protect him from the tavern. I don't want him here, exposed to the noise and … and the people any more than you do."

Daniel huffed. "And you think that's easy on him? Not being with you every day?"

She turned her head, not wanting him to see the emotion threatening to overwhelm her.

"It's hard on both of you, I know."

There was that gentle tone again. If he kept on like this, she'd be bawling on his shoulder in a few minutes.

"It can't be helped. I really did dance all over Europe. I built up a nest egg, but not enough to live on that nice street in Manchester and pay for Westover Academy. Managing the tavern supports me. And I'm close to the school in case Timmy needs me."

"How do you manage this subterfuge? You think you can get by and not have people see you around town?" He uncrossed his arms and picked up the coffee cup once more.

"Michael knows me only as Eve Star because he saw the name on my paintings. I didn't know he attended Westover or I would have explained myself as Mrs. Knowles."

Daniel snorted his disbelief.

"I have plenty of experience proving that people see what they expect to see." She crossed her arms and looked up in challenge. "I rarely leave the tavern or my apartment, unless it's on an outing with Timmy."

Endless nights of noise punctuated with the odor of whiskey and beer, followed by long, solitary hours in the apartment, flashed through her mind. She pushed them away.

It didn't matter that she hated every inch of the apartment she'd come to know intimately in the days and nights alone, or that she'd tired of working around the drinking and smoke that pervaded taverns and dance halls alike. She longed for a different life but wanted something better for Timmy's future more.

Daniel shook his head. "You've obviously thought this out, but I have a feeling you're going to get yourself and Timothy into trouble. Lies always catch up."

"We'll manage. I just want him to get through this year. Westover Academy is one of the best schools in the country. From here, he can transfer anywhere. At least this year, when he starts his education, there's a respectable reason for why he doesn't have a daddy, and no one has to know that his mommy manages a bar. *This* year we can pretend he's just as good as any other boy there."

"Based on a lie."

"Yes!" She threw her arms up. "A stupid lie, perhaps not as good a lie as you could have composed, but it's done. He's been at school for two months and, so far, everyone but you is happy. Perhaps I'll consult you before I make up my next fantasy family."

She dropped her hands. Her expression grew hard, her gaze determined. "My son is six years old. There's plenty of time for him to face realities."

Daniel formed his lips into a moue. "I believe kids should be allowed to be kids, but..." Turning, he rinsed his coffee cup and set it in the sink. "Okay, let's examine where we are. You: unmarried, former stripper—"

"Exotic dancer."

"—mother to a six-year-old boy. Timothy could be discharged from the academy, not because you're an unwed, former stripper, but because you lied on all of your forms. Instead of a pleasant house in Manchester, you live over a bar, which you manage under your stage name."

Here he stopped and looked to Eve for confirmation. She hesitantly nodded, and he continued.

"Again, this information would get Timothy discharged because this bar is strictly off limits to each and every student. Teachers and even maintenance staff at Westover think twice before coming here. Then there's Michael. You have entertained a teenaged boy in your apartment. Innocent as it is"—he narrowed his eyes and glared at her—"*probably*, it could get you arrested and Michael discharged for being here. Michael was drunk tonight, which would also get him tossed. I'll try to handle the problem with your name tomorrow, when he can remember what

I tell him."

Daniel studied the floor silently and then spoke as though to himself. "Then there's me. Tied by contract and duty to enforce the rules of Westover Academy and morally bound to protect Westover students, I'm thrust into the middle of all this. And circumstances forced Jeffrey Torrington into the mess, too. If I come clean with the front office about everything, I can probably salvage my job but my appointment as headmaster will be forfeited. But if I say nothing, *and* if everyone else plays their part, we can all skate by. Maybe."

He nodded to the floor and scraped his hand over the back of his neck. "Christ. I can't believe I'm even thinking this, but it might work."

Facing Eve, he looked determined. "A few things have to change."

"Like what?" Her heart hammered. All she'd worked for, all she wanted for Timmy was now in this man's care.

He shook his head. "Hell if I know right now. We'll have to feel our way through this mess. I'd better get the boys back to school. I'll call you later and make sure we're straight."

She shouldn't trust him. Every man she'd ever known had an agenda or an angle of some kind. "If it wasn't for this headmaster job you want, you'd come clean with the front office and we'd be out. You're only willing to go along for your own gain."

"Lady, I should *have* that headmaster job. I've worked hard for it, and I'm making sacrifices you can't begin to understand. But if we're caught, I'll most likely end up beside you in jail for contributing to the delinquency of minors, so forget my career goals. I'm doing this for two reasons only. One, for the boys. They don't deserve being punished because of our foolish decisions."

Could she believe him? "And the second?"

He blew out a breath and shook his head.

"For some reason, I kind of like you. I think you're an idiot for taking chances with your son's success and happiness, but I understand your motivations."

She couldn't believe what she heard. Hard experience had taught her not to trust men, but Daniel Goodman inspired trust. In her heart, she knew. This man who'd come into her life under the strangest of circumstances, this tall, good-looking man, with the dark brown hair and even darker brown-green eyes, was worth his weight in gold. Just like his name, he was a good man.

Without thinking, Eve strode across the floor, rose on tiptoe and kissed Daniel's cheek.

His eyes narrowed. "Be careful. A woman like you is bound to have noticed a man's reaction to you."

Fury rushed through her. Disappointment followed on its heels. She'd thought he was different. "A woman like me? Has it ever occurred to you that there are only women like me because there are men like you?"

Daniel's gaze softened and he gave a quick shake of his head. "That came out wrong, but you have to know how beautiful you are. Nothing would please me more right now than to explore who you are in every way a man can explore a woman. But, as a patron, you're off limits, and at least *some* of the school's rules should be obeyed."

He smelled of coffee and spice. And more—something woodsy and fresh. Despite good sense telling her to back away, she wished he'd hold her.

"What if I don't want to be off-limits?" she whispered.

His gaze rose to her hair then dropped to her mouth. Fire flared in his eyes."I must be out of my mind, but maybe we'll discuss that later, too."

Her hands went to Daniel's shoulders and once again she rose, this time for a full kiss. First brushing his mouth, she dipped her tongue through his parted lips and tested the heat. His hands clasped her waist then slid around and down to her butt before pulling her against his erection. His lips devoured her mouth.

God, how long had it been? Years since Timmy's conception, years since his father had cursed her for getting pregnant and thrown her into the streets. Years since she'd trusted any man, even for casual relief of her needs. Not until this man, whose compassion for her son and Michael outweighed his own desires. She wanted him with a fierceness she'd never known.

He broke the kiss, saving them both from an unforgivable situation if any of the children had awakened. Something else she had to thank him for.

"I need to get the boys back to school." He bent to nibble her neck.

She pulled her hair away, giving him more access. "I suppose so."

He straightened and pushed her back a few inches. "Too bad it's not up to only us, what we'd like to do." His lopsided grin melted her heart. Then he slipped by her to wake Michael and Jeffrey.

For a second, she leaned against the counter. She didn't know where their kiss would lead. An affair? A relationship could only complicate things further, but she was so ready to be held again, to pretend there were happy-ever-after endings and real Prince Charmings.

Yes, she'd be happy to have an affair with Daniel Goodman, but there was no need wishing for more. She knew the odds were small that she'd find a man willing to marry a former exotic dancer with a son in tow. Considering that Daniel Goodman's ambition included a high position at one of the most prestigious schools in the country, a woman of her background would not be an asset.

For now, things had to remain as they were. Before she'd jeopardize Timothy's welfare, she'd do far more than lie about her background or go without the comfort of a man.

After all, she had before.

Chapter Five

"Right there ... right there. *Oh, yeah, that's it."*

Daniel reached for Eve's breasts, full and heavy in his hands just as he knew they'd be. Her nipples stiffened at the merest brush of his thumbs. He lifted his head and took one dusky tip in his mouth. She arched into him, offering more. He accepted, swirling his tongue around the pebbled nipple after lightly scraping his teeth over it.

His hands gripped her hips, guiding her, steadying her as she rose and fell over his dick. Her hands wandered all over him—across his shoulders, down his arms, through his hair, around his ears. She was driving him senseless. Her pussy was tight and wet and fiery *hot, branding his dick with every thrust, making every other pussy in the world seem unappealing. He never wanted this to end.*

"You're off limits," he mumbled, hating to relinquish her breast to speak.

"What if I don't want to be off limits?" she whispered. "What if I want to fuck you every which way to Sunday?"

"Do it," he moaned. "Oh, baby, just do it."

Her knees bracketed his waist, opening wide to allow him the deepest penetration, and, God! He thought he touched the back of her womb. She ground against him and he shot off, filling her with everything he had.

Groaning her name, he ... woke himself.

Half sitting, fully groggy, Daniel looked to see the time. Three o'clock. He'd been in bed only a couple of hours before she'd invaded his sleep. He couldn't remember a more realistic wet dream. Good thing he'd worn pajama bottoms to bed, in deference to the two boys sleeping on his pullout sofa. Steady, deep breathing coming from the living room assured him he hadn't woken Michael and Jeffrey with his dream. Well, *he* was awake. He stumbled to the bathroom and cleaned himself.

Hell, all he'd wanted was a little free time to himself over the weekend. Instead, he had two boys sleeping on his sofa, a very real chance he could lose his job and damage his career, and a female invading his thoughts and dreams. Not a female he could pursue, nor one good for his future—in fact, just the sort he'd sworn his whole life to avoid. He loved his mother, but dealing with one free-spirited, uninhibited woman was quite enough. Been there, done that, looking to trade the tee shirt for a button-down Oxford.

That's what made the instant attraction he'd felt with Eve Star/ Lauren Knowles so dangerous. Forget an affair, he couldn't afford even a friendship with her. She managed a bar, she'd proven she was a liar—regardless of her justifications—and no one associated with the academy would approve.

He cringed at the last reason for keeping his distance, feeling like a prick. But even in her "respectable" persona, as Lauren Knowles, she was a school patron, putting her firmly in the unavailable column.

The plain fact was, he trod a very thin line when it came to his possible appointment as headmaster. Jonah didn't understand how much the appointment meant, how hard he'd worked, how much he wanted to do at the academy. Perhaps Daniel should have described it in racing terms. His becoming headmaster was equivalent to Jonah's team winning every race in the NASCAR circuit—every year.

But he was far from a shoo-in. Ethical standards at Westover Academy were very high, and the board unbending. Anything could topple his chances. The last thing Daniel needed was a relationship with Mrs. Knowles, a patron of the academy. Then there was Eve Star. Every day, she risked recognition as manager of one of the area's most disreputable taverns, and as a former stripper, with a fabulous body and sensual moves.

Eve Star or Lauren Knowles, she wasn't for him. On that finality, he collapsed on his bed and fell back to sleep.

***

"Jonah? This is your brother. If you're there, pick up."

Daniel cast an eye to the coffee pot. Almost ready. The oatmeal simmered and thickened as he watched. He lowered his voice, hearing the boys in the living room.

"Okay, you're not there. I'm calling to be sure you haven't forgotten about Jeffrey Torrington's NASCAR cap. He's had kind of a hard week, so I know he'll appreciate a treat. Also, in case I didn't make it clear last week, let me reiterate that I won't be attending the nuptials at

Thanksgiving. I'm letting you know in case Mom asks you. I'll call her myself and tell her, but you might talk to her before I do. Okay, take it easy."

He hung up just as Torrington charged into the small space followed by a much more reluctant Michael. The toaster popped. Placing the toast on the table, he pointed out the butter to Torrington and the carton of orange juice to Michael.

"I spoke to someone named Joseph last night, Mr. Haynes, and let him know you were here. But have you called your parents?"

He spooned oatmeal into three bowls. Michael Haynes looked as though he'd seen much better days. Daniel hid a smile. There was nothing like the morning after being drunk. He only hoped this was Michael's first experience and that it taught the young man a lesson.

"I talked with Joseph."

Daniel looked up.

Through his paleness, Michael reddened. "Joseph is the head of household staff. He said he'd tell my parents where I am when he spoke with them." He put the juice carton in the refrigerator. "No one would have realized I was gone all night if you hadn't called."

Fucking hell! Why do some people even have children? He didn't let anger for Michael's parents inflect his voice when he spoke, trying to save the kid from further embarrassment. "Okay, we're covered then."

He finished distributing the oatmeal and set the pan on a cool stove burner. "Good job, Mr. Torrington," he said, approving the buttering job. "Gentlemen, let's have breakfast and then we'll set our plans for this glorious autumn Sunday."

At the word *breakfast*, Michael's face lost color again.

"You're going to feel really lousy for most of the day," Daniel informed him with a grin. "But you'll do better than you think after some food, followed by lots of fresh air and exercise."

"Thanks," Michael said in a low voice.

"Any time," Daniel said cheerfully.

They took their seats and began the meal, Torrington and Daniel with more enthusiasm than Michael. They ate in silence, forgoing the tasteful discourse the boys were encouraged to join while in the dining hall.

"What are we going to do today, Mr. Goodman?" Torrington asked, emptying his juice glass, then taking his final spoonful of oatmeal.

Daniel placed the empty bowls and glasses in the sink. "What would you like to do?"

Michael looked as though he'd like nothing better than to return to bed. *No chance, hotshot.*

Torrington's eyes lit up. "Could we go biking at Great Glens? My uncle keeps saying we'll go when he comes for the weekend, but we never find time."

Daniel considered for a moment. He'd ridden the trails near the town of Gorham many times. He knew of a few that wouldn't be too strenuous for Torrington and would provide exactly the kind of exercise Haynes needed.

"That's a good idea. Would you enjoy that, Mr. Haynes? The foliage is beautiful, the day is beautiful, and it'll be totally different than anything we could do here at school."

"I guess." Michael's voice exhibited even less eagerness than his expression.

Daniel resumed his seat and wrapped his hands around the warm cup filled with coffee. "Before we do anything, though, we must have a serious talk and come to a few understandings."

Michael, evidently feeling Daniel's wrath was about to descend, dipped his head.

"Michael, I want you to look at me while I'm talking. This mostly applies to you." Daniel's heart twisted at the look of misery on the boy's face, but he kept his emotions to himself. What the boy needed now was firm guidance, not friendly sympathy.

"All of us are in a bad situation right now because of actions taken last night. When you chose to stay with those boys and drink, you thought you were doing something that would only affect you. But in the end, what happened involved Mrs. Knowles and her son, and Mr. Torrington and me. It's put us all in the position of having to keep quiet about where we were and what we were doing, or risk punishment."

"I didn't mean to cause any trouble." The boy's eyes sparkled with tears, though he kept them under control.

"I'm certain of that and I'm not saying you did it on purpose. But I want you to learn that actions—all actions—have consequences, good or bad. In this case, the costs could be very high. You're an underage boy, you were drunk in the apartment of a grown woman who happens to live above a bar."

Michael's brows puckered in thought. Daniel saw the look in his eyes the moment Michael realized what he was leading to.

"But … but Miss Star didn't do anything wrong. Honest! She's the nicest lady and—"

"Who's Miss Star?" Torrington asked. He slid an innocent look from Daniel to Michael and back.

"I'll explain in just a minute," Daniel said. He focused on Michael again. "I know you didn't intend it, but Mrs. Knowles would still be in a lot of trouble while you and she were trying to explain the situation."

Daniel glanced to make sure Jeffrey Torrington was paying attention, too. He was, with a rapt expression.

"Plus, for reasons of her own, she uses one name for her job and another for her son, who's enrolled here at the academy. Do you know why she might do that?"

Soberly, Michael nodded. "Because they probably wouldn't let Timmy come if they knew she ran The Bare Moose." He looked up with a flare of passion lighting his eyes and tingeing his cheeks pink. "And that's so unfair. Just because she works there doesn't make her any worse than someone who owns a software company."

"*Someone*" *who owns a software company*, Daniel thought, *like Michael's father.*

"At least she loves her son and wants to spend time with him," Michael continued, morosely.

"You're right," Daniel agreed. "She seems like a nice lady, which makes it doubly wrong that any of us would do something to hurt her or her boy."

Torrington nodded, as though he understood completely. Michael compressed his lips and nodded, too.

"What about you, Mr. Goodman? Are you in trouble, too?" Torrington asked the question quietly.

"Yes. I took you with me last night, into an uncertain situation." He gave Michael a long look. "And I decided to forget what I saw and heard at The Bare Moose, which would have serious repercussions here at the academy if it came out."

"You mean you could get fired," Michael whispered.

Daniel nodded. "Yes, I would be let go. But more importantly, you would be expelled and so would Timothy Knowles, for different reasons."

He looked at each boy and finally let a smile touch his lips. "So, men.

We must agree to forget about last night. No telling our friends what we did Saturday; no bragging about drinking." Michael shook his head violently and then seemed to regret it.

"No talking about going out late and ending up in Mrs. Knowles's apartment."

Torrington shook his head, his eyes sparkling, probably with the thought of being included in something so adult.

"No telling people we know anyone named Miss Star."

"I know Tim Knowles. He's on the lacrosse team."

"Well, Mr. Torrington, you might someday meet his mother around school. She's Mrs. Knowles, and that's all you should ever call her."

"Yes, sir. She's nice. I liked her last night."

Daniel smiled openly at the boys for the first time that morning. "So, are we set, guys?"

"Yes, sir," Torrington said, excitedly jumping up and racing off to dress.

Michael placed his hand on Daniel's arm. "Thank you for helping me, Mr. Goodman, but why are you doing it?"

The boy sat rigidly. Questions filled his eyes and he appeared to be holding his breath. Daniel carefully worded his answer.

"Because you're a good man, Mr. Haynes. Your judgment could have been a little better last night, but you didn't do anything most guys haven't done, myself included. The trick here is to learn from what you did wrong. I hope next time you're disappointed and at loose ends, you'll think about what you *should* do as well as what you *want* to do. If you'd called me when you arrived home and found your plans changed, I would have come to get you."

"You would have?"

Moisture sparkled in the boy's eyes once more. Daniel wanted to punch Michael's father in the worst way. He had a fine son and he treated Michael like dirt.

"Of course. You could have watched the baseball game with Mr. Torrington and me. It wasn't as exciting as your evening perhaps, but you'd feel a whole lot better right now."

Michael stared a moment then solemnly nodded his head before standing.

Forty minutes later, Daniel rented bicycles for the three of them. By the time they set off on the Cascade Falls trail, both boys were laughing.

Jeffrey Torrington was full of jokes second graders found hilarious, and Michael's coloring and disposition were much improved as he laughed at the silly things, despite himself.

Remembering his dream of the morning, Daniel wished his own needs and desires could be satisfied as easily. Unfortunately, it would take more than a bike ride to make him feel better.

***

"Mrs. Knowles!"

Eve raised her head, looking beyond Timmy's dormitory to see who called. From the adjoining dorm, Michael Haynes and Jeffrey Torrington walked at a fast pace. They looked very different this Monday evening than they had Saturday night, dressed as they were in academy uniforms of dark blue blazers with matching trousers, white shirts, and gray and blue striped ties. She always had to brace her heart when she helped Timmy get back into his uniform for the return to campus. He morphed immediately from an adorable ragamuffin in his ratty tennis shoes and jeans into a little man. It surprised her how much she hated seeing that change, and how much Timmy seemed to take pride in it.

"Look, Mommy, it's Michael and Jeff."

She looked down and stroked her son's hair. "I didn't realize you knew Jeffrey Torrington."

"He's on my lacrosse team." He looked at her with warm brown eyes and smiled. "He's not any better than I am and he's a year older."

She smiled back. How could she not? "I'm sure you'll both get better the more you practice."

By then, the two boys had arrived.

"Hello, Mrs. Knowles," Michael said with a shy smile, then looked down at Timmy. "Hi, Tim."

Jeffrey Torrington grinned. "Hi, Tim. Hi, Mrs. Knowles. Mr. Goodman told us to look out for you in case you needed any help. Tim, do you know what we did yesterday? We went biking up at Cascade Falls and afterward we went to this really neat restaurant where the river actually flowed under us. It was so cool." Unlike the sleepy, reserved Jeffrey of Saturday, this boy was full of life and energy.

"Wow. That sounds so neat. We just walked around Riverside Park and went home for hot dogs." Tim picked up his overnight suitcase and he and Jeff started slowly toward Tim's dorm. "Where's Cascade Falls, Jeff? I know how to ride a bike but..." Their voices faded as they strolled off.

Eve watched Timmy walk away without a backward glance and had to blink to keep the tears at bay. This is why she'd brought him here. For an excellent education and to gain independence. As an only child growing up in a single-parent household, Timmy could too easily come to lean on her. That's what she told herself. What she really feared was that in centering her world around her son, she'd smother him. Letting go, though, was so damn *hard*.

"You look very pretty today, Mrs. Knowles," Michael said with a shy smile.

With relief, Eve turned her attention back to the young man standing beside her. "Thank you very much, Michael." The teal silk pantsuit had cost her a fortune in Paris, even on sale. The only fun in coming to the Westover campus was dressing in the clothes she'd purchased in Europe, when she'd had money to burn.

Michael fell into step with her as she started a slow walk toward the door into Timmy's dorm building.

"Did you enjoy this amazing bicycle trip?"

"Yes, ma'am. It was great. Mr. Goodman is a lot of fun."

"So you had a good weekend after all. No ill effects?"

"I felt pretty rough yesterday morning, but Mr. Goodman got us up early and made us eat oatmeal." The tone he used made her smile. "Then we drove up to Gorham and after a little while I felt better."

Michael stopped. She took a couple of steps then turned back when she realized he was no longer walking. He shuffled his feet, staring at the ground.

She tilted her head. "Michael? Are you all right?"

He let out a hard breath. "Mrs. Knowles, I want to apologize for what happened. Mr. Goodman explained that I could have gotten you into a lot of trouble. And Timmy, too. I'm really sorry and I want you to know I'll use much better judgment in the future."

Eve wanted to hug him but instead, linked her fingers and stood calmly.

"Thank you. I know you wouldn't do anything to purposely hurt Timmy or me."

He pressed his lips together and nodded. "You and Mr. Goodman won't have to worry about me again." He started forward.

Before they reached the doorway, Timmy and Jeff burst out.

"Mom, Jeff says they might go biking again before it gets snowy. If Mr. Goodman says it's okay, can I go, too?"

"What?" Taken aback, Eve looked from Timmy's face to Michael's, Jeff's and back to Timmy's. His eyes were wide and shining. "I don't know, Timmy," she said, "we'll have to see."

"Let's go ask him now if it'll be okay," Jeff said in a rush, and before Eve could say anything, they started for the grass separating them from the other building.

"Jeff, stay off the grass," Michael called out softly.

Jeff turned and grinned at Michael. "Oh, yeah. Thanks."

Timmy ran back and threw his arms around Eve's waist. "Bye, Mom. I had a great time this weekend."

She bent for a quick kiss and before she straightened again, the boys were off, down the sidewalk this time.

"Do you want to go over and ask Mr. Goodman yourself?" Michael asked.

"No, I'll wait and see what happens. Thanks."

She'd planned to extend the holiday by offering to take Timmy to a local grill for an early dinner, but now that he had found a friend and mission, she had no further business to keep her. Slowly, she turned and started back toward the parking area. Michael accompanied her, chit-chatting on the way.

"Oh, look. Here comes Mr. Goodman," he said when they'd almost reached her car.

She hadn't realized how much she'd hoped to see Daniel until Michael made the announcement. Pivoting, she watched him approaching at a fast pace. Their gazes connected even at the distance of several yards. She had a general impression of a suit and some kind of dark robe that billowed behind him with his stride, but mainly what she noticed were his eyes, filled with heat, and his mouth.

Their kiss from Saturday night came to mind. He'd tasted of spice and smelled of the woods. His hands holding her against his arousal had been firm and warm. Hell, all of him had been warm and he'd sparked the same in her. After so many years away from the flame, she craved the heat.

"Mrs. Knowles," he said, standing before her. Then he smiled at Michael. "You and Mr. Torrington did a great job. Perhaps you'd better check in with your dorm master now, Mr. Haynes."

"Yes, sir." He glanced at Eve and back at Daniel, hesitant. "I want to thank you both for what you did for me. You rescued me. And I won't forget what you said, Mr. Goodman."

Daniel put his hand on Michael's shoulder. "I'm glad you spent your weekend with us, Mr. Haynes. I had fun. I'll see you in class tomorrow."

"Bye, Michael. Have a good week," Eve said.

The boy raised his hand in farewell. He had that wistful look in his eyes, the one that had called for her to befriend him to begin with and which had gotten them all in hot water. The boy nodded and walked back toward campus.

A car passed along the drive and two students, already changed into sports clothes, walked by, bouncing a basketball between them. Still, Eve wondered what the possibility was Daniel would kiss her. *Slim to nil*, she decided.

"I hope you don't mind. I asked the boys to watch for you, thinking it might be hard for Timothy when you left."

"He usually starts to cry when I go, though he tries to hide it." She felt her own tears again and blinked them away. "It's as hard on me, I'm afraid."

"If nothing else, Mr. Torrington can talk someone's mind off a problem."

Laughing, she said, "He is a good distraction."

"He drives me *to* distraction sometimes but he's a good boy."

"I could see your affection for him the other night."

"Which brings me to why I followed you. I meant to call sooner, but we've been busy."

"So I heard." Being so near to him set her heart pounding.

"There are a few things, actually." He smiled lightly into her eyes, took her elbow, and turned her. "I'll walk you to your car. I have only a few minutes."

Once traveling in the right direction, he removed his hand. "First, I had a talk with the boys. They understand the need to forget Saturday night happened, and Michael knows he's not to visit you. Second, Jeffrey and Timothy just asked about Timothy's joining us when we take another outing. I don't know when that will be, but of course he'd be welcome, with your permission." He frowned. "Third, we have that kiss to discuss."

They reached her car and faced each other. "Kiss?" It took every bit of stage presence to act as though she'd forgotten.

For a moment, he looked nonplussed. Then he smiled, seeming half embarrassed. "My mistake."

She couldn't leave him thinking she'd forgotten. Indeed, she'd lain awake for hours Saturday, reliving it until she could almost feel his hand on her breast and then his weight on her body. But an imagination could only take her so far.

"Sorry, I was teasing. What is there to discuss?"

He searched her eyes then looked away at the sound of boys' voices heading their way. "It shouldn't happen again. You're a patron of the school. If I am promoted, we'll be working together on a business level."

Eve didn't look away as the three kids passed nearby. "But..."

The smile he gave was primal before he brought it under control. "I think you know I want to explore where such a kiss would take us. But it's not a good idea. I have ... things to consider."

"You mean your promotion."

"Yes. I need to set an example. But more than that, there's your reputation. I wouldn't want to risk questions being asked. You have as much to lose as I have." He studied her eyes. "Or maybe much more. How could I take the chance of harming you or Timothy?"

At that moment, she'd have given him anything within her power. No one in her adult life had worried over her reputation or her dreams. Only, as in the case of Timmy's father, their own prestige.

"Can we meet and discuss this further?"

His lips pressed together, and his face set in a hard expression. She imagined this was how his dormitory wards felt, willingly doing penance for their wrongdoings, not out of fear but from knowing they'd disappointed Mr. Goodman. She'd made things harder for him by insisting they meet instead of accepting gracefully that they shouldn't.

"It's really not a good idea. I'm thinking of your reputation here, as well as academy rules. The more you're seen around town, the more questions will be raised. Being seen with school personnel can only make speculation worse."

"Please. I have no real friends here. No one but you knows who I am." She saw his deep breath, the indecision cross his face, and she continued. "I plan to be at the farmers' market in Overbridge tomorrow at four-thirty."

His smile was slow. "Believe me, if things were different, *you* wouldn't have to ask *me*. I've never known anyone else who could tempt me to color outside the lines, Mrs. Knowles."

She imagined he used her "married" name in order to remind her of where they were. Of *who* they were.

"Please call me Eve. It's been a very long time since I was known as Lauren Knowles. I hardly think of myself that way."

Daniel smiled. "To tell the truth, I do think of you as Eve. But as Eve or Lauren, our meeting again outside school activities is not a good idea."

Eve smiled. "Well, thanks anyway." She stepped back. "I do appreciate your including Timmy in your next outing."

"It will be my pleasure to have him with us. He seems like a fine boy." He also stepped back. "Take care, now."

He held the car door for her, then turned and strode back to the dormitory as briskly as he'd come.

Eve watched him with regret. If the real-life Daniel Goodman was half as good as her dream Daniel, letting him go could be the mistake of a lifetime. In this case, she had the feeling real life surpassed her dreams by a wide margin. Only knowing that being with her would destroy his dreams kept her in the car.

For the first time while driving off the school grounds, tears stung from leaving more than her son.

Chapter Six

Stan Baxter walked beside Daniel as they made their way from the English building to the dorm area. "Friday, and classes are over at last! After a short day tomorrow, most of the little monsters go home for Sunday and leave me in peace."

Daniel snorted a laugh. "Your dedication truly amazes me. Don't you have any duties this weekend?"

"Only—Oh my God, there she is again." Stan looked as though he was going to cross himself in reverence. Daniel followed his friend's gaze and his heart about stopped. There *she* was, indeed, walking toward the dorms at a leisurely pace. In a minute, maybe less, their paths would intersect.

On a hanger, the suit she wore wouldn't be the least bit alluring. On Eve, it screamed S-E-X. A rich, royal purple, the long-sleeved tailored jacket hugged her hips. A thick black leather belt cinched her waist until he thought he could encircle it with his hands. The skirt stopped just above her knees, after molding her thighs into a perfect column. A scarf that matched the color of the golden autumn leaves drifting to the ground around them covered one shoulder, and her glorious auburn hair, brushed to one side and left loose, draped over the scarf.

The men stared in sheer admiration. Eve seemed not to know they were there.

Stan rubbed his hands as though anticipating a feast. "What a body. I can see her now, naked, with her legs spread and her hair all over my pillow—"

"Knock it off," Daniel scolded. The younger man turned a surprised face toward him. Daniel frowned to back up the harsh tone. "She's a student's mother and deserves respect, not you undressing her in your mind."

"Sorry. She doesn't know, so no harm done." Stan waited a beat before adding, "How do women walk on those spikes?"

"Practice."

Her heels did seem impossibly high, bringing his gaze from her ankles up, up, up, impossibly higher, past the hem of her skirt to the bottom of her jacket. His imagination normally could have had her undressed in a matter of lust-induced moments, but with the Eve-inspired wet dreams he'd been having all week, his imagination didn't have to strain much. Instead, he struggled to display a genial, friendly expression. The way he would for any patron.

Every day, an upper form boy watched each dormitory, allowing the dorm master some free time. Daniel normally spent his interlude grading papers and preparing for the next day's classes, but sometimes he went off campus for dinner or shopping. Last Tuesday he'd taken advantage of his free hours to stroll around the Overbridge farmers' market, despite having lectured himself all morning about why it was disastrous for him to go. For a man with the single-minded goal of achieving headmaster status, he showed an amazing weakness for the woman he'd termed *Evening Star* in his fantasies. There she shone bright and true, guiding his lust and imagination to that heavenly place he just *knew* lay between her thighs.

At the market, he'd seen her from the back as she picked through a bin of pears, and known her immediately, even without the sexy sway of her luscious ass. Unlike today, her clothes had been loose-fitting, her hair covered in a scarf, and the softness of her shoulders hidden beneath a leather bombardier jacket.

As though they'd met by accident, Daniel had picked out a ripe pear and glanced her way. He'd spoken a friendly hello and she'd turned. Her smile could have lighted the whole state of New Hampshire. After that, he'd rambled with her through the displays of pumpkins and apples and all manner of other things, stopping to appreciate a color or shape, but really unaware of anything except her scent, the warmth of her hand when she touched his arm or the way her voice fell over him like a gentle spring shower.

They'd had a quick cup of coffee at one of the stalls, and just as he'd moved closer, just as he'd seen a welcoming gleam in her eyes, just as he'd imagined his dick inching through her pubic hair, plowing the furrow of her pussy lips and finally—greedily—sinking shaft deep inside her…he'd heard his name called.

He'd flashed Eve a warning look, gritted his teeth and turned to greet Sydney Thomas. End of afternoon tryst. End of fantasy.

Just as well, he'd thought at the time. Having anything to do with Eve Star except in his dreams spelled career meltdown. He'd be crazy to take the risk.

And maybe that was why he'd pursued her, conservatively but steadily. In his whole life, Daniel had never been crazy or taken risks. Wild and woolly, letting-go-of-the-reins-of-life had been the purview of the rest of his family, except Mark, who seemed not to know or care about such concepts. At times he'd wished he could be more like Jonah, and even his parents, but until Eve he'd never acted on the desire.

Daniel had called Eve several times since their farmers' market meeting, but with Sydney in town and complications with work, he hadn't been able to get away again that week. With each explanation of why he couldn't leave campus, her tone had become cooler. And now here she was, and he didn't know how he'd be able to contain his rampant libido.

Stan slowed their progress. Daniel suspected his unhurried gait was to postpone their arrival at the crosswalk and ensure their meeting Eve. And it worked.

"Hello," Stan said, showing bright eyes and sparkling teeth. "I saw you last weekend but didn't have the chance to introduce myself. I'm Stan Baxter, an English teacher here at Westover."

Eve smiled back and took his outstretched hand. "Hello. I'm Lauren Knowles."

Then she turned her gaze to Daniel. Her eyes flashed, and her cheeks hinted at a lovely shade of pink. His cock started rising and he fought it down by mentally listing Shakespeare's tragedies. At the same time, he noticed how utterly kissable her lips were.

"It's nice to see you again, Mrs. Knowles," Daniel said smoothly.

"You know each other?" Stan shot him an accusatory look.

"Not well." *Not nearly as well as I want to.* "Her son asked to come along on a trip I have planned, and I needed to ask Mrs. Knowles' permission."

"Oh."

As though prearranged, Eve took her place between the men and they strolled slowly toward Daniel's dormitory, which was next to Timothy's.

"Have you gentlemen had a busy week?"

Was that a backdoor question to determine if he told the truth when he begged off seeing her?

"I certainly have," Daniel said. "There don't seem to be enough hours in the day, sometimes."

"You had time for dinner with the daughter of the chairman of the board on Wednesday," Stan chided.

I'm gonna kill him. He stifled the urge to see Eve's reaction.

"That was business."

Stan snorted. "I use my precious free hours for relaxation." He sighed loudly. "I hate eating alone on nights I go off campus. *I'd* like to dine with a beautiful, intelligent woman once in a while."

If he doesn't die in my first attempt, I'll keep at it until I get the job done. "Next time I'll send you to dinner with Sydney." Daniel finally looked at Eve. "That's Sydney Thomas, the daughter of the board chairman."

"With whom you had time for dinner, when you were so busy." She smiled but it appeared false.

"I *was* busy," he muttered, his previous good mood souring.

Eve seemed to shift her whole body and attention closer to Stan. "I do sympathize with your dining problems, and I wish I could help. I've been known to enjoy a good meal with a nice-looking man who can carry on a reasonable conversation. Unfortunately, no such man has invited me to dinner since I moved to your lovely state."

Daniel could almost see Stan's chest puff out. "I'd love to take you to dinner, Mrs. Knowles. I'm a native of the area, so I could give you the cook's tour, too."

Idiot! As if she needs a good tour guide. "I'm sure Mrs. Knowles doesn't need any of your help—"

"I'd *love* to be shown the town by a real native, Mr. Baxter. How wonderful of you to suggest it. You're the very nicest person I've met here"—she cast a cold glance at Daniel—"not that everyone at Westover Academy hasn't been very nice. You promise now, don't you? I've found people sometimes say they'll do something but there's no follow-through."

"Stan..." Daniel's tone was meant to warn off his friend. It didn't.

"You worry too much, Daniel." Stan looked at Eve. "There's an unspoken rule against fraternization between patrons and staff." Stan looked around her to Daniel. "But it's not written anywhere, and we're talking about a friendly, helpful gesture here. It's not as though there's a conflict of interest. I don't have your son as one of my students."

"You sound quite reasonable, Mr. Baxter."

"Call me Stan, please."

"Well, Stan," she said on a sigh, "I live in Manchester, quite a distance away, and most often I spend all of my time with my son when I'm here, but perhaps I can find the time on one of my trips…"

She slowed and then stopped at the sidewalk leading to Timothy's dorm. "Thank you so much for the pleasant walk. Lucky me to have two handsome men escort me across campus."

Eve held out her hand. "Goodbye, Stan. Maybe I'll see you on my next trip."

"I hope so, Lauren. May I call you that?"

She smiled. "Of course."

Still smiling, she faced Daniel. "It was nice seeing you again, Mr. Goodman. Please let me know when you need my permission for Timmy to accompany you on an outing. And I do hope you find a few minutes in your busy schedule to relax this weekend."

"And you, Mrs. Knowles."

"Oh, I usually find weekends are my busiest times, so I doubt I'll have a free moment. If you'll excuse me now…" With another wave at Stan, she turned and walked away. Her hips swished as each long leg stretched out to eat up the distance to the building.

Only after she entered the dorm did the men continue toward Daniel's apartment in the adjacent building.

"That was a stupid thing to do," Daniel said.

Stan chortled. "You're just sorry you didn't think of it first."

"Yeah, right," Daniel muttered.

"To tell the truth, she seemed a little cool to you. This is a first. Me—shorter, dorkier, master's degree instead of a doctorate. Usually you're the one women go for. I like being on this end of the stick for a change."

"This has nothing to do with attracting women in general," Daniel said, opening the private door to his apartment, "it has to do with *that* woman. Don't get involved."

Stan shook his head and patted Daniel's shoulder. "Envy does not become you, my friend." He crossed the small room and opened the refrigerator for a Coke. "So, what *are* you doing this weekend?"

"This weekend," Daniel repeated, trying to get his mind off Eve and back to business. "Well, Sydney came to town this week for something. She never was clear what she had in mind, though her dad was supposed to join us for dinner Wednesday—"

"Ha," Stan said, dropping into a chair. "She wants your body, that's why she was in town, and I'm sure she made up the story about her dad being here in order to get you to dinner."

Secretly, Daniel feared Stan was right. "Whatever. She promises he'll join us Sunday, so I'm driving to Boston."

"Ouch! Lots of driving for a dinner."

"It'll be an early afternoon brunch but, yeah, I'll be tired for class Monday. To tell the truth, Mr. Thomas spent a lot of time talking to Andy Worth at the headmaster's tea last weekend. I know I was late, but he didn't even say hello."

"Andy Worth hasn't got a chance. Besides your qualifications for headmaster—which are many—you've got another thing going for you, buddy." Stan took a slug of soda. "Sydney wants you, and if she gets you, she wants you to be more than a lowly department head. You'll be headmaster because she's thinking of her future as well as yours."

"Hell, Stan, that makes me sound like I'm sleeping my way to the top."

Stan's eyes widened. "You're *sleeping* with her?"

Daniel shot a look at the door into the dorm. "Shh! Keep your voice down. No, I'm not sleeping with her, but you know what I mean."

Stan shrugged. "Hey, if you were, no one could blame you, I guess. She's gorgeous as well as influential with her father." He waggled his brows. "Not as gorgeous as Lauren Knowles, though. Woo-hoo! That woman is hot with a capital H." He snapped upright. "Hey, I've got an idea. You'll be driving right through Manchester on your way to Boston. I can call Lauren and see if she's free. You can drop me off and pick me up on your way back."

Shit! He was afraid just this sort of thing would happen.

"Not a good idea, Stan. Besides, she said she was going to be busy all weekend."

"She might make time for me. I'm going to call her." He looked at his watch and sighed. "Almost time to gather the angels together and find out who has plans to go off campus this evening. You've got it easy being dorm master with little kids, Daniel."

"Yeah, remind me of that when I'm up all night with a little guy puking his guts out and crying for his mama."

Stan huffed out a laugh. "You think that doesn't happen with the high school kids?"

Daniel laughed, too, as he showed Stan out. Then he made his plans for the evening. His dorm assistant would arrive in an hour and he'd be free for three hours after that. Rather than spend the time doing what he should—writing a parody based on *Romeo and Juliet* that his junior level students would appreciate—he'd wait for Eve. She'd taken Timothy to dinner, but he had to be back by five, giving Daniel two hours afterward to talk some sense into her.

She'd played with fire today but not the kind he desired.

***

Daniel was waiting by Eve's car after she left Timmy in his room. He looked grim, which somehow made him appear adorable rather than fierce.

Head high, she unlocked the door and tossed in her purse before facing him.

"Aren't you too *busy* to be standing here waiting for me?"

"Eve, don't you have any sense? Flirting with Stan will cause problems."

"Don't talk to me about having sense. I understand men, and I know if your girlfriend hadn't interrupted us at the market there would have been more than an embarrassed goodbye between us."

He clenched his jaw.

"You called all week but couldn't find time to get away. I know your kind all too well, Mr. Goodman. There's nothing wrong with having dinner with a nice man, and your friend seems nice."

"Dinner is different than calls or meeting at the market."

"How?"

"It just is." He raked his fingers through his hair, then looked surprised he'd done it. "Stan wants to … He thinks you're… Oh, hell. Forget it."

He looked away. She stood quietly. The parking area was almost empty. Sounds of cheering floated to them from the other side of campus. There was a nip in the evening air and over the natural fresh, clean smell the scent of wood smoke floated.

"Stan is going to want more than dinner some evening. He's thinking of calling you and arranging a date in Manchester when I drive to Boston on Sunday."

"You're going to Boston on Sunday? I thought you were busy."

"It's *business*," he hissed.

Eve sucked in a breath. "God, Daniel, I'm sorry. I'm acting as though there was something between us and of course there's nothing. It's just…" She looked away, unable to face him. "I keep thinking of that kiss, and you're so nice and reliable, and I guess I hoped maybe there could be something. I know I should forget it, and I've tried. I'd never fit into the kind of life you have planned."

"Lauren. *Eve*." He was quiet until she raised her head. "You'd fit into any life. I've never known a woman as selfless as you, or as beautiful. And I'm not as nice as you think. I've dreamed about you ever since that kiss last week." He smiled crookedly. "Why do you think I had a sudden craving for pears when I knew you'd be at the farmer's market?"

"When your girlfriend showed up, beautiful and sophisticated, she proved just how different we are."

"Sydney can't hold a candle to you. And she's not my girlfriend, she's the daughter of the academy board chairman." He lifted his hand as though to touch her, then dropped it. "I had dinner with her Wednesday because she said her father would join us, and any chance I have to discuss my ideas with him, I take. That's why I'm going to Boston on Sunday."

More than anything, she wanted to rest her head on his chest and feel his arms around her. Leaving Timmy was always hard. She'd thought it would be easier when he made friends and became involved in the school. Now he had, and going home alone was harder yet. Today he'd acted as though he didn't care if she left because he was going off to do something with one of the boys in his dorm. How much easier leaving would be if she were a couple instead of a single. She was lonely and feeling pathetic, but Daniel's solid, steady chest wasn't one she could lean on. She needed to rely on herself, as desolate as that made her feel right now.

"Look, you don't owe me any explanations. I know I shouldn't have flirted earlier—it was a throwback to another time. To Eve's time, not Lauren's. I'll let your friend know, if he does try to reach me. And now you need to know that I don't expect anything of you. Really, I don't. I hope you won't let my actions affect how you treat Timmy. He's got noth—"

"I'd never do that."

She took a breath, plastered on a smile, and faced him directly.

"Thanks. I'd better go now. 'Eve' is already late for work."

He opened the car door for her. With another smile of thanks, she drove home.

***

After ensuring her regular bartender didn't need her, Eve had just settled down to go over the books. The past month had seen an increase in income. She'd steadily been improving the way the place looked, hoping to make it more appealing to women as well as men. When word got out, women did come, for after-work happy hours and ladies' free nights.

As more women patronized The Bare Moose, the male clientele improved, and she had fewer sloppy drunks to contend with each night. Happy hour ate up the alcohol inventory, but increased food sales. Since people tended to stay after happy hour, the additional business had started increasing the profits. The changes pleased Eve, and the word from the bar's owners indicated they were happy also.

"Eve?" Jed, her bartender, called through the closed door.

"Come on in, Jed."

He opened the door and stuck in his head. "There's a guy here to see you. Dressed too good to be a regular and turned down a beer while I came to get you."

She frowned. "An inspector, do you think?"

Jed shrugged.

"Okay," she said. "I'll be right out."

Jed closed the door. She made a notation of where she'd left off and rose, putting the books away and tidying her desk. Crowds packed the Moose on Fridays. Soon, she'd be needed behind the bar and to serve and bus tables. On busy nights, she did anything that needed to be done. Her qualifications didn't include business manager, and she'd had to spin her skills in order to convince the bar owners to give her a chance. Through hard times, she'd learned how to serve tables and handle the bar, as well as come-ons, wandering hands, and drunken propositions. Dancing alone on stage was a breeze compared to working a busy tavern.

She checked that her hair was still in its neat braid and that her blouse was tucked in. The top two buttons were undone, and the collar flared out. Tendrils of hair floated around her face. Many of the guys would think she was hot—and she knew the tips she earned by looking hot would be appreciated by the waitresses when she added them to the common tip jar.

Stepping from her office into the tavern felt like catapulting from a peaceful meadow to the foot of a raging volcano. The heavy beat of a song playing on the jukebox punctuated the noise of the crowd that already filled the taproom, although it was only a little after six o'clock. Several regulars greeted her as she came around the bar, and she stopped and laughed with a few of them as she searched for the man Jed mentioned.

She turned and there he was, against the wall. Daniel Goodman. The smiles she'd showered on her customers faded. Like tackling an obstacle course, she made her way to him.

"Is everything okay? There's nothing wrong with Timmy?" She had to yell to be heard.

"No." He shook his head to confirm the word instead of shouting. His hands slid around her waist and he pulled her close. His breath was hot on her neck and her hair tickled when he spoke into her ear. "I want to tell you something. Can we go to your apartment for a minute?"

She nodded, then pushed away and led him to the office. From there, she silently opened a second door which went into the small foyer he and Jeffrey Torrington had entered almost a week ago. The stairs to her apartment were to the left, the door to the outside in front of them. A good bit of noise from the bar disappeared when she shut the door, but the bass from the song on the jukebox pierced the walls. At least they could talk in a normal tone and be heard.

"If there's nothing wrong, I'm surprised you came," Eve said, starting up the steps.

Daniel grabbed her waist when she'd risen but two steps.

"This is what I needed to tell you," he growled. "Regardless of what's best, I can't forget that kiss. I want more."

He took the first step. Her lips were slightly higher than his, but he took them, too. He was rough, pressing his mouth tightly to hers. His tongue didn't ask permission, but drove into her, brooking no argument, taking command. With a groan of need, she slanted her mouth to allow him even greater access and raised her leg to his hip.

"Need to get upstairs," he said against her lips.

"Yes."

She dropped her leg and tried to turn but he was kissing her again, eating her lips, plundering her mouth with his tongue. His hands held her captive against his body. His heat branded her. Or was that heat all hers and she shared it with him?

When he finally pulled back, they stared at each other. The sounds of their heavy breathing filled the stairwell. Her heart beat in time to the bass coming from the bar, fast and primitive, making her body pulse with a rhythm as timeless as the first joining of men and women. She ached to give in to it.

"You know what this means, my going upstairs with you?" His voice was hoarse and deep. His eyes never left hers.

She shook her head, wanting him to spell out the terms of the relationship. She'd put her son's future at the school in his hands once before and he'd proven himself worthy of her trust.

"It means no dinners with Stan. No endangering our positions at the school. Just play the part you've set for yourself. I'll be with you as much as I can, but we have to be careful—we both have a lot to lose."

Daniel rubbed his thumb across her bottom lip and his eyes traced the path. She licked the tip of his thumb and then sucked it into her mouth. His eyes widened and darkened, the brown encompassing the green.

"I want you more than any woman I've ever known. I can't sleep without dreaming of you, I can't work without seeing you there beside me. I need you so much I ache." Now he gazed back into her eyes. "I can't lie to you, I won't jeopardize years of work for a temporary relationship and temporary is all we can have."

"I understand."

In a way, it hurt to have everything laid out so impersonally. He might have *said* she'd fit into any life as a way to bolster her ego earlier, but she'd always known who she was, where she came from. She'd done well over the years, considering. But Daniel Goodman represented an arena she wouldn't suit. Respect for him would be lowered were she by his side. She could accept this as a temporary arrangement if it meant having time with Daniel. Some part of her knew he would alleviate her loneliness, if only for a little while. She trusted him to do that because she trusted her own instincts. Something about this man was different. Despite his harsh words, he'd treat her heart gently.

She took his hand and led him to her apartment. When she closed the door and locked it behind them, they entered a place untouched by the world's opinions and mores. There, they were just Daniel and Eve, two people who needed each other.

For now, for her, it was enough.

***

Daniel couldn't wait to get Eve to the bedroom. When he heard the click of the lock, it was as though they'd pushed the world away and existed alone in that island of an apartment.

What are you doing? Are you out of your fucking mind? He was where he shouldn't be and with a woman he shouldn't be. And he didn't give a damn.

He backed her against the door. "Take off your clothes."

Locking onto his eyes, she started unbuttoning her blouse. She must be as crazy as he. If he said the wrong word at the academy, her son would be out, yet she—

"Wait a minute. Swear you aren't doing this to keep your son in school."

Eve's eyes narrowed then widened. "Are you using his position at Westover as a threat?"

"Hell, no."

"I want you as much as you want me. That's the only reason I let you in this apartment."

Satisfied, he nodded. She loosened the last button and let her blouse fall to the floor. Still watching his eyes, she reached behind and unhooked her bra. Her breasts were large, but not overly so. He cupped one. The stiffened peak of her nipple scraped his palm as he massaged her. He removed his hand and raised his eyes back to hers.

She unzipped and unsnapped her jeans. He crowded her but in a great stripper move, she slithered down the door, pushing her jeans and panties with her. On her haunches in front of him, she unbuckled his belt. He reached in his pocket for the rubber he'd brought and let her free his cock as she pulled down his trousers and briefs.

Her breath was hot on him, and her tongue like a branding iron striking across the crown, licking up his pre-cum and dipping into the tiny slit as though digging for more. Her mouth surrounded the head of his cock, hot and wet and so inviting. He closed his eyes and pushed forward, letting the heat envelope him, burn him. He withdrew and the cold air on his tender flesh sent a shiver through him, a shiver she sensed because she surged forward, covering him in heat again. When she pulled back, she wrapped her warm hand around his exposed rod. His cock twitched, gliding like a snake into the recesses of her mouth, sliding ever so slightly past the entrance to her throat. His balls tightened, so ready to let go. Daniel pulled back.

"Here," he said, handing her the condom. It took her no time to apply it, then, unbelievably, she stood in the tiny space he allowed.

This time, Daniel crouched before her, removed her shoes and slipped the jeans over her feet. He parted her legs and licked his way from ankle to thigh. Her skin smoothed over his cheek, a length of silk leading to the apex, an amazing thatch of soft curls. He nuzzled, and her aroma overtook him, the warm, musk scent making his dick pulse with need. With a groan, she widened her stance. He parted her lower lips and studied her. Already, dew drops of her essence glistened along her lips and the entrance to her pussy. His tongue lapped it up, stroking a path to her clit.

"Oh, God!" She slapped her hands against the door.

She was wet enough, especially after his brief exploration. Another time he'd take more care. Right now, he only wanted to feel her around him, to be lost in her touch, her scent, her woman's heat that could bring the strongest man to his knees.

He stood and lifted her over him. "Are you ready?" His voice was hoarse, the taste of her still on his tongue spurring his desire and emptying him of all reason.

"More than ready."

In a single stroke he drove into her. She cried out.

"Did I hurt you?"

She wrapped her legs around his waist and her arms around his neck, pulling him as close as he could get. His hands kneaded her ass. Her hips undulated, grinding into him.

"Harder," she whispered in his ear.

"Oh, God," he moaned.

Feeling like a man of iron, he pounded her back against the door. Someone had started another song in the bar below and the steady bass beat a feral rhythm to which he stroked. Steel sheathed in liquid fire, he drove in and pulled out. In and out, in and out, to the beat from below, to the pounding of his heart, to the grunts of pleasure Eve made while he hammered her to the door.

And then his balls clenched against her butt and he came, hard, strong, for what felt like forever. At the same moment, Eve moaned, holding him tight while her muscles clamped, seeking to trap him deep within. No problem there. He was deep and long and right where he wanted to be. She was tight and strong and hard around him.

They stood there until he had nothing left to give and the ripples of her orgasm died away. His mouth sought hers, drinking and sipping and nuzzling. For the first time, he noticed her hands tangled in his hair. Her tongue invaded his mouth, taking command in a way he found arousing. Incredibly, his heart raced and his breathing quickened. Damn, he couldn't wait to have her again.

"I have to get back," he finally mumbled against her lips.

She spread tiny kisses across his cheek to his ear. "Me, too."

He leaned them against the door. "When can I see you again?"

"Not over the weekend. I'm usually dead from work." She sighed. "Next week?"

"My assistant usually arrives by four unless he has a game or something that delays him. Four-thirty? Here? What time do you have to be downstairs?" Daniel sucked the tip of her earlobe and gently nipped it.

"We're open at four. I usually take care of the small number of people who trickle in until five, then Jed takes over. Can you come at five?"

He was still inside her. His hips rocked forward. "With you? I can come whenever you want me to."

She chuckled softly. "I could say the same right back. You were wonderful."

That was what he wanted to hear. "Have you ever fucked a man in a three-piece suit?"

"Not men who were wearing them at the time."

Disappointment stabbed him. She'd been a dancer. That didn't make her anything else. Of course, a woman as beautiful as Eve Star would have attracted any number of men. She could have had her pick and would have been within her rights to sample any of them. She had a son—she hadn't been celibate. Still, he wished she'd said no.

He must have tensed because she added, "None like you."

A common line for a woman. Question was, was she a common woman for the line?

Dropping her legs and raising her head, she tugged on his hair, forcing him to meet her eyes. "Now you're wondering just how many men I've slept with."

"No, I was—"

She shook her head. "Don't lie. I'll tell you, Daniel Goodman. More than I should have, though I was very particular. I was in demand, so there were no quickies in the alley behind the dressing rooms. The men I chose were more into caviar than tuna salad. You can make of *that* what you want."

Daniel studied Eve's eyes, searching for any hint of guile. He found none. But he did see a woman with a past he couldn't condone, understand or accept. His mother had danced. She'd been in demand. Had she also sampled men as though they were different vintages of wine? Eve may have selected only the finest, but she'd still sipped from any number of bottles. His mother and Eve were two of a kind, even down to having children without marrying the father. At least his mother had stayed with the man she loved, and they'd provided a stable home for him and his brothers. Well, except for when their dad was in prison. *Can't duck history.*

Firmly, he pushed thoughts of his parents to the side. The person in question here was Eve Star.

Suddenly, he saw anger in her brown depths.

"I'm sorry if my past bothers you. You're the first man since Timmy was born. And you can make of that what you want, too." She pushed him away and scooped up her clothes.

Turning, he removed the rubber, holding it awkwardly while pulling up his pants. Still unzipped, he walked to the bathroom.

He splashed water on his face and stared at his reflection in the mirror above the sink. What difference did it make if she'd slept with a thousand men? Timmy was six, and Daniel was the man with her, here and now. What happened before, well, happened. His past wasn't exactly lily white, though he'd gone a very long time without finding sweet release in the way only a woman provided.

And what about the risks? He was finally within an inch of getting his dream job, Headmaster of Westover Academy. He would be the leader of the finest private school in America, and he had ideas he'd been dying to implement. Continuing to see his Evening Star put his dreams at risk.

"Hell," he said to the man in the mirror. "You have a lot to lose. She has a lot to lose. So, you'll be discrete. What's the problem?"

Nothing, he decided.

Walking back into the living room, he was straightened and neat and looking very much like an instructor at Westover. Eve was also put back together, her auburn hair tucked back into a braid, her blouse opened enough at the collar to give a hint of sin, and in jeans and high heels.

Nodding at her feet he asked, "You work in those?"

She tossed her head back, haughty and regal. Not at all like a woman who'd just been pounded into a door until she moaned in ecstasy. "Men are strange creatures. They give bigger tips to waitresses in high heels."

Their eyes met and locked. "Will you wear them for me next time?"

"You're certain you want a next time? I am who I am."

"I can accept that." He smiled and saw sparks flare in her eyes. "Because for now, you're mine."

Chapter Seven

"Hello?" Eve's voice sounded as smooth and sexy as it had last Friday when she'd whispered *harder* into Daniel's ear. Then, he'd been driving into her. Now he was passively listening over the phone, and still her voice had him hard in seconds.

Unfortunately, the sex had been on Friday, and this was Monday. A long, lonely weekend had intervened, making his cock twitch in protest that he was on the Westover Academy campus and she was miles away in her apartment above The Bare Moose tavern.

"Did I interrupt you? Are you already at work?" He hoped not. He wanted her in her apartment, wearing nothing but silky stockings and heels.

"No, I was changing and thought you might call, so I stopped dressing. I'm stretched out on the bed right now."

He couldn't believe she meant what he thought she meant. "You're *naked?*"

"Naked, hot and wet. Dripping wet, wishing your cock was deep inside me." Her voice dropped an octave; his dick grew an inch.

"God, you're going to kill me."

Imagining her with no clothes, spread wide and aching for him the way he ached for her, he unzipped his trousers and released his cock from his briefs. His cool hand caressing the shaft didn't begin to lessen the fiery desire fueling his erection.

"Baby, it's what you do to me," she purred. "My nipples are at attention, hard and peaked, and I can feel you sucking them. Your mouth is so hot, your tongue is rough on my sensitive skin."

"I love your tits, God knows I do, but I want to taste your pussy."

"I'm open and waiting. But I warn you, I'm so close, just a lick will make me come."

She thought *she* was close? He couldn't remember the last time he'd jacked off, and he'd never had phone sex. Jonah had told him once how fucking hot it had been. Daniel hadn't been able to imagine that it could compare in any way to the real thing—and he was right, of course. But in lieu of the real thing, Jonah was right. It *was* fucking hot.

"Put your lips on me, Daniel. Lick me."

Titillating nuances, double entendres, maybe a hint that he might get lucky at the end of an evening—that had been the extent of his sensual telephone experiences. Those experiences were as far from this as, well, North Carolina small town life was from Westover Academy. Eve was inviting him to eat her, and there was no way he'd disappoint.

"Sweetheart, I'm gonna do more than lick." Scrunched down in his leather armchair, still dressed in his suit and gown from class, he stroked his length, only vaguely aware he'd slipped into his Carolina drawl.

"You're so sweet, Eve, your cream is like honey. And your smell." Closing his eyes, he inhaled as though his nose could really detect the bouquet of her arousal. "I think in a room of women I could find you just by your scent if you were aroused."

"If you were looking for me, I'd be aroused."

Faster and harder, he pumped his dick.

"Is your clit sensitive? I've sucked it into my mouth and it's swollen and thick against my tongue. And don't worry, I've slipped a couple fingers in your sweet, wet pussy, and we're jammin', honey. Most of my face is covered in your juices."

"God! Can you come with me?"

"Yeah, oh yeah, one second." His breath caught. He jacked his strokes until his hand was a piston. "Now, sweetheart, now!" Daniel growled the words as his cock pulsed, shooting cum into his palm, which deflected it away from his shirt and vest.

Caught up in his release, he wasn't too far gone to hear Eve's panting breaths and soft whimpers. He wanted her to scream, to wrap herself around him and let the sounds and convulsions of her orgasm reverberate through him.

Finally, he heard her soft breathing. "Eve?"

"Yes, Tony, thanks *so* much. I'd better go now before my friend Daniel calls."

He shot up half-way. "What the fu—" Her laughter stopped him dead, and he caught the joke. About to rake his fingers through his hair, he took a look at what covered his palm and reached over to pick up an unused napkin from the coffee table. With some difficulty, he wiped his hand and cleaned himself. "Please tell me you're really naked and that wasn't an act."

"Believe me, Mr. Goodman, that was no act. That was incredible."

"Thank God. I'll have to have this suit dry cleaned and I'd hate to think it was for a one-sided hand job." He chuckled but his voice and tone were once again Daniel Goodman, Ph.D., all trace of North Carolina gone.

She laughed again. "I like that you called before you even changed clothes. You're not going to stick me with the cleaning bill, are you?"

"When I stick you with something, it won't be a bill." He smiled at her chuckle. "How did you know it was me calling?"

"Well, let's see..."

In his mind, he pictured her lying on her back and staring at the ceiling, one leg bent and the other across it, swinging as she talked. One finger would be twirling a long strand of her hair, her cheeks would be pink and glowing, and her eyes sparkling with satisfaction. How could he be so in tune with a woman he'd met barely a week ago? It seemed a miracle. For the millionth time he wished she had a nice, respectable job, where she'd fit into the academy culture and he wouldn't be risking his career to date her openly.

"Daniel, am I talking to myself here?"

"Oh, no, I'm..." He chuckled an amused admission. "Tell me what you said again." He could almost hear her smile.

"I said, you called at four-thirty on Saturday and Sunday, so I took a wild leap that you would today, too."

"Ah." Smiling to the empty room, he squirmed to get into a more comfortable position. "A woman of logic."

"Absolutely. You don't want to play me in chess. I think five or six moves ahead."

"I'll remember that. There's nothing worse than seeing a guy cry when he's been beaten at chess by a girl. Why are you lying naked in your apartment instead of working?" Then a thought occurred to him. "You *are* upstairs, right? Not in your office with that puny lock on the door?"

"Yes, although I might get a discount from my beer distributor if I conducted our meetings like this. What do you think?"

He huffed a laugh. "I hope you don't try. Now answer my question.

I know you don't have a lot of help this time of day."

"I'm paying Jed extra to come in a bit early."

Her voice was low, as though she didn't really want to tell him. The words struck his heart.

"You don't have money to be paying Jed extra, Eve. I'll start calling later, after dinner and before I grade papers."

"No, don't. It's quiet this time of day and I want these few minutes to myself. Jed doesn't mind, and he can use a few extra bucks."

"Well, okay."

"Besides, you won't be calling forever. Soon you'll be head of the school and won't have free time for the likes of me."

Daniel hadn't promised her on Friday that he'd call. He'd simply felt the desire and acted on it. Then, by unspoken agreement, they hadn't mentioned what might happen next in their relationship. They'd spent time sharing that day in their respective worlds.

Today, he'd discovered the desire to talk to Eve wasn't an "at loose ends" feeling that sometimes came over him on weekends. After his dorm assistant had arrived, Daniel had locked his doors, put his books and papers away, and picked up the phone. Only after they'd been well into the fantasy did he remember he hadn't even removed his gown and jacket before pressing her number. He'd wanted to hear her, find out what her day had been like and communicate his own. He felt seventeen again, with an infatuation about to drive him crazy. Except men his age didn't have infatuations. They had obsessions.

"Hey," Eve charged, "I didn't mean that the way it sounded, like I was hunting for compliments or reassurances. I was simply stating a fact, the way we both know it to be. I want this to be short term as much as you do, so don't worry."

"I'm not worried."

But he was. How long did obsessions last, anyway? Daniel had never allowed himself to be distracted by a woman or anything that might waylay his goals.

"Okay, good. So"—her voice dropped to that sexy purr she'd used earlier—"did you like the little fantasy?"

"I did, yes. Until today I was a phone sex virgin."

"No!" He heard the smile again, but she didn't laugh. "And you liked it. Well, know what I liked?"

"What?"

"That really sexy Southern accent. Talk like that again? Next time?"

"Just for you."

Daniel looked across the room at the stack of senior term papers he had to grade by the weekend. Another set of sophomore class essays waited in his office, and the ninth-grade book reports were neatly rubber banded in his brief case. All of that, plus tests to create and lessons to put together, needed his deft hand and whole attention to complete. Hours and hours and hours—

"Eve, do you think Jed would mind coming in early again tomorrow? And working alone for a couple hours after that?"

She hesitated, but not for long. "I don't know what I'll do without my phone call."

Daniel smiled and tried out his best North Carolina twang. "Darlin', I'm sure we'll think of somethin'."

***

Why was Eve so nervous? The bar was in good hands. Jed had been happy to come in early again and had assured her he'd be fine without her help.

"It's a Tuesday, for God's sake. If I can't take care of an early Tuesday night with one hand tied behind my back, you should fire my ass. *You* just worry about that relaxation program your doctor prescribed." He'd given her a knowing wink. "And tell Dr. Goodman that he's doing a good job. You *do* seem less stressed."

He'd laughed and jumped out of swing range, then left the office before she could ask what he suspected about her and Daniel, or how he even knew Daniel. He hadn't known him the first time Daniel came into the bar, of that she was certain.

Jed had been there when Daniel called Saturday and Sunday, but instead of just asking him to come in early, she'd said she needed a bit of time in the afternoon to relax. *Doctor's orders*, she'd joked. As nervous as she felt now, minutes before Daniel's arrival, she wasn't sure her few private moments weren't having the opposite effect.

The choices she'd made since becoming pregnant with Timmy had been all hers, with him the center of her attention. She didn't regret those choices—most of the time. But it had been years since she'd been desired for the sexual creature she was. That's not to say she hadn't been propositioned. She had, thousands of times. But what she needed—what she longed for—was a man who would appreciate *her*, not just what she had to offer in bed. And someone who was safe to be with, who wouldn't hurt Timmy. How ironic that the man making her heart race right now was someone who could destroy all she'd worked for with one word whispered to the wrong person.

Then again, maybe that's what drew her to Daniel: her belief that no matter what happened between them, he'd never purposely hurt Timmy. In spite of their clandestine affair—if one episode of sex and a handful of phone calls rose to the level of "affair"—she knew Daniel was one of those men who cared, really *cared* about people. Especially those under his protection, like the boys at the academy.

A knock sounded. She'd left the door at the back of the building unlocked, so he could enter without having to go through the tavern. She glanced in the mirror, patted her hair, checked her lipstick—a bright red gloss she'd dug out of her makeup kit for this occasion—and went to answer.

"Hi," she said, smiling into his face after she swung the door wide.

Wearing a russet striped Oxford-cloth shirt, pressed trousers, and a tan corduroy jacket with leather patches on the elbows, he couldn't have looked more Establishment if he'd tried. In contrast, her jeans were old and worn, with holes and frayed cuffs, and her silky top hung carelessly off one shoulder. Her three-inch heels brought them eye to eye.

"You look amazing," he said. "Just as I thought you would." He extended a bouquet of white mums.

She took them and closed the door behind him. "Thanks, for the compliment and the flowers."

He followed her into the kitchen, where she found a vase and dropped the stems into water.

"I'm glad you like the way I look." She glanced over her shoulder— the bare shoulder—purposely licking her lips. "I wanted to play the slut, to tell the truth."

His eyes narrowed, and he smiled. Crossing his arms, he leaned against the counter. "And as I said, you look amazing."

She faced him, back slightly arched, shoulders back, knowing the pose showed her breasts off to best advantage and made her nipples stand out like the poles of a tent. His gaze dropped from her face to stare. How many men had she seen do exactly the same thing? Too many to count. How many had made her sizzle when they did? Only two. Timmy's father and Daniel Goodman.

When Daniel's eyes met hers again, she reached up and removed the combs capturing her hair. She watched his gaze follow as it cascaded over her shoulders and around her face; she shook it back. His nostrils flared, the only sign that he'd noticed.

"If I look so damn amazing, what are you doing over there?"

"My dad would say I was holding up the wall."

Years of male attention assured Eve she owned a sultry look she could use when desired. She desired now. In her best imitation, she adopted a Southern accent to match her expression. "Hey, boy. What're you doin' holdin' up the wall over there when I want some lovin' over here?"

"I guess I don't rightly know." His smile faded, and he pushed away from the counter. In two strides, he braced her with his arms and crowded her against the sink.

"By the by, back home, with your tattered jeans and zebra-striped high heels, we wouldn't call you slutty. We'd say you were a loose woman lookin' for trouble."

Too close to the truth, but where names like that had hurt at times in the past, tonight she relished the label. As long as Daniel didn't believe it, as long as this was just a game, she would be all right. The first time he hinted that was how he thought of her, he'd be a thing of the past no matter how great he made her feel.

She pursed her lips. "I feel like a loose woman. Are you gonna be my trouble?"

He inched his head forward and his chuckle rumbled in her ear. "Count on it."

"For you, I wanna be trashy as all get out."

"That's my girl."

He swooped to lift her over his shoulder, amid her shrieks and laughter. With sure, unhurried steps, he carried her down the hall to her bedroom, kicked the door closed and dumped her on the bed.

The mattress bounced when she hit, leading to more laughter. Daniel shook his head then gave in to her mirth. He draped his jacket over a chair in the corner and then looked down at her with his hands on his hips.

"What's so all-fired funny?"

The laughter finally ended, but she couldn't erase the smile from her face or the butterflies from her stomach. "I don't know. I think I'm nervous."

"Nervous? With me? No need, sugar."

With one knee on the bed, he leaned over until their lips met. Soft and gentle at first, the kiss grew stronger with every passing moment.

Daniel stretched out and pulled her to him. His hand roamed freely over her butt and then up under her top, stroking her back, tracing the line of her spine and at last skimming forward where his thumb teased her nipple. She strained her hips toward him while unfastening the buttons of his shirt. When his chest was bare, she ran her palm from his stomach through the soft coating of hair to his nipple. He moaned and broke their kiss.

"Are you ready to get naked with me, Professor?" Scooting down on the bed, she let her tongue swirl over the nipple she'd just caressed.

"Ah, Miss Star, you say the nicest things. You take care of getting yourself naked, sugar, and I'll watch."

A striptease for one. It had been years since she'd thought of stripping, and when she did think of it, it was with the sure knowledge she'd never do it again. This was different, though. This was for her as much as for her audience.

Eve stood and locked gazes with Daniel, making sure he watched her, that his mind was on nothing *but* her.

Some women strutted on stage and closed their eyes, performing for themselves. Others danced and smiled at the crowd, but only because they thought they should. Eve looked into the eyes of each man, saw his desire, and silently promised that she was the answer to his every wish. Because she truly believed in her ability to fulfill dreams through her dance, *they* believed, and followed her like puppies after kibble. She couldn't best some of her friends in the craft of dancing, but she excelled in promising dream fulfillment. That made her a star in more than name. Now, confidence filled her. Laughter bubbled up from deep within. She felt happier than she had in a long time.

Silence cloaked the room. Suddenly, "Fever" played on the jukebox below them. The strong bass pounded steady and solid, and strains of the melody drifted through the floor. Eve smoothed her hands over her hips and down her legs to her knees. Slowly, very slowly, she straightened, running her hands back up her legs, across her stomach, her breasts, shoulders, neck, until she lifted her hair and then let it fall.

In a swift pivot, she turned on a beat, spreading her legs and bending at the waist. Reaching around, she rubbed her butt, which she knew

showed tight and smooth, encased in fitted jeans. Daniel's breathing
could be heard over the music. Eve smiled.

She stood up, swaying her hips. Walking her hands up her back, she
took her shirt hem with her. When her back was exposed, she turned
enough to reveal one breast, then let the shirt drop back into place. She
took a moment to look over her shoulder and make eye contact with
Daniel again. His eyes were dark and hooded. He reclined on his side,
leaning on one elbow. When he met her eyes, he gave her the slow, sexy
smile she loved.

Smiling in return, she unbuttoned her shirt and whipped it down to
her waist, turning to face him at the same time. She snapped the edges
together to cover herself and then whipped them away, playing an adult
game of peek-a-boo before finally dropping the shirt to the floor. The
flare of Daniel's nostrils and rapid rise and fall of his chest told her she
hadn't lost her touch.

She strutted to the end of the bed and flipped her foot in the air,
sending her shoe flying toward his head. He caught it and tucked it next
to him. He caught her second shoe, too, then sat up to watch the action.

Unzipping her jeans revealed the edge of lacy, red panties. She gave
him her back again and inched her jeans over her hips while adding
grinds, swings and gyrations with each measure of progress. After
stepping out of the pants, she swung around, bent, letting her hair
provide a temporary veil, then snapped to attention, sending her hair
flying. She knew she looked wild and wicked—every man's dream—
wearing only panties and sheer, thigh high stockings. She thrust her
hips forward, back, gyrated for another snap forward, all while holding
her hair off her neck.

Daniel's eyes moved from her hips to her breasts, to her eyes and back
again. He licked his lips and reached for her. Her pussy moistened at the
same time her mouth dried. She'd made implicit promises to thousands
of men, but to this man she'd pledged more than imaginary satisfaction.
Much more. The very thought thrilled her. While he watched, she
slithered out of her panties, spread her legs wide and waited for him to
tug her down beside him.

Instead, he motioned for her foot on the edge of the bed. She waited,
doing nothing more than watch from beneath her lashes. He tapped
the edge of the bed again. In no rush, she placed her left foot where
he indicated. He ran his hand over her instep, back to the heel and up

her calf. Desire crawled up her spine and dampened her pubic hair. Her arousal filled the air.

Daniel's fingers trailed up the inside of her thigh until they reached the dew drops coating her lower lips. One finger spread the moisture around, and then inched into her pussy. Need twisted and coiled, molten hot inside. Her hips swung forward to meet him. He tickled her passage, rubbing and stroking, before removing his hand and painting his lips with her juices. Crooking his finger, he held up his face. Eve bent forward, licking his lips with the tip of her tongue, taking back her taste and scent.

When she backed away, he handed her the heels.

"Put these on."

Then he stood and got naked, himself.

Aroused and sheathed, he sat on the edge of the bed and held out his hand. Eve took it, allowing him to tug her around so she stood before him.

"You don't look like a loose woman anymore."

"No? And I tried so hard. Not even in my zebra-striped heels? Or with this bright red lipstick I wore so you could watch me swallow your cock?"

"Damn!" He smiled. "Well, maybe a little bit."

His hands settled on her hips. His cock pulsed and bobbed, but still he didn't pull her onto him. Her need became a living thing, but she wouldn't make the move to bring them together. This was his show.

"It's okay, you know. I love the idea of a trashy woman stripping for me, but I like making love to a lady." He pulled her down for a kiss. "And, baby, you're one hell of a lady."

He fell back on the bed, lifting and carrying her with him as though she weighed nothing. She straddled him, and then guided his hard thickness into her. They rocked slowly at first. She leaned forward to kiss him and the friction of her breasts on his chest pushed her toward the orgasm she'd dreamed of since the last time he'd been there. Their kisses deepened; his tongue explored and conquered her mouth and then he sucked her tongue into his mouth. Her hands tangled in his hair. Their moans mingled, separated, joined again.

By the time Daniel took control of her hips and their pace, she was more than ready to come. But completion wasn't the important part of this afternoon, making love was. Daniel had made love to her with his words, before they came together. He wanted to make love to a lady and proclaimed her to be one. Her earlier nervousness about where their relationship was headed came rushing back, tenfold. This was a man she could love. She'd recognized the attraction and the danger the night he came to collect Michael Haynes. Was the certainty of heartache worth the reprieve from loneliness? Could she stand the pain when—

He touched her clit and sent her where nervousness and worry had no place.

Chapter Eight

Two days after Eve's striptease and the subsequent two incredible hours spent exploring each other's bodies and minds, Daniel took his seat in the academy dining room with a few of the boys from his dormitory. Each table sat six, with a permanent place for a dorm master or table monitor. Each month the boys rotated tables, assuring they spent casual dining time with their dorm master and others, and learned proper table manners. Usually, Daniel enjoyed meals with his young charges. They were more willing than the older students to talk about what had happened during the day, and he often picked up on budding problems by listening to their conversations. For this reason, even though late afternoon-early evening was the part of the day he had free, he usually liked to attend dinner.

However, he'd changed his calls to Eve from four-thirty to after dinner, and now Daniel counted the minutes until the evening meal ended. He urged the boys not to tarry after dessert and then cursed the fact he had to walk sedately rather than sprint back to the dorm. Once there, he made sure to lock the doors and get comfortable before punching her number on the telephone face. A minor dorm crisis requiring both him and his assistant had prevented their saying much more than hello yesterday, and today, though he'd just eaten, he felt like a starving man.

"Nothing a little sugar won't cure," he muttered, using Southern slang for kisses.

At the same moment, a deep, male voice answered.

"Well, honey, you ain't getting' it from me." The man laughed. "Hey, doc. Eve told me to tell you she had to go out, and if she missed you, she'd call back as soon as possible."

"Hi, Jed."

Of course, Eve shouldn't be hanging around waiting for his calls, but he couldn't help the disappointment that hit like a sledgehammer.

"Say, why'd you call me doc?"

Jed laughed. "Ask Eve."

"I'll do that. Thanks."

Well. Daniel set the phone back on the side table. *All dressed up and nowhere to go.* He looked at the remaining term papers he had to grade but reading the opinions of high school boys on any subject, much less *Romeo and Juliet,* a love story that ended tragically, didn't appeal. What he wanted was to hear the voice of the woman who'd ridden him hard and put him away wet on Tuesday evening.

Eve had been right. Seeing her bright red lips travel the length of his cock, taking all of him into her hot, wet mouth and then slowly relinquishing him as she drew her head back, had been as erotic as anything he'd ever known. When he'd had blow jobs before, he'd closed his eyes, enjoying the sensation without visual input. But Eve had proven that sometimes seeing was every bit as good as feeling. Or at least seeing added to the pleasure—he didn't think anything could compare to how she made him feel. When he would have pulled out, she thrust her head forward, taking him deep in her mouth and swallowing his cum, something no other woman had ever done.

Daniel was no novice when it came to sex, but in the short time they'd known each other, Eve had shown him one or two things that took his breath away. Literally. Instead of lessening, his compulsion to be with her grew. In the coming week it would be put to the test, and that was one of the things he needed to talk to her about tonight.

For such a physical relationship, they talked a lot. He'd been friends with women with whom he enjoyed banter and conversation, and maybe occasional sex. And he'd had hot and heavy physical relations with women he didn't care to talk with at all. But with Eve, he found intense, amazing sex, and a funny, charming partner easy to talk with—a perfect woman.

He wanted her. No, God damn it, he *needed* her. *And* he wanted her.

Shit. No doubt about it, he had it bad.

The phone rang, and Daniel snatched up the receiver.

"Hello?"

"Daniel, hello."

His heart settled back into a normal rhythm. "Hi, Sydney. How are you?"

"I'm fine. I just wanted to call and say I was happy to hear you were coming to Boston next week with the group from the academy. When we heard that one of the teachers scheduled to accompany the boys was sick, I called the headmaster's office and suggested you take his place."

So that's why his whole coming week's schedule had been turned upside down. *Thanks so much.*

"I wondered how that change came about. I mean, I'm a lower form dorm master but I teach upper form. We do have parent volunteers for emergencies like this, Sydney."

"Of course," she said, "but I knew you'd want to pitch in and help. First, it'll bring you to Boston, where we can get together for dinner at least once or twice during the week—"

Oh, great.

"—and second, it'll help repair a little problem that came up this week with Daddy and the board."

He sat up, instantly alert. "What problem?"

"Well, it seems Andy Worth saw you pulling out of a bar. He says it's a place with a horrible reputation and nobody with any sense goes there. You turned onto the road ahead of him and were driving erratically." She stopped for a pregnant pause. "Or at least that's what Andy said when he called Daddy Tuesday night."

That bastard. He'd known all along that he risked everything by seeing Eve and he'd chanced it anyway. That phone call could end it all. A part of him whispered that if so, he'd be able to see Eve without as much worry.

Wait a fucking minute, he *wanted* that job.

"Andy said he saw me? I can't remember what I do from day to day, but I can tell you I rarely go out in the evenings. And you know I almost never drink. How could he be sure?"

There was that pause again. "He noticed your car. He says you have a brother who sells sports cars or races them or something, and he thinks it's funny that you drive an old Volvo station wagon. Really, darling, if your car is so distinctive, you should be discreet where you drive it." Pleasant words, but his ear detected a sharp undertone.

Okay, so it wasn't the kind of vehicle Jonah would appreciate, but he loved that car. He'd bought the classic used, his first year of college, but no one would think it was that old, listening to the way the engine purred. He might not repair and tune top racers for a living like Jonah used to, but the time they'd spent rebuilding their Pacer as teens hadn't been wasted. The tinkering did more than give Daniel a decent car, well situated for working with boys; it had provided lots of non-academic mental challenges over the years, as well as mindless time to give his brain a rest. Now it could hang him.

"I won't be tried and condemned for something no one can prove I did. I've never had as much as a drop of alcohol while around the boys, and I certainly was on duty Tuesday night and every other night since school started. If the board is going to take the word of Andy Worth over mine and all I've done for the past ten years—"

"Daniel, darling—"

"Please stop calling me 'darling,' Sydney. You and I are friends, not lovers."

The silence from the other end of the line deafened him.

"I know that. And you've known for years I'd like to change our status. I only called tonight to give you a heads-up on what happened this week. Daddy will probably want to meet with you while you're in town. I know you won't need to be with the boys every minute, so I hope you'll save some time for me, too."

"Sure, of course. I'm sorry I flew off the handle."

"That's okay. It's just … I know how important it is for you to be appointed headmaster. I want it for you, too, Daniel, I really do. But Andy has a few friends on the board who think your ideas are a little too progressive. They're afraid you want to stir the pot. Any little thing could push the decision in Andy's favor. As *your* friend, I don't want that to happen."

"I appreciate your letting me know, Sydney. I guess I'll see you next week."

The euphoria Daniel felt earlier had worn off. Dragging himself to the desk, he tried to psych himself for grading the Shakespeare papers. How bad could they be? He'd been over everything—the play, Italy's society, and Shakespeare's England. He'd even written a parody and had members of the class act it out. Still, he read the first few paragraphs of the first paper and lost all interest.

Then, about half an hour later, the phone rang. "Daniel?" Eve's voice acted as a balm and immediately his focus returned.

"Hi. How was your day?" He settled into the leather chair again and put his stockinged feet on the coffee table.

"Very hectic. Sorry I missed your call, but I ran out to get something you're going to like this weekend."

Her laugh, low and wicked, hit him right in the cock. Eve hummed, like someone who'd just tasted a delicious treat. He wished she was tasting him.

She continued, "And I can't wait for you to see me in it."

"Whatever it is, I can guarantee you'll look better in it than any woman deserves to look. I also guarantee you'll look better out of it than any woman should dare to dream."

"God, I love it when you talk like that. It makes me feel so..."

He smiled at a piece of lint on his wool slacks before he plucked it off. "So *what?*"

"So happy," she whispered. "Actually, it scares me a little. Being this happy invites trouble."

Oh, God. This is bad, really bad. Not the way things are supposed to go at all. Daniel rubbed his temple and tried to think. Being with Eve was going to get his ass fired. He'd lose his job and everything he'd worked for, all for sex. Great sex, true. Fabulous, best-ever sex with the greatest, most interesting woman he'd ever known, sure. But...

Shit! What was wrong with him? Bad? This was nowhere near bad. In fact, it was so fucking good he couldn't believe he ever considered sitting there grading fucking, stupid papers when he could be with someone who made him smile.

"Eve, I have a little over an hour. I've got to see you."

Damn Andy Worth and his blabbering mouth all to hell. A phone conversation wasn't enough to cool his blood, not from the anger he'd felt talking to Sydney or from the need he had to be with Eve.

His heart skipped two heartbeats before she answered.

"Please hurry."

"On my way." He slipped into his shoes and then went to tell his assistant he'd be going out for a short while, after all.

Starting the engine of the Volvo, he revved the engine. The irrational thought crossed his mind that the sound of the V-8 carried across campus to Worth's apartment, announcing Daniel's intention to go back to the bar and be with the world's most gorgeous woman. *Take that, asshole.*

Big and clunky and priggish it might be, but he'd built the Volvo for speed and reliability. His classic handled the curves and left the newer, stamped-out Detroit clones in the dust. Maybe Jonah was right. Maybe cars did reflect their owners. He was his Volvo—strong, dependable, able to take the hills and enjoy the valleys.

Andy Worth would lose out to Daniel for the coveted headmaster job. His confidence and focus were back. How much of that was due to his natural optimism and how much to his speeding to see Eve, he wasn't sure.

At the moment, he didn't really care.

***

Eve heard Daniel's car before it pulled around to the back of the building and she ran down the stairs. She flung open the inside door just as Daniel took the three porch steps in one stride and yanked open the screen door. In the next second, he held her so tightly she could barely breathe.

And he was kissing her. His lips moved over hers until he found the right fit, his mouth hot and wet, the kiss hard and long. His tongue invaded, caressed, pressed for a response. Just as suddenly, her tongue pushed forward, and he sucked, pulling her farther into the heat of his mouth.

His hands caressed her everywhere, up and down her back, her arms, linking with her fingers, tangling in her hair while he positioned her head, her lips, her tongue. Every spear of contact sent all manner of sensations through her and cut off rational thought.

Finally, his tongue took control of her mouth again, hungrily pushing past her teeth and stroking the roof of her mouth, brushing her tongue, breathing his need into the recesses of her mouth.

His hands flew down her back to cup her ass. She still wore a skirt from when she'd gone out and he pleated it up to her waist before lifting her over his erection. Her arms wrapped around his neck, her legs around his waist. Hard steel pressed insistently into the vee at the apex of her thighs. At the same time she reached out to push the door shut, he ripped off her panties and backed her against the wood.

"Those were expensive French lace," she moaned into his mouth.

"Fuck French lace," he growled.

Eve raised her head and smiled, brushing her hands through his hair. "Oh, yeah."

Rocking her hips forward, she lowered her head and continued the kiss. Beneath her butt she could feel Daniel fumbling with his belt and zipper and then—thank God!—he was inside her, driving in all the way with one stroke.

"Yes, yes, yes," she groaned, grinding against him even as he pounded into her.

Her nostrils filled with the heady aroma of sex and Daniel's fragrance—his aftershave, fresh as a morning at the beach, his shampoo, outdoors-like in its own woodsy way, and something that was solely Daniel. Indescribable, overwhelming, completely seductive.

The door to her office opened.

"Let me see if Eve— Oops, sorry."

The door closed, shutting off Jed's voice and that to whom he spoke.

She threw her head back. Daniel's mouth slid along her jaw, up to her ear and down her neck. His hips jerked forward and back; his cock slid in and out, sending the most delicious friction through her pussy, around her clit and skating along every nerve she had. Synapses burst like fireworks all over her body and she lost control. Her lips locked with his and she screamed her release into his mouth. He thrust into her, moaning with her, kneading her butt cheeks and pressing her closer. Was closer possible? Could there ever be a close enough?

A long time later—such a long time later—their kisses turned gentle. His breathing was heavy, but he nibbled her lower lip then softly kissed the corner of her mouth, her cheek, her nose, her eyelids.

"Ah, Eve. I'm sorry."

"For what?"

"Being too hard, too fast. Mostly for taking you without protection." He held her easily with one hand and cradled her cheek with the other while he looked her into the eyes. "Is that going to cause you a problem? I sure never in hell intended—"

"Shh. It's okay." She met his lips again, softly, and too quickly for any meaning to be exchanged. "I won't get pregnant, and I already told you I haven't been with anyone for years."

"I should have taken more care."

"I was just as greedy." She dropped her legs and moved away in the tiny space. Daniel pulled up his pants and refastened them while she watched. "Do you have time to come upstairs?"

"Not as long as I'd like, but for a few minutes. I need to talk to you."

Eve laughed, picking up her ruined panties. "I have to say, I like the way you start a conversation."

"And you know how to carry on a great dialogue," he said, smiling. "Come on up."

In the kitchen, she dropped the panties in the trash. "Want some coffee?"

"That'd be great. I'll be up late tonight trying to finish class work before I leave tomorrow."

She stopped and turned with the scoop brimming with coffee grounds half way to the filter. "But, I thought the boys in your dorm were going away and you were staying here. Did I mix up the dates?"

"No, that was the plan." He leaned against the wall separating the kitchen from living room. "One of the teachers who was supposed to go on the trip has flu and I was drafted to take his place. I just found out this afternoon."

Her shoulders slumped, and she turned back to the coffee pot to hide her disappointment. She hated to admit how much she'd looked forward to spending time with Daniel next week. He'd told her about the week's reprieve from evening duties on Tuesday when they'd snuggled in bed recuperating from a delicious bout of sex, and she'd thought of almost nothing else since. With the boys gone, he'd have been freer. Since Timmy would also be away on the trip the following week, she'd even called in a former tavern employee to cover for her, so she'd have available time, too.

Speaking over the sound of the tap as she filled the pot, she said, "No problem. It's not as though we had anything special planned."

"Maybe we had more planned than I thought. Didn't you say you'd gone out to get something I'd love?"

She pressed the switch to start the coffee perking. "That's nothing. It'll still be here later." She walked past him to the sofa. "When do you leave?"

Daniel sat beside her and stretched his arm along the back. "I have an abbreviated schedule tomorrow. We leave right after lunch. I'll be back a week from Sunday."

"So long?" That hadn't really been her, had it, sounding clingy and needy? "I mean, who will handle your classes? How can you be away that long?"

He exhaled heavily and frowned.

"I wish I wasn't going to be gone at all. I could have gotten so much work done without the boys in the dorm. Now I have twice as much to do, getting lessens ready for the substitute and grading papers before I leave." His fingers slid beneath her hair and caressed her nape. "Staying here also meant I'd have had a hell of a lot more time with you."

Hiding her frustration, she shrugged. "Work is work. I'm sure the kids will love having you with them."

"That's the other thing I wanted to talk to you about. It's not just the other teacher who's sick, several of the kids are, too, and can't come. That means we have extra spaces for the weekend part of the trip. I checked, and saw that Timothy is scheduled to spend the weekend here and just take part in the academic segment of the trip, next week. If you don't have plans scheduled, I'd love for him to come with me for this weekend and next."

Timmy's class would be in Boston with the rest of the lower form for the five weekdays. She'd planned to bring him home Friday and meet his class in the city on Sunday. She'd even hoped Daniel would drive down with them and that they could have a leisurely trip back up by themselves.

"The weekends are for fun," he added. "This weekend they have a cruise on the Charles River planned, and one of the board members scored us tickets for the Patriots game. Next weekend, most of the parents will pick up their kids in town, but for the rest, we'll do something fun. I'm betting the zoo, the movies, or someplace most of us adults would rather not be with forty kids in tow. All I know for sure is, I'll be dead tired when I get back, and Timothy will have a good time if he comes with us."

No! She saw so little of her son, she begrudged every moment they weren't together. "Are you sure you want to add one more kid to your responsibilities?"

"One more on the weekends won't matter. I thought we might have the chance to know each other a little better if he came during this more relaxed time."

That's what had her worried. She found her own thoughts becoming tangled with Daniel. Did she want her son to know him better and face the same thing? To rely on his friendship only to have it end when Daniel became head of the academy would be super hard for her. It could be devastating to Timmy. He'd never had to endure rejection. Still, when else would he see a football game or spend so much time with a good male role model? And Daniel was exactly the kind of man she wanted Timmy to know and emulate.

"That would be great, Daniel. I appreciate it and I know Timmy will be thrilled. What do I need to do?"

"Can you come by the front office early tomorrow and sign the permission slip? I promise to watch him well, and Jeffrey Torrington will keep him occupied. They've become pretty good friends."

"Oh, believe me, Jeff is all he talks about. How can I thank you for thinking of my son?"

"It takes no effort—he's a great kid. However, I know a way, if you're interested."

His smile dazzled, but she only saw it for moments before she closed her eyes as he leaned forward for a kiss.

As opposed to when he arrived, now he touched her with nothing but gentleness. He pulled her onto his lap without breaking the kiss. She managed to straddle him, struggling to balance as she unbuckled and unzipped his pants. He groaned when her questing hands found his cock and drew it out, but he trembled as she positioned him and then impaled herself.

He pulled her sweater over her head and placed it beside them on the sofa. Eve rose and slid down the length of his shaft, letting his total possession of her senses wash over her. She smoothed the straps of her slip off her shoulders and down her arms; he unhooked her bra and tossed it aside. Arching her back she offered him her nipples. His mouth sought and found one, transferring his heat with each swirl of his tongue and suckle of his lips.

And all the while she rose and fell. The muscles of his flat abdomen rippled against hers, his legs tensed with each surge of his cock. His hands grasped her hips and took control of their speed. His thrusts stroked her clit as well as her pussy, and soon she panted with every breath.

"Daniel, take me over."

"Go ahead, baby."

"Come … come with… Oh, God!" She shuddered with her release, shaken to the core.

He pulled her against him, cradling her on his chest like a tightly held baby while he shot into her. Her world disintegrated and then reassembled. When she came back to herself, her breathing and heartbeat slowed, she found herself safely guarded in Daniel's arms. She licked the pulse beat in his neck, then nuzzled him. He rubbed his cheek against her hair and sighed.

"I've never known anyone like you," she murmured against his skin.

"I hope that's good," he said with a smile in his voice. His hands touched every inch of her bare back, spreading fire.

"Very good." She straightened but didn't attempt to cover herself. Daniel's eyes caressed her face, her neck, her breasts, and she was proud. Her body had pleased so many men over the years—more mentally than realistically—but she'd never been happier to satisfy anyone.

With a tiny shake of his head he straightened his clothing and then glanced at his watch. "I have to go. Don't worry about Timothy, I'll make sure he stays safe and has a good time."

She closed her eyes. Until taking him to Westover Academy she'd never spent a night away from her son. Even at that, he'd never been gone for days at a time when she didn't know where he was and generally what he was doing. Her heart ached with the changes, happening all too suddenly. She opened her eyes and gazed at the man before her.

"You know Timmy is my heart." Daniel nodded, and she thought he understood her fears.

"I wouldn't let him go with anyone but you."

Daniel moved her off his lap and stood. Smoothing Eve's hair from her face, he said, "That means a great deal. Having Timothy around will give me a good reason to call you every night."

He kissed her, then smiled and winked. "As if I needed any more of a reason than just wanting to talk."

Another quick kiss, a fast straightening of his clothing, and he was gone.

Not for the first time, Eve no sooner saw him go but she wanted to talk to him again, laugh with him, joke with him, feel their bodies merge, and form the perfection she'd come to expect whenever he touched her. She had enough experience to know what she had with him was rare indeed. The symmetry of their bodies and the synchronicity of their desires and needs combined to make their few times together more than memorable. Good thing, since tonight would have to last her for more than ten days.

There'd be ten days until she'd see Timmy again, too. How would she bear being without her guys all that time?

Her guys. She moved down the hall and into the bedroom, pulling her hair back in preparation for work. Okay, so it was dangerous thinking of Daniel in those kinds of terms. But she loved being with him; obviously he liked being with her. He could have explained about the trip over the phone, but he chose to see her.

He wanted to bang you. Don't go thinking it's anything more.

She yanked open the drawer. There was more than sex between them. How many years had she played her cards, deciding when to ante up her body and emotions or when to pass? It hadn't taken long to develop a sixth sense for when guys liked her for more than T & A—tits and ass. This time with Daniel felt right. Not forever, but for a little while. Enough time to enjoy a fantasy. When he decided to call their affair quits, she'd have these weeks to live on until she met another man as compatible. Maybe another seven years would elapse. Maybe it would never happen again. So she had to make the most of her opportunity.

Hopping as she pulled up her jeans, she heard the jukebox from downstairs. Judging from the voices rivaling the music, she guessed it would be a wild and long night. She checked her hair, her makeup and an open-necked shirt that had become her tavern uniform. Then, before closing her dresser drawer, she touched the new teddy she'd bought that afternoon as a surprise for Daniel. Soft green satin with ivory lace trim, it was almost too feminine to be sexy. She'd fallen in love with it immediately.

She sighed, then rushed to switch off the coffee pot and hurry downstairs.

"Sorry, Jed. I appreciate your taking care of things."

"No problem but we're both going to be in bad shape by the end of the night, I'm afraid." He reached under the counter and brought out an envelope. "So, before we get too busy and I forget, this is why I interrupted you and Doc earlier. There was a guy to see you. A foreigner. He said to give you this."

Cold dread flooded her. Jed answered a call from the end of the bar. Without thinking, Eve replaced an empty bottle with another longneck for a man lounging on the bar in front of her. Hearing no other immediate demands, she tore open the envelope.

Signorina.

Forcing herself to focus, she read the rest of the fine Italian script.

I am sent by my employer to politely request your presence at the Ritz-Carlton Hotel in downtown Boston. A room is reserved in your name for Wednesday night. He wishes to discuss the well-being of his son.

Signor Donatello knows the circumstances of your living arrangements and his son's schooling and implores that you will not force him into doing something you will regret.

Your most humble servant,

Giorgio Salvetti

Her hands shook when she slipped the note back into the envelope, and her heart hammered inside her breast. There was no question of how he'd found her. She used her stage name here and her real name on the school's paperwork, after all. No, what she wondered was why he'd *bothered* to find her. Without a look back, an offer to help, a single word of care, he'd tossed her out of the Florence apartment she'd thought hers, leaving her to find a way to support herself and their son. For more than seven years she'd heard nothing. Now, he appeared out of nowhere making threats. Luigi hadn't realized at the time what a strong woman she'd been. The years had only made her more so.

Fear lodged in her mind, though. She wouldn't be able to put it to rest until she saw him and discovered what he wanted.

What can it be but Timmy?

God, he couldn't—wouldn't—expect to take her son. She wouldn't let him.

She spared one small thought to Daniel. If her background as a simple stripper and unwed mother proved impossible for him and his career, being the former mistress to one of the leading industrialists in Europe tripled her unsuitability.

Forget Daniel! Her only concern now had to be Timmy, and how to keep him away from his father.

Chapter Nine

"All right, men," Daniel said, clapping his hands. "Are we all ready for bed?"

"Yes, sir!"

The response came back in a somewhat chorused form, with a few voices coming in a little late and others trying to yell their answer over their neighbors.

"Brushed your teeth?"

"Yes, sir!"

"Put on your pajamas?"

"Yes, sir!"

Each answer gained volume and by the time they finished this answer several of his charges were doubled over in giggling fits.

Daniel lowered his head and focused on Torrington and Timothy, two who had lost control, laughing. Daniel crooked his finger at Torrington who stumbled forward, still giggling. His doing so sent Timothy into even deeper paroxysms of laughter. Who could understand the mind of a six- or seven-year-old? Shaking his head, Daniel unbuttoned Torrington's pajama top and correctly rebuttoned it. Jeffrey was a smart boy, but he did have difficulties with his buttons. With a ruffle of the boy's hair, he sent him back to his friends, all of whom had shaped up marginally and now looked at him like an army waiting for his orders.

"Okay, troops. I have to go out for a few hours, but I expect you to behave for Ms. Allen just as you would for me."

God, he hoped they behaved for one of the school mothers *better* than they did for him, but he wouldn't expect too much. Thus far, the week had gone surprisingly well but now, Wednesday, he could see cracks in the boys' behavior. They were tired and out of their routine.

"Remember, bedtime is in one hour. As long as you're good, I'm sure

Ms. Allen will let you watch television for part of that time. But no more eating and no drinks. Do you know why?"

"Because we've brushed our teeth," said everyone but one boy.

He burst out with, "So we won't wet the bed."

That started the giggles again and several of the kids turned to point at little Robbie MacAdams, who did still wet the bed now and then if he drank anything beforehand.

"That's right. You've brushed your teeth and we don't want any accidents."

He focused on each one of his charges, loving the sparks of intelligence, the humor, the absolute innocence, and the decency he saw in every face. He would miss being this close to the boys when he became headmaster.

"Are there any questions before I leave?"

From the other side of the room came a small, "You'll come back, won't you Mr. Goodman?"

That was George Allington Longman. Another little kid whose parents had no time for him.

"You bet I will, Mr. Longman. I'll be back in a few hours and then I'll be in to check on each one of you, so don't worry. Be good, but have a good time, too, okay?"

"Good night, Mr. Goodman!"

To his relief, they turned to each other and began talking and, yes, giggling over something only they could understand.

"You have my cell number?" he asked Debbie Allen.

"Sure do. Don't worry. My youngest may be in upper form now, but he's the youngest of five boys. I've handled this age group before."

Daniel smiled. "I know. It's just…"

She smiled back. "You worry about them."

"I do."

She patted his shoulder. "That's why you're one of the most popular teachers at Westover."

He was?

"Boys know who cares about them and who's just giving lip service." She leaned forward and lowered her voice. "You'll make a fine headmaster, but I can tell you, the boys will miss having you in the classroom and in the dormitories."

Daniel couldn't help the shock he felt at her words. Or the pleasure.

"Now on your way," Debbie said, shooing him out the door. "See you in a few hours, after you've had a nice dinner with your girl."

"Thanks, Debbie."

He grabbed up his coat, not bothering to take the time to tell her that Sydney was not his "girl." No, as much of a girl he had was up in New Hampshire, managing a joint where he couldn't afford to be seen.

Just the thought of Eve set his heart racing. Six days had passed since he'd last seen her, and he had four more to go before returning home. Add a couple more days to catch up, and he'd be ready to burst from sexual tension. He hoped she felt the same.

In the lobby, he pulled out his phone and called up her number. They'd talked every night except last night. She'd said she would be busy, and though Tuesdays were generally slow at The Bare Moose, from what he'd gathered from Jed, she must have had something special happening. Eve had told him how she was working hard to change the character of the place to increase business by also widening the clientele. *Smart woman, my Eve!*

Not for the first time, he marveled at how easily those words came to him these days. *My Eve.* He liked it. Too much, actually, but he didn't quite know what to do about it. The thought of giving her up sent panic caroming around his mind like a stainless steel sphere in a pinball machine. He wasn't ready yet.

After the fifth ring, Daniel gave up on the call. He hadn't received her voicemail, either, so she must have the phone turned off. Surely she wouldn't, not with Timmy far from home. She would want to be available.

Pressing "End," Daniel made his way to the street and turned right to walk the couple of blocks to the Ritz-Carlton where Sydney and her father—Daniel hoped!—were meeting him for dinner.

With the sounds of traffic and the city energy guiding his steps, he made the trip in no time. Just as he reached the hotel, the doorman pulled open the door and Daniel stepped behind him to allow the party coming out some space. He glanced up, away, and then jerked his head back around. What the fuck? Eve, as he'd never seen her, exited on the arm of a man. She wore a gold lamé gown so tight it left nothing to the imagination. She couldn't have underwear on under that getup. He'd seen her in heels that high before, but not when she walked as regally as she did now.

The man was tall, olive-skinned, and with white hair that brushed the top of his collar. Daniel didn't know clothing labels, but the suit had to have cost several grand, regardless of who designed it. He had his hand on Eve's elbow, possessively guiding her to a stretch limo at the curb where the driver held open their door. Fortunately, they climbed into the car without Eve's having seen him.

What could he have said to her if she *had* seen him? "What the fuck are you doing here with him when you're mine?" Only he had no right. Daniel had never made any promise to her other than they would have fun.

That's not quite true. He'd as much as promised they had no future together because he had a goal that could never include her.

And what could he say to the man? "Get your fucking paws off my woman?" Except…she wasn't his, despite what his feelings had been leading him to believe.

Or what his heart screamed that it wanted.

***

Eve followed the maître d' to a table far from the kitchen and along the window. Once seated, she allowed herself a moment's excitement to view Boston through the window in her sparkling illuminated finest before facing the man who sat across the table. He was the reason she was here in town instead of serving patrons in The Bare Moose and counting the hours until Timmy was back in town. And Daniel, too, though she couldn't afford to let down her guard and think about him. Luigi would notice any weakness, any lapse of attention.

She accepted the proffered menu only to have Luigi take it from her and hand it back. "We will have your finest champagne and afterward I will consider if we will order dinner."

The waiter jerked back and stared from Luigi to her.

"No need to check with me. I have no idea what he's about," she said in a low voice. The man nodded and turned away. "And what *are* you about, Luigi? I thought we were here for dinner. It is after eight and I'm starving." She held out her hands. "And I don't dress like this just for a quick glass of champagne."

"You look satisfactory, but I haven't decided how long this meeting will last yet. If we don't eat, you can stop by a vending machine back at the hotel. I'm sure it's the kind of fare you are used to now." He lifted his chin towards her. "I'm guessing it's that kind of food that has added the pounds, also."

Eve narrowed her eyes. "You bast—"

She stopped and took a deep breath. It wouldn't serve to show anger before she even knew what he wanted from her. *Please, God, not Timmy. Please, don't let him want custody.*

She was saved by the arrival of their champagne. The server twisted the cage from the bottle neck and cut and then removed the foil. Deftly, he removed the cork, allowing only a sigh of sound. Eve only barely managed to avoid tapping her foot with impatience, but she recognized the ceremony attached to champagne. The server wrapped a white napkin around the neck, held the bottle at the bottom and tipped a small portion into each of their glasses, only adding more when the bubbles had subsided. Then he placed the bottle in the ice that filled the bucket next to the table.

Luigi picked up his glass, held it to the light and examined it closely.

"You were calling me a bastard, I believe?" His voice was pitched low, but Eve saw the woman at the table next to theirs turn to look at them. "It's strange that you should say so, when it is in actuality your son—*our* son—who is the bastard, is it not?"

"Only because of you."

Luigi lowered his glass and smiled at her, a cold smile that came nowhere near his eyes. "Come, come. You were there, too."

He sipped. "Quite delicious. Drink, why don't you?"

"No thank you." Nonetheless, she twirled the glass by the base and watched the light play through the glass and onto the white tablecloth.

"Why are you here, Luigi? What do you want?"

"What do you think I want?"

"Tell me." Instead of fear weakening her, she gained strength. Until he told her he wanted custody, she could believe that he didn't. She could handle anything else.

"I find that I want my son."

Eve was struck with a sharp pain that radiated from the vicinity of her heart.

"You can't have him."

Nausea followed the pain. She wanted to bend over and scream out both the pain and nausea, but the battle hadn't yet ended.

"I can. I have put aside my wife and the three sniveling girls she says belong to me. I find now that I need a son, someone I can train to take over for me in the business as I took over from my father. I need a son, you *have* my son." His eyes took on a calculating gleam. "Or so you tell me. As soon as I have proof of his parentage I will bring him home to Italy."

Slowly, with victory in his expression, he took another sip of the sparkling drink.

"Of course he is yours. Why would I lie?"

He shrugged. "I have money, prestige, power. Why would I believe that you would *not* lie?"

"I don't know. Maybe because I could care less about your power or prestige and because I never asked you for a dime after you threw me out of my home?"

Luigi threw her a cold smile and wagged his finger at her. "My home, Eve. You lived there for a time, but it never belonged to you."

Of course, he had told her just the opposite, but that didn't matter now.

"Timmy is a long way from the age where he can be 'trained' to take over your business, Luigi. You don't know him at all and he doesn't know you. Why would you rip him away from everything he loves?"

"You mean you. He has only been living in this village where you have him and at that school for a few months, so *you* can be the only thing he knows and loves."

Again, he shrugged as though his words and actions had no meaning. "You will accompany him, of course. He will live with me, but I will provide a small apartment nearby. He will visit with you there once a day."

"No," she whispered. "I will fight you."

"I would expect nothing less." He leaned across the table and this time made no pretense of niceness. "But I will prevail in this, Eve. He is my son. He *belongs* to me, much as you did at one time. I let you go easily, but I will not relinquish my only son."

The maître d' arrived at the table looking nervous. A woman stood beside him. She bent to kiss his cheek.

"*Ciao*, Luigi."

What the hell?

"*Ciao, bella.*"

Luigi fixed Eve with a stare.

"I will allow you one week to prepare our son for my visit. He may finish the autumn term at his school. At that time, I will provide tickets for your flights and I will expect him before Christmas. My family will expect to meet him then, also."

"By family, I know you don't mean everyone in your family. You can't be divorced. When a family counts cardinals among their friends, divorce is not allowed. Will your 'family' welcome my son? I don't think so."

"We shall see. Now, I am dining with a *beautiful* woman. Giorgio will bring the car around and see you back to your hotel."

With that, he stood and took the other woman's hand, completely dismissing Eve.

Despite the rude dismissal and the slight, Eve preferred a hamburger alone to the finest dining sitting across the table from Luigi. How had she ever thought she loved the man? Following the maître d' back through the tables she stopped to gather her wrap before venturing out to the street and to find Giorgio.

"I am so sorry, ma'am," the embarrassed maître d' said in a low tone. "Please accept this with my compliments and apologies." He pressed a foil wrapped package into her hands that smelled delicious. "We cannot control what kind of person comes to dine with us."

"This is most kind of you," Eve said, accepting the package. "I could have controlled who I associated with, but I was young and stupid, and believed his lies."

She thanked him again and stepped out to find Giorgio waiting for her.

She *had* been young and stupid. Now Timmy was going to pay the price.

Chapter Ten

Three nights after the class trip to Boston, Daniel sat in his apartment trying to concentrate on grading papers from the week he'd missed class. He wanted to chuck it all and take off for parts unknown—a feeling alien to him. He loved teaching and normally didn't mind the paperwork, but lately he'd been restless.

Monday's and Tuesday's classes had left him frustrated since the substitute—the headmaster, himself—hadn't covered the material outlined in his lesson plans. Two tests and a homework assignment had been skipped altogether, and he found himself trying to catch up the class work and his sleep, and also perform his regular duties.

The boys were at dinner, so no noise rang down the hall of the dorm, but Daniel was still unable to concentrate on the work stacked in front of him. Picking up half the peanut butter and banana sandwich he'd prepared for his own meal, he looked at the next test paper and read his essay question: *Discuss similarities between the protagonists in the tragedies* Hamlet, King Lear, Othello, *and* Macbeth. The answer, written in neat script, was *"Billy used their names for play titles"*.

What? He looked at the top of the page. The student's name didn't register with him. Searching through the notices he'd folded together in his briefcase, he found one regarding the boy, a new student. A personally penned note from the headmaster indicated tutoring might be needed. *Well, no shit, Sherlock!* Furious to have something else piled on, Daniel shoved his fingers through his hair and then snatched his red pen from the desk, ready to slash through the answer. Even without the same lectures and readings the rest of his junior level boys had, this kid should have known better than to—

Rife with tension, his fingers poked through the bread of his sandwich. A mind-clearing breath made him realize the boy was simply being a smart ass. The academy had rigorous entrance exams, so the kid had met some kind of academic standards. This test answer represented nothing more than a student pushing the envelope—and the teacher. Daniel gave him a fraction of a point for imagination then shoved the papers away. He wasn't up for more mental wrestling tonight.

Setting the remainder of the sandwich in the kitchen, he let his mind wander. He might as well face facts. His trouble was Eve. Much as he wanted to forget what he'd seen last week at the Boston Ritz-Carlton, he couldn't. Since knowing her, he'd risked so much, broken so many rules—both the academy's and his own—that an objective observer might think standards didn't matter to him. Of course, they did. Though he'd been willing to bend the law where it applied to seeing Eve, he'd still understood relationship rules. First and foremost, monogamy during the time they were together. They'd had unprotected sex, for Christ's sake.

She'd not only come out of a hotel with a man, she'd been dressed like a wet dream. With each step, her slinky, shimmering dress had reflected the city lights in flashes of golden rays. Her hips had beckoned, the way a woman's did when she walked in high heels—a twist left, a flick back to the right, a seductive sway left. Daniel had stood stock still, entertaining a mental image of Eve wearing nothing but her stockings and heels the next time they made love.

But then he'd noticed that her hair, adorned with sparkly clips to keep it back from her face, flowed over her shoulders. Down, the way a woman wears her hair when she wants a man to touch it, to wrap it around his fingers, to use it to bring her close for a deep, long kiss.

He'd been stabbed with lust and jealousy in equal portions. Her hair was *his* to entangle, her lips *his* to nibble, her mouth *his* to plunder. At least for now, his *alone.*

Or so he'd thought. That she didn't agree showed the gulf between them in how they viewed relationships and, he feared, life. Eve's roaming wouldn't have surprised him when they first met. Now that he'd come to know her so well—and, he admitted warily, come to care for her so much—the discovery disturbed him a great deal.

He paced his room, wondering what to do. He hadn't called her since his return for fear of saying something he'd regret, but he had to deal with his suspicions sooner or later.

A tentative knock came at his door. He sighed inwardly. Such a feeble effort usually indicated a young man facing punishment who hoped Daniel wouldn't hear if he kept the sound to a minimum. Thinking to surprise the miscreant, Daniel swung the door open, looking down. Down, where a seven- or eight-year-old head should have been. Instead, he found himself staring at the shirred waist of a softly feminine suit. He raised his gaze to Eve's luminous brown eyes. Eyes filled with questions.

"Daniel, I hope I'm not intruding."

"No."

For two beats he simply drank in the sight of her. The scent of delicate perfume floated by, pushed by the breeze coming from the doorway at the end of the hall.

"No, not at all. I was grading papers." He stood back. "Come in."

She walked past. The way her hands clutched the rectangular bag she carried contradicted the confidence of her graceful carriage and the tilt of her head. Her suit fit with classic styling. The design was conservative in a shade between mustard and gold. The scarf defining her shoulder in shades of russet, dark chocolate brown, and gold, and the traditional upsweep of her hair, didn't offset the effect of her fuck-me heels. What could? Their height would have sent any mortal woman tumbling to the ground. Eve glided by him as though she'd been born wearing heels. She stopped and turned, and for a moment she was more goddess than human.

He couldn't speak with his breath hitched and his heart racing out of control. Closing the door, he took the opportunity to try to make sense of his scattered thoughts. Guess he'd have to deal with those suspicions sooner.

Eve spoke first. "I saw Timothy for a few minutes before his dinner. He couldn't stop talking about you, and Boston, and what a good time he had."

She sat on the sofa where he indicated, but on the edge, back rigid and knees tightly together. He spun his office chair and sat facing her, saying nothing.

She fidgeted with her purse, though her expression showed no tension. "I don't think you realize how new and different last week was for him. He's never been away from me that long."

Daniel only raised his brows and she rushed on as though to fill the void.

"I don't mean here at school, I mean"—she waved her hand and blinked her beautiful eyes as though holding back tears—"out in the world, where I couldn't pick up a phone and call whenever I wanted."

"I'm sure Timothy misses you when he's here but it's harder on you, isn't it?" He smiled, the friendly schoolmaster, making courteous comments as he had to countless mothers over the years. What a fraud. "All mothers go through separation trauma at one time or another."

She let go a sob-laugh, opened her pocketbook for a tissue and dabbed at her eyes.

"God, it was awful. I think I drove this direction two or three times before remembering he wasn't here. Thank you so much for letting me talk to him last week. I'm sure that broke some rule of the academy's," she said with a rueful smile. "It seems every time I turn around I'm bumping into one of the damn things."

Daniel smiled and saw some of the tension leave her shoulders. Truth to tell, some of his own strain let up as he allowed the pleasure of seeing and hearing her wash over him.

"I agree they can be annoying at times, but rules do serve a purpose."

Eve's gaze met his and held. "And not just where they concern my being with Timmy."

Her hands clenched her bag and it didn't require a good ear to recognize a slight tremor in her voice. "While I appreciate your calling so I could talk with Timmy, I was a little confused as to why you and I didn't have more to say. When you left, I was under the impression you enjoyed talking to me. I know it seemed we did more and more of it—"

"Between episodes of sex in the few hours I've had away from here, you mean. We really haven't had much time together."

"No, but we used it well. I needed what you've given me, and I don't regret anything. I had thought there was more, that's all. That we'd become friends of sorts."

Friends? More than friends. His feelings for her had grown passionate, beyond where he should have allowed them. Almost beyond where he could control them. He'd risked years of time and effort in the last few weeks. Each time they'd met or talked he'd weighed all he'd worked for against his increasing feelings for Eve. He thought she'd moved a bit past their initial, physical needs, too.

Then he'd seen her in Boston. Eve hadn't shown any blatant sense of intimacy, but the man's air of possessiveness hadn't been concealed from any who looked their way. Though Daniel had no claim on Eve's affection or body, her betrayal had shocked him. The sophisticated, chic woman on the well-dressed man's arm had opened Daniel's eyes to how she must have been at the height of her career as the toast of Europe, before closeting herself in small-town New Hampshire.

There might be a way to finesse loving Eve Star, tavern keeper, but not his Evening Star, famous exotic dancer. Even if he could afford her, which he couldn't, based on the looks of the man escorting her, would he want to be with that Eve? He wanted and needed the woman he'd come to know. A woman more like his mother than someone who aspired to be every man's sinful desire.

Daniel decided to ignore her subtle plea for answers and instead share his own news. "I met with Sydney Thomas's father while I was in Boston. Mr. Thomas is calling the board together this week to make a decision about the headmaster's position. He thinks I'll hear good news by the end of the weekend."

"Oh, Daniel." Her eyes sparkled with excitement. Excitement for him. Hell, how could he not love her?

The truth slammed into him. He loved Eve Star, God help him. When he first met her, his nights had been filled imagining her legs over his shoulders and his dick deep inside her. Last week he'd thought as much about holding her and sharing his thoughts and mundane events of the day. He'd begun to want the moon *and* the star. Daniel's amusement over his pun was superseded by confusion. How could he have let himself feel so much for her knowing their unsuitability, and now, what in hell difference did it make? She obviously didn't feel the same about him.

"Of course they'll appoint you headmaster. No one else cares for the boys as much as you do. You'll be very good for Westover Academy. And Westover will be very lucky to have you in charge. I can't believe there was ever any doubt about whom to select."

He grinned. "Thanks. I had fences to mend though. My major competitor for the position saw me pulling out of The Bare Moose parking lot last week and reported me."

Eve jerked to attention. "Do you mean they might not have considered you because they thought you'd been in the bar? How dare they! It's a perfectly respectable place now."

Laughing, he enjoyed seeing the affront in her expression and hearing the indignation in her voice. All for him and his dreams.

"Not only would they dare to pass me over, they almost did. Fortunately, Sydney and her father are in my corner. I was able to convince Mr. Thomas that my vision should prevail, and I think his support will be enough to secure the appointment."

"So, Mr. Thomas didn't mind that you were at the tavern? At least there's one open-minded—" She stopped, studying his eyes.

"I see. You told him you weren't there."

"No, I simply evaded answering the question. Andy Worth—he's the guy who reported me—can't prove it was me he saw."

Silence reigned for a few moments. Then, "I understand, I think."

She stood. "And I'd better go. As Lauren Knowles I've been invited to help with the Halloween party this evening. I only came by to say thanks for all you've done for Timmy. Spending time with you has been wonderful for him."

She turned and strode to the door. "And for me," she said in so low a voice he almost missed hearing her words.

Daniel jumped to his feet. "Wait a minute!" Something just happened—this sounded like goodbye. He took her hand and held her back.

"You're disappointed that I didn't own up to being at the bar."

She raised her head high. "Yes."

"Should I have explained to Sydney and her father what I was doing there? Do you think it would have helped my case to confirm Andy's accusation?"

"I don't know. But that you're ashamed showed in your lack of comment."

He thought back to Sydney's call alerting him to Andy's tattle. He hadn't felt guilt, only anger.

"Not ashamed, prudent. You sound like my brother."

He shook his head at her quizzical expression. "I've worked here for ten years, Eve, and I know something about Westover. Perceptions and appearances are important. Sometimes more important than facts."

"I'm surprised you'd even want to be in charge of a place like this, then."

"It's not a bad place. I love my boys and want to make a difference in their lives. For that, I have to be in a position to implement my vision, and that means picking my fights. I don't have full support of the board, or the faculty and parents. As soon as I admit being at The Bare Moose, the statement would be used against me and I'd have a fight on my hands that has no bearing on my abilities as headmaster. If I'm going to defend myself, I'd rather it be over something that matters to the job, not over my personal life."

"I see that," she said. "But what if you'd been seen leaving my apartment? Am *I* worthy?"

His hesitation was bare. He hardly noticed the tick of time between her question and his answer. Surely Eve didn't either?

"Well, yes." His thumb stroked her palm and he looked into her eyes. "That's not to say I'm going to rush out and advertise that we're seeing each other. I'll be plain. I won't get the job if the board knows about you, any more than Timothy would be allowed to stay if it came out you run The Bare Moose. We've both marked our lines in the sand, and for the same reason. Because we want what's best for someone else."

Eve's expression softened under his scrutiny. And saddened a little, too. He wanted to take her in his arms and reassure her that he cared. But the image of the tall stranger and the way he'd acted toward her intruded in his thoughts. Daniel wanted to know who the man was and why she'd been there with him.

"The solution to both our problems will present itself at Christmas break," Eve said. "I've decided to take Timmy back to Europe."

***

"*What?*" Daniel took a step back.

Eve knew he might expect her to agree that being less than honest was acceptable just because his motives were pure, or he might even have thought she'd disagree. But she figured he didn't expect her to cut and run.

"What are you talking about?"

She tried to turn to the door. He stopped her and made her face him. His fingers dug into her shoulders, though she wouldn't have moved if he'd let go of her. She didn't want to leave, didn't want to give up seeing him. But his half-hearted reassurance showed he didn't feel the same.

They had agreed at the beginning—had that been only a few short weeks ago?—that a physical relationship was all they could afford. She'd tried, she really had, not to let emotion interfere with the amazing way Daniel made her body feel, but it had.

Damn! Once before she'd been willing to give up her life in order to be part of someone else's, regardless of how small a part. Never again. Romantics were all full of shit. The non-romantic reality of what she'd accepted with Timmy's father had almost killed her.

"It's complicated."

"I have a Ph.D. I can understand complicated. Just be honest with me."

Daniel's eyes seemed to change color with the emotion running through them. Brown to gold to a mixture that made her warm all over. From the hallway came the sounds of children entering the building.

"I can't talk now, Daniel, there's no time. But whatever the reason, don't you think it's for the best?"

"Probably. No." His jaw tensed. "Hell, I don't know." He let out a breath. "Who was the man I saw you with in Boston, Eve?"

She jerked back but his grasp provided no leeway. "I don't know what you mean."

"I saw you with him at The Ritz-Carlton Hotel where I was meeting Sydney for dinner. There you were, all dressed up for a big night out with a very wealthy-looking guy whose hands were all over you."

Clutching at any straw to turn the conversation, she blurted, "So it's Sydney you met for dinner, not her father."

"That night, yes."

Her eyes narrowed. "In a hotel. How convenient. It was obvious even the one time I saw her that her interest in helping you gain the headmaster position is for more than goodwill. She wants you."

"I think that's true, but we aren't talking about me."

Eve shoved his chest, hoping he would anger enough to make her do what she couldn't do on her own, leave his apartment.

"When she saw us at the farmers' market a few weeks ago, she looked as though she wanted to fuck you right there among the pumpkins and apples. How much more must she have wanted you in the confines of a hotel room? I can see the two of you now, tangled in the sheets, hot and satisfied in each other's arms. Do ladies in Boston *allow* themselves to get hot and sweaty in sex, or is that something left to—"

His mouth came down on hers before she could move. His hands framed her face so there was no way to avoid his hot mouth or the searing breach of his tongue past her lips. He explored, probed, tested.

She dropped her bag so she could use both hands to hold him, her arms wrapping around his waist and stretching up his back. He slanted his mouth, moving his lips over hers and making low groans deep in his throat when she pressed her tongue past his teeth. He trailed his fingers over the rim of her ear, along her jaw line and down the column of her neck.

A hair wouldn't have fit between them. Her breasts crushed against him with each heaving breath. She felt his heart hammer as though there were no shirt and suit keeping her skin from his. He radiated heat like a blast furnace and she absorbed it as she did his breath.

Daniel broke the kiss and rested his forehead on hers. The quiet noise of well-behaved boys filtered through the door.

"Who is the man, Eve?"

She shook her head, fighting to regain enough composure to exit his apartment and walk past the boys crowding the halls. "I wish we could ... I need—"

"I know. Don't move. I just want to hold you."

"I want so much more."

"*Who was the man?*" His hands swept down her back and up. "Be honest. I'll understand."

Dropping her hands to his waist, she pushed, but met perfect resistance. "I have to go."

"Not until you tell me."

"Timmy's father," she blurted.

She knew the moment he realized the importance of her words. At the same time, she caught the meaning of what he'd said. *I'll understand.* He'd believed she found a man, a quick fling to serve as diversion. How little he thought of her.

Sadly, she watched the play of emotions on his face. He could have handled her cheating. He would have dug down deep and found a way to forgive her a fling.

Would he even believe what had happened between her and Luigi? Sex had been the furthest thing from either of their minds. After acquiescing to Luigi's arrogant high-handed demand that she drop everything in her life to meet him when and where he said, she'd spent time before their meeting worrying about what he wanted, and the time since worrying about how she would escape falling back into the chaos that had once been her life. That Daniel was ready to *understand* meant he'd already made up his mind about what she'd been doing in Boston.

Now, the joke was on him. Instead of a nameless man and meaningless sex he could *understand*, she'd spent time with someone who mattered, in that Luigi was the one person who'd given her everything that meant anything. The man whose touch had once lighted her afire and whose body had given her the only prize worth having. Her son.

Daniel's arms dropped away and he moved back. Without a blink or another word, she stooped for her bag, rose, and left.

***

Snagged from a shadowy half-sleep by the ringing phone, Eve knew a moment of gripping fear. She glanced at the luminous face of the clock and her breath hiked. A call at one-thirty in the morning couldn't be anything but bad news. *Timmy!*

She grabbed the receiver. "Hello?"

"Eve, it's Daniel."

"Is everything all right?" she demanded, at the same time that he said, "Don't be nervous, there's nothing wrong."

She slumped back on the bed and rubbed one eye with the heel of her hand. "Thank God. It's uh … it's kind of late."

"Or early, depending on how you look at it."

"Very clever," she said drolly.

"I wanted to catch you before you went to bed. I'm sorry if I woke you."

Settling under the covers, she held the phone to her ear, closed her eyes and savored the smokiness of his voice curling through her.

"You didn't really. But if you'd waited ten more minutes…"

"How was the Halloween party?"

"Wonderful. Not like the trick or treating I used to do when I was Timmy's age, but the boys enjoyed it."

"My brothers and I used to go out trick or treating, too. It was fun in a small town."

"I lived in Chicago. But neighborhoods were like small towns in themselves." Moving the receiver away, she tried to stifle a yawn. "Did you call to compare costumes?"

"Were you serious about leaving after Christmas?"

"Yes."

"Is it possible to find someone to work for you this weekend?"

She sat and pulled up her knees to rest her chin on, suddenly awake. "Maybe. Why?"

"I know you must have good reasons to be making plans like that, but I don't get it. I want you to explain it to me. And I'm selfish. I want to see you. I need to, even though it would probably be the worst possible thing for me right now."

Hurt pierced like a hot poker but she controlled her voice. "Look, I don't want to be the cause of trouble for you. Especially since I won't be around much longer."

"That came out wrong. I want time, Eve, and I want you, all to myself. Because I had to take that class trip I'm pretty sure I can get away this weekend, from Friday afternoon through Sunday. We could go somewhere and talk. Would you be interested?"

"I'm not sure." She heard his breath, soft against the receiver.

"You're not sure because you think it would be bad for me or because you don't want to be with me?"

"We both know our meeting again wouldn't be good for your position, so let's leave it at that."

"God, I wish I could."

She gave a hard laugh. "Has anyone ever let you in on the secret that your lines suck?"

He didn't laugh. He just stayed quietly on the other end, breathing. Shaking her head, she almost said goodnight and hung up.

"Have you ever been in the position of wanting two different things? Having one means losing the other, but you just can't bring yourself to let go?"

If only he knew. "Yes."

"Then you understand how I feel right now. For the whole first half of my life I was an outsider, looking in. Odd man out, always. Until I started teaching, and especially since coming here. For the past ten years I've known who I was and where I wanted to go in life. What I wanted to do. I reached for the prize and found it at the tip of my fingers." Awe sounded in his voice.

How could Daniel ever have felt on the outside of life? He was so smart, decent, and caring, it seemed impossible to believe anyone wouldn't take him to heart.

"Then I met you. I never knew fire could burn so hot, that need could be so great."

His voice lowered and rasped into her ear. She grew wet just listening.

"I never experienced jealousy until I saw you with … Timothy's father. Or felt as empty as when you left tonight. You said who you were with in Boston, and I knew there was nothing I could offer as great as what he'd already given you. He must have meant a great deal to you at one time because, Eve, I know you're not the kind of woman to have a cheap, easy fling. I *know* it. And I'm sorry for my smug assumption earlier."

"Daniel—"

"So forgive me if I'm ambivalent. I shouldn't see you. I shouldn't want you."

He stopped, and Eve pictured him in the clothes he'd worn earlier, sitting in a darkened room, talking to her. A phone line connected them, the only two people in the world.

"I shouldn't need you. But I do, Eve, all the same. Will you come away with me this weekend?"

"Yes."

His sigh came through the line. "I'm still up to my neck in work so I won't be able to get away this week, but may I call after dinner each night?"

"I hope you will. I've missed you."

"I've missed you, too, sweetheart. Make the arrangements. I'll pay Jed's extra salary and whatever else the costs are"

"That's not nec—"

"Eve?"

"Yes, Daniel?"

"I can hardly wait until Friday. Goodnight."

"Good *morning*."

His chuckle sounded before he hung up, but Eve sat holding the phone for long minutes after.

"I love you," she whispered.

Placing the phone on the night stand, Eve lay back. What in the world was she doing? When she'd left his apartment, she'd thought the break was made, that she and Daniel would most likely not see each other again, and that had been for the best, as she'd told him. As hard as it had been to leave Luigi before Timmy was born, that event didn't equal the pain she already felt at the thought of never seeing Daniel again. She loved him. Loved his steadfastness, his humor, his caring attitude, the way he acted with Timmy. The way he made her feel, as though no other woman existed.

He was high-handed sometimes, but he didn't seem to mind ceding control, either. She didn't understand why his position at the academy was so important to him, but he'd revealed a little of himself tonight, enough to let her know the two of them were more alike than she'd thought before.

It had never occurred to her that she'd be spotted in Boston. Thank goodness Daniel hadn't approached her in town. Explaining Luigi to Daniel would be much easier than explaining him to Luigi.

She wasn't sure if she could get across to Daniel why she had decided to give in to Luigi's demand that she and Timmy return to Italy. In truth, she wasn't sure she quite understood it herself. She would make things easier for Timmy by being there and easing his way with Luigi's family. If he turned out to be happy, she would be, too, regardless of Daniel's living thousands of miles away, leading the boys in a posh school. She'd find some way to let him know she was glad for him. His happiness mattered a great deal to her. More than her own, truth be told.

That's what love was, after all.

Would he ever think of her? She'd do her best over the weekend to make sure he did. And then she would *not* see him again. She would be leaving in seven weeks. She needed to prepare herself for the break. A woman can't wean herself off love. A fast break is always best.

She'd said from the beginning that she would store memories for when they left each other. She hadn't known then how soon that time would come. Or how deep the leaving would cut.

Chapter Eleven

Friday took its sweet time arriving. At last, Daniel dumped his books and papers in his apartment, changed clothes and grabbed the case he'd packed the night before. He could hardly believe it, but he was skipping school, and this time he wouldn't be spending his precious freedom with Jonah, stuck in some crappy "art" theatre like he had the only other time he'd escaped his academic responsibilities.

Stopping at the hall mirror to check how he looked before walking out the door was a habit he'd developed years ago to ensure he set the best example for the boys. Clothed casually in slacks, a button-down shirt and a tie, topped with a sport jacket, he quickly approved his appearance.

While the assessment had become *pro forma*, his appearance today wasn't really a matter of great concern. He saved all of his interest in appearances for Eve and whatever she'd be wearing. He'd bet it wouldn't be anything conservative. In actuality, because it had been over two weeks since they'd been together, he didn't care what she wore. He only cared about how soon she'd be *out* of whatever she wore.

With barely a wave to the substitute dorm master, Daniel rushed for the car and then for the train station. In a far corner of the lot, he pulled up beside Eve's green Honda Accord. She rolled down her window when he exited his Volvo. He leaned down, one hand planted above the driver door.

"Why, Mrs. Knowles. Fancy meeting you here. Taking a trip?"

She smiled, and his heart started pounding. No other woman he'd known could do as much with just a smile.

"Just waiting for the train to Maine, Mr. Goodman. Thanks for asking."

"Here's an idea. I'm driving to Maine. Why don't you ride along and keep me company?"

"Oh, how lovely. I'd like that."

He stepped back, and she opened the door. Taking his proffered hand, she murmured her thanks.

"I only have this overnight case." She gestured to the backseat.

He raised his brows. "You do realize we won't be back until Sunday evening?"

"I don't have big fashion plans." Her lips tipped up again and God help him, he couldn't wait any longer to dip his head for a taste of her sweet mouth. Damn anyone to hell who saw them and cared.

Their kiss was fast and hard, not coming anywhere close to what he wanted, but it would have to do for the moment.

"You look beautiful," he said as she walked around the front of the Volvo to the passenger side.

Daniel had been wrong. He *did* care what she wore because she looked so damn beautiful. Demure and feminine, she wore soft-looking, sand-colored slacks, a pale green blouse and beige blazer. With her mass of auburn hair in a soft braid, and the collar of her blouse open, a simple gold necklace and earrings showed off her neck to perfection. If there was anything to complain about, it was her shoes. Attractive and dressy, but low-heeled. Daniel sighed. This was Lauren, country club mom. But surely, with only an overnight bag for three days, Eve the sex kitten would emerge at some point.

He retrieved her case. She hit the remote lock for the Honda and placed her coat and gloves in the Volvo before settling into the passenger seat. He tossed her bag next to his in the back and they headed off.

Daniel put her past and his planned future from his mind. For three hours, they talked and laughed about little things. They brushed fingers and shared a secret smile full of heat in a McDonald's.

Once more Daniel experienced a flashback—or can you have a flashback to something that never happened? Here he was, acting like a high school kid in love with his first girlfriend, anxious to get in her pants and even more anxious to make a connection. This was an adventure like he'd never allowed himself in his teens. In this fantasy, he and the gorgeous woman beside him would be fucking like bunnies for the weekend. Something else totally unlike high school.

At dusk, Daniel pulled into the parking area of a stately Queen Anne perched on a hill in Boothbay, Maine. Only two other vehicles occupied the lot. Standing beside the car, Eve looked up at the house and then rotated to gaze toward the ocean. He watched her expression change from wonder to joy.

Finally, she fixed her sight on Daniel over the top of the Volvo. "It's beautiful. Just beautiful. How did you ever discover this place?"

"Research. It was listed in the top ten most romantic inns in New England." He examined the near empty parking lot. "Not much romance this time of year, I guess."

"That depends on the people, I'd say."

Daniel shifted his focus back to Eve. In the quickly fading light, her features had softened and her eyes were heavy-lidded. Her full, moist lips turned up in a beguiling smile and one brow arched. The wind whipping off the water and up the hill plummeted the temperature, but he was heated from the inside out. Better than any radiator, better than any fire, all it took to send his thermostat off the charts was a single, evocative glance from Eve.

He looked at his watch. "We have just enough time to check in and see the room before dinner. I made reservations at a place that's highly recommended."

Her face glowed. "You really have this all planned, don't you?"

"Just through dinner, darlin'." He stepped to the back to retrieve their bags. "We've got the whole weekend. There's lots of time to improvise."

"Good." She took her coat from the back seat and slipped into it. "It is kind of cold, so I'm hoping you have ideas on how to warm me up."

"I'm from the south. Heat is in my blood," he said, and she laughed.

The proprietor of the B&B didn't bat an eye at two people without wedding rings checking in with only one bag and one overnight case between them. Maybe it happened every weekend. But the experience was new for Daniel. He'd hooked up with women once in a while, away from the academy, but he'd never sought a quiet, romantic place to spend a weekend alone with anyone. He recognized how dangerous his feelings were becoming. Every moment he spent with Eve—hell, every moment he spent *thinking* of her—only increased his desire. He wanted more time. He had more dreams of holding her, kissing her, sensing the balls-deep satisfaction of being inside her.

The weekend was more than playing hooky with Eve—it was a test. Their normal circumstances ensured he was teased. They'd spend a couple of hours together maybe once a week, then heat each other to a lustful inferno on the phone. Eve was like a cookie being held out and then snatched away after he grabbed a meager crumb. This weekend was an Eve immersion—the whole batch of ginger snaps, hot and spicy with a definite kick after the first bite.

If being with her a straight fifty hours or so didn't end his obsession, he had some serious thinking to do about his future. Weighing his choices would be difficult. One side of the scale held his precious career, to which he'd devoted himself for several years. On the other side hung what could very well be love. Of course, it could also be only a powerful, consuming physical attraction, one that had every chance of proving temporary. That's what he had to determine, and quickly. Eve said she was leaving in a few weeks, so he didn't have time to casually explore the hunger for her that conquered more of his life every day.

Career or Eve. There was no way in hell he'd be able to have both, of that he felt certain.

***

Peals of Eve's laughter rang through the lobby. Daniel carried her in his arms, matching her laughter as he started for the stairway.

"Damn it! Stop making me laugh or I'm gonna drop you. I should have attempted this before you ate two pounds of lobster." He faked puffing, for emphasis.

"Hey, you made it just fine from the car and up all those porch steps. There are only three flights to our love nest. Surely a big, strong man like you can do that…?" Her smile teased and challenged.

"Don't be too sure," he said, but he took the first flight of stairs at a dash. "You dancers may look shapely, but you're all muscle and that weighs a lot, you know."

She took one arm from around his neck and slapped him playfully on the shoulder. "Are you insulting me?"

"No way."

The second flight was dispatched with the same speed.

"Good, because that muscle allows us to do so many other things. Things you'll be happy to discover."

"Oh, yes?"

"You don't sound suitably impressed."

"All of my brain is concentrating on getting to our room before I collapse."

She leaned her head back to take a look at him. "Pshaw. Your face isn't red. You're not even breathing hard."

"Trying to seem manly in front of you."

Laughing, she said, "I know better ways to show you're manly than tempting a heart attack on the steps."

"Huh," he grunted. "Me caveman. Me do both." He turned to the left at the top of the final flight of stairs. "The room, thank God."

Eve slapped at him in playfulness again as he set her on her feet at their door.

He kissed the back of her neck. "Madame, our room awaits."

She turned the knob and stepped inside. He closed and locked the door, tucking them into a room under the eaves that served as their own special paradise.

The third floor housed two suites, each covering a side of the house. Thus, both had sitting rooms facing the ocean and bedrooms overlooking the back garden and distant hills.

"This is the loveliest inn," she said. Removing her coat, she hung it on a coat tree in the corner. Then she turned to Daniel. "And very romantic."

When they'd dropped the bags off and freshened up before dinner, he'd made a quick appraisal of the suite. The rooms were better than the inn's website depicted. The sitting room contained two focus areas—one toward a double-sided fireplace, and the other a loveseat and chair arrangement in the bow window overlooking the rocky beach and ocean. A folding screen, covered in a flowered print that matched the furniture and complemented the pastel paint and delicately-patterned wallpaper, hid a tiny kitchenette. Opposite, a doorway led to the bedroom where a canopied, queen-sized bed facing the fireplace waited for them. The bathroom opened into both the bedroom and sitting room. Sexy more than romantic, it boasted a dressing table, glassed-in shower stall and a whirlpool tub, large enough for two.

"I'm happy you came up here with me." He tossed the room key on the coffee table between a sofa and the marble-fronted fireplace and took her in his arms. "And I'm glad the trip was problem-free—it was much better with you along than if I'd had to drive by myself—and that dinner satisfied you. But all of that begs the question … what now?" He added a little tactile stimulation to his teasing words, skimming his hands down her back and across her ass.

"I've given that some thought," she answered. "Let's make this a fantasy weekend. Tonight, you can tell me a fantasy, and, if it's in my power, I'll fulfill it."

"You always do."

"But this is special and specific. Let your imagination run wild."

"Hmm."

He examined the room, wondering what he could ask her to do, how she might perform for him. Draping her shoulder with his arm, he walked to the bedroom. A few feet from the bed stood an antique wardrobe. He'd seen earlier that half the cabinet provided room to hang clothing and the other held a television, VCR, and stereo. *As if we'll be spending any time watching TV.*

The doors, covered in mirrors, gave him the idea.

"I'd like for us to watch you make yourself come."

Eve followed his gaze to the mirror and smiled. She turned and rose to kiss him, slowly, deeply, her tongue delving into his mouth and out, in and out, licking his bottom lip with each stroke. When he reached for her, she stepped back and started undressing. His attention followed every move, his cock at attention, his hands fisted at his sides lest he reach out to help.

She opened the armoire door and hung her jacket on a padded hanger. Her blouse, released from the waistband of her slacks, flowed like liquid over her hips. Slowly, she unbuttoned the sleeves and then the front, and hung it beside her jacket. Each piece of clothing found its place in the makeshift closet, handled with care. Daniel found her actions erotic and wondered what could possibly be sexy about watching a woman undress slowly, carefully, with no purposeful attempt to seduce. He decided Eve made the actions sexy. Hell, watching her wash dishes would probably make him hard.

He caught his breath when she left her lacy panties on the floor—she'd shaved her pussy. Eve closed the wardrobe door and Daniel raised his eyes to see her watching him in the mirror. Smiling, knowing his surprise, she broke the stare and padded the few feet to the bed.

"Don't you want to join me?" Her voice was low and throaty.

"Sure," he said, already beginning the process of getting naked.

"Come and sit behind me. That way you'll have the best view."

Daniel, divested of clothing, settled on his knees directly behind Eve. They didn't touch, but she radiated heat. He detected her perfume, light and flowery, and, amazingly, a slight whiff of her arousal. He was already hard as steel, and sorry he'd ever suggested this fantasy since now he wanted nothing more than to bury himself in her.

Light from the living room filtered into the bedroom, lending just enough illumination to show her expression and body distinctly. She sat back from the edge, knees bent, her toes just hanging off. Daniel watched the silvered glass in the armoire door; Eve watched him.

Her reflection spread her knees, revealing her pussy glistening with moisture.

"This is from just being with you," she whispered. "I haven't even touched myself and I'm wet."

It could have been nothing more than a come-on. Daniel didn't care. He loved hearing her refer to him that way, thinking he affected her the way she did him.

Her lids dropped, as though keeping her eyes open took more energy than she had to give. She sucked two fingers into her mouth, then used them to stroke the lips of her labia, rubbing the ridges of skin and then plowing the furrow between. She took long strokes, from the tiny puckered rosebud of her backside, over the juicy opening to her channel and up to the nub tucked under its hood at the top of her lips. Her fingers were long and slender, her nails neat, though not long or painted. She popped two back in her mouth, sucking, licking, sending them wet from the heat of her mouth to the fires of her sex, stroking again the full length of her pussy lips, circling and swirling around her clit.

Daniel glanced at her face and saw her parted lips, heard her ragged breathing. Burnished cheeks matched the rosy blush making its way over her breasts, where her nipples pebbled hard and pointed. He wanted to suck them, take them in his mouth and lave them with his tongue, but this was Eve's show, and he'd let her finish it. Dropping a hand to his dick, he stroked once, smoothing the droplet of cum on the tip over the crown.

Musk filled the air. He inhaled, letting the scent push him to a new, harder level of urgency. He scooted forward and pressed his cock against her back, skimming his hands from her shoulders to her elbows then back up and across her back, tracing light patterns on her skin.

"Open your eyes."

She leaned into him and moaned as her fingers delved inside her channel, then up and around before burrowing back into her wetness. Her lids lifted as though being dragged. She stared at herself for a moment. Heavy-lidded, she met his gaze in the mirror.

Slowly, he licked her shoulder then turned his head and took her earlobe between his teeth. He felt her breath hitch more than heard it. His hips thrust forward, streaking a drop of cum from his dick a few inches up her back.

Once more she made the trip from pussy to mouth and back, for that long stroke. Instead of encircling her clit, she sank both fingers into her heat. Slowly, they disappeared then reappeared, each time wet and glistening. Again and again she thrust her fingers into her sheath, then up and around her clit, bringing moisture and fragrance along.

A light sheen of perspiration coated her upper lip. As though he kissed her, he tasted the salt of her sweat on his tongue. He licked her neck again, nuzzling the crease where neck met shoulder.

"Oh, God," she cried, tensing. Her eyes widened in surprise, but never left his.

He dropped his gaze briefly. The muscles at the mouth of her pussy convulsed around her fingers. Creamy moisture leaked around them, coating the folds of her labia and running down to the pink, tight ring of her ass.

Daniel raised his gaze and struggled to maintain his control. His hips rocked. One arm snaked around her waist and pulled her tight. He sucked air. She pushed back, even while her fingers coaxed more cream from her pussy. His cock felt molten against the satin of her back. He wanted to let go; he wanted to shoot his wad right there, even without being scorched from the slick heat inside her. But he wouldn't. Not until she finished and he could bring her off again, this time inside her. God willing, that wouldn't be too long.

Her fingers and breathing slowed at the same time. Daniel covered her neck in hot, open-mouthed kisses. Eve moved away and maneuvered around to stretch out. He lay beside her, his head at her hip. Raising up, he placed his mouth where her fingers had just stirred her essence.

Immediately, her aroma overpowered him. Her juices flowed freely, coating her labia generously where no soft curls of hair remained to capture it. He lapped at it, harvesting her essence in long swipes and dips. Using his elbows as wedges between her legs, he spread her thighs farther and ran his hands along the silk of her skin. Using his tongue, he stroked her inner thigh and nipped her with his teeth.

So engrossed was he, Eve maneuvered his thigh over her head and licked his cock before he realized what she'd done. As he coaxed her clit to life again and reveled in her openness against his mouth, she wrapped her lips over his cock and took him all the way. His hips thrust and withdrew naturally. He licked her cream and swirled his tongue around the little nub at the apex of her labia; she licked and circled his crown with her tongue, and lightly dragged her teeth along his length of his shaft.

Her arms wrapped around his thighs to grasp his ass. Gently at first, and then with more force, she kneaded his cheeks, pulling him closer, making him work to withdraw. He grunted, dipping deep to take more of her spicy-sweet taste, inhaling and filling his lungs with her scent that drove him wild. His hips plunged, fucking her mouth, slapping his balls against her forehead and rasping his stomach across her tits. When he was deep, tapping the back of her throat, she fingered the tight opening of his ass and hummed. He heard the sound as though from a distance but felt it all through him.

Like a burst of fireworks, his restraint broke, and he shot into her mouth and down her throat, pulsing madly. At the same time, Eve came again, convulsing in strong ripples against his lips and tongue. He thought he'd die of pure pleasure. This woman would never be boring, never be just another body in bed.

Never be just another woman out of bed, either.

When he could tell where he was, and Eve's body had cooled to a simmer, he rolled to the side. He kissed the soft flesh of her leg and propped himself on his elbow, looking up the length of satiny skin to her face.

"Did that satisfy your fantasy?" Her smile was languid and sexy.

"More than. It might take a few minutes before I can satisfy one for you, though."

Eve's smile widened. "How do you know? Maybe you just did."

That caused him to smile, too.

Hell, Daniel thought. *I might just be smiling the whole damn weekend long.*

Then the position at the academy shoved its way into his mind along with the knowledge that Eve planned to return to Europe, and the smile faded.

***

At least three times during the night, either she or Daniel had wakened and moved against the other, leading to sleepy touching and kissing. They'd come together as though they had lots of time, moving with an easy rhythm that suggested a long, intimate knowledge of mutual satisfaction. Even after years with Luigi, Eve hadn't known this passion mixed with familiar comfort. It made their lovemaking just that—making love instead of having sex. For her part, anyway. Daniel hadn't hidden his pleasure in their physical relationship but had said nothing about anything more.

That was another reason she had to break things off after this weekend. Until then, she would impress each glance, each lingering touch, each sigh, each and every moment he surged inside her, onto her mind. He was a part of her, though he didn't know it. She might be moving back to Italy, but she would not be returning to her old life with Luigi. Nothing could ever compare to what she knew now. Intimacy such as this, with Daniel on the rocky coast of Maine, would have to keep her warm for a very long time.

***

"Are you sure this is your fantasy?" Daniel asked, raising his voice to be heard over the wind whipping off the Atlantic.

"I'm going to miss the ocean." Eve tucked her hands in the pocket of her camel hair coat and shrugged against the bite of the wind on her neck. She looked up, smiling. "Did you think I'd ask you to do something sinful and kinky?"

He grinned. "A man can hope."

"Hold that thought." She spoke to herself as well as to him. "Eventually, all things come to pass."

Playfully, he took her arm and acted as though he would turn her back toward the B&B. "Maybe we should head back in case the urge strikes?"

She laughed. "I'll let you know in plenty of time."

He relented, and they continued their walk high above the shingled shore and cresting waves of the ocean.

"Don't you like strolling along a bluff overlooking crashing waves?"

"Sure, in May," he said, though his jacket hung open. The wind ruffled his hair, but he didn't seem to mind. With a sea-green crew-neck sweater topping a button-down shirt and jeans, he looked like he'd stepped right out of an L.L. Bean catalogue.

"Let's see what's over there," he suggested, pointing to an antique shop across the street.

Crossing meant waiting for one car to pass, and then they were looking through the window of a shop crammed with more trinkets and whatnots than Eve had ever seen. Daniel caught hold of her hand and pulled her through the door.

"Just call out if you need anything," came a woman's voice from the back.

"Will do," Daniel called back. "Look at this," he said, holding up a piece of crockery.

"What a pretty little pitcher." She examined the rest of the bric-a-brac on the table. "I don't see any matching pieces, though."

"It must be the only part of the set they have." He smiled and his voice took on a wistful quality. "My mom would like this." He stared at the crockery as though lost in thought.

The pitcher wasn't sophisticated or delicate. A dark red-brown with a small gold band of fleurs-de-lis below a simple gold rim. The inside shone with a white pearlescent glow. The whole piece couldn't have stood more than four or five inches. Eve tried to remember if she'd ever seen anything so pedestrian on Luigi's table, or anything as nice on her mother's when she was growing up. Neither, she decided.

"Your mother had the set?"

Daniel snapped out of his reverie, smiling boyishly.

"Sorry," he said, setting the creamer back on the table. "Yeah, she had the teapot, coffee pot, cups, all of it. Damn, was she ever proud of that set. My brother and I knocked the table one day when we were horsing around teasing our other brother and the creamer fell off and broke."

"I'll bet she was mad."

He thought for a moment.

"Not really. She was upset, we could tell that. But we were just kids—seven years old, maybe—and she knew we didn't mean to do it."

How different from her home, then. Breaking anything of her mother's would have meant a beating for sure. Hell, just playing in the house would have earned her and her sister a whooping.

"You must have a good mom."

"The best." He cast a curious look around the rest of the store. "Do you like antiques?"

"I had a few good pieces in Florence."

She stroked the fur of a fox stole and thought of her apartment in a former palace not far from the Ponte Vecchio. When she first moved in, she'd been amazed and thrilled to live in such a beautiful place filled with beautiful things. She'd been so in love with Luigi; everything had been roses and laughter.

For almost three years, like millions of foolish women in love with married men, she'd let him set the rules. She hadn't expected him to leave his wife and daughters, but neither had she expected him to throw her out and disclaim their son. During her time in Florence, she'd studied and learned what it took to live in Luigi's circle. And, she'd examined her love.

By the time she left—evicted by note, delivered by the same emissary who'd come to The Bare Moose last week—she'd still been in love, but only with her apartment and the city. Now she dreaded the thought of returning, even for the chance to live once more in the shadow of the *Duomo.*

A cloud passed over Daniel's face. "Is that where you'll go?"

"To Florence, yes."

"To be near Timothy's father."

"Yes." She reached for a porcelain figure of a Siamese cat in order to avoid meeting his gaze. "I've been selfish to keep Timmy from his father. Luigi wants to know his son."

In her mind's eye she saw Luigi's penetrating gaze as he explained he'd left his wife and now wished to acknowledge Timmy—once he had proof that Timmy was his. Anger still simmered over that remark. There had been no love in his gaze when he explained he wanted them back in Italy, only a casual possessiveness. She feared what the courts would say about custody if she dared to take things that far and so she'd been happy Luigi had said he would give her a few days to get over her shock. Would he be surprised to find she'd return without a fight? Not really. Men like Luigi always expect to get what they want.

"Family is important," Daniel muttered.

"Yes." Though her family had never professed that belief. "Especially to Italians."

Maybe that's why, out of all the men who had pursued her, she'd been drawn to Luigi. He'd never hidden his deep affection for his parents and two brothers. She'd wanted that for herself, and then for their son. It was too bad it had taken him so long to realize what he owed Timmy, but at least he'd come to the truth eventually. Her parents had never expressed the first interest in seeing their grandson.

His mouth firmly set, Daniel wandered away, picking up an ivory queen from a chess set then putting it back. A few steps farther, he stopped to check the price on a quilt. She watched him wander, smiling at the way he kept glancing back at the little pitcher he'd first picked up. Finally, he circled around to pluck the creamer off the table and took it to the cash register. A woman emerged from a back room, wiping her hands on an apron and bringing the scent of furniture polish. Daniel chatted with her, causing a smile and then a laugh, in little time. Eve wasn't surprised. After all, she'd given in to Daniel's charm right away herself.

Eve turned toward the large front window and stared across the street where the ocean charged the shore, always the same, always changing. The far-off water soothed the slight tension stemming from talk about Italy. Eve didn't want to go back to Italy, but this weekend reinforced her decision to do so.

The last twenty-four hours, the casual passion she and Daniel had shared throughout the night and the contentment she'd felt waking up beside him, gave tangible evidence of how much she'd come to care. She was exactly the wrong person for him. And because of that, he was the very worst man for her—the last thing she needed was *another* man who would set her aside. Luigi had done so to protect his family name. Daniel would walk away to protect his position at the school.

Before, when she'd left Italy, she didn't have Timmy's feelings to worry about, since he hadn't yet been born. Now, he already liked Daniel far too much. For his sake, she couldn't afford to let her feelings for Daniel grow any deeper.

"Ready to go?" Daniel appeared beside her, a shopping bag in hand.

"So, you bought the pitcher."

"Yes. It's a gift for my parents. Mom will be surprised. Dad probably won't have any idea of the significance, but Mom will remember."

They walked outside and strolled toward the B&B, the wind in their faces. Daniel reached out and took her hand, but Eve felt a chill even the warmth of his fingers couldn't dispel.

She shivered and hoped he didn't notice. "Is it still my fantasy time?"

He grinned down at her. "Sure."

"Well, I still want to look at the ocean, but it occurs to me that we can do so from our bedroom balcony. And we can see it just as well without clothes."

"Do you feel the temperature, woman?"

She wrapped her arm around his waist and looked up through her lashes. "Do you doubt you can stay active enough to keep us warm, Mr. Goodman?"

His arm draped her shoulder and he pulled her tightly to his side. "No, darlin', I most certainly do not."

"Good." For one more night and day, she could keep the thoughts of leaving and Daniel's job at bay.

Then, his cell phone rang.

Chapter Twelve

"Hello, Headmaster Goodman."

Daniel stopped mid-step, speechless. He'd hoped for the appointment, he'd half-expected to receive it, but hearing that he had the position of headmaster at the most prestigious private school in America still stopped him in his tracks. His heart pounded; his mouth went dry.

"Sydney?"

Eve had taken two steps before Daniel tugged her to a halt. She turned, an expectant look on her face.

"The board made a decision?" Damn. He could barely get enough air into his lungs to speak.

Sydney Thomas laughed on the other end of the phone line. "They have. I asked Daddy to let me tell you the news." He heard the smile in her voice as she continued, "So, how do you feel, *Headmaster?*"

He laughed, too, and squeezed Eve's hand when she smiled with him.

"Amazed. Humbled. God, I don't know … honored."

"But not surprised?"

"Yes! Surprised, too."

A gentle pull brought Eve close enough to wrap her in a one-armed hug. "I got the headmaster position," he told her. It couldn't be true. No, saying it aloud *made* it true.

"Of course you did!" Eve beamed as though she were proud of him, and how much he liked that ambushed him.

"Congratulations!" she said at the same time Sydney said in his ear, "Who are you talking to?"

"Sorry," he murmured back to Sydney. Then, "I don't suppose it was unanimous?"

"No, but Daddy kept on until enough members saw the light." She hesitated only a moment. "Where are you?"

"After the weekend in Boston I decided to take a couple days off."

He and Eve started walking again, stepping off in synch, as though each knew the other's mind.

"Why didn't you tell me? I would have loved to get away for a few days." She took a breathy pause. "We could have celebrated together." It came out a purr more than a statement.

Sydney's suggestive words poured into his ear, but Daniel was only aware of Eve's arm sliding around his waist. They strolled in unison, two puzzle pieces fit perfectly together. She squeezed lightly, sending shafts of heat to his groin. If this were his turn for a fantasy, he'd find a spot right now and share his joy, physically and emotionally. He'd never done it in public before. He wondered if Eve—

"Daniel, are you there?"

He needed only the sound of Sydney's voice to remind him that his being there with Eve could still spell disaster. The position wasn't firmly his. The board giveth and the board could still taketh away.

"Yes, yes, I'm here. I didn't tell anyone where I was going, Sydney, because I just wanted some time alone, you know, worrying a little about the appointment and everything."

"But weren't you just talking to—"

"Sydney, I think I'm losing signal. Thanks a lot for—"

He pressed the little hang-up button to end the call and then slipped the phone into his pocket.

"Coward," Eve said, shooting him a meaningful look.

"Yeah, I know. It's not an attractive quality in a headmaster." He grinned. "I'll have to work on that."

"Lucky for you, you have so many other attractive qualities," she said, smiling. "The mantle of power will sit very nicely on your shoulders."

"Thank you, ma'am."

"What shall we do to celebrate?"

He pressed her closer. "No need to change our plans. Dinner, an evening in front of the fireplace, then another night with you beside me sounds about perfect."

She stopped, and he swung around. Her eyes rounded and her mouth formed an "O" of surprise. "What a sweet thing to say."

"I'm a sweet guy."

"Yes," she whispered, "you are." Her eyes shone wet and bright.

"Hey." He brushed the back of his fingers across her cheeks.

A quick glance showed they were alone on the street. He bent his head and took control of her lips. Her intake of breath sent a thrill of possession through him. He wished he didn't, but he wanted her, all of her, for more than one more night. For more than a weekend.

He needed time, though. A chance to solidify his position at the academy and initiate his plans. Eve would have to change her mind about going to Italy. She needed to forget about Eve Star and adopt her Lauren persona all the time. And she needed to stay in New Hampshire and give him a chance, something longer than the few weeks they'd had. In their short time together, he'd changed from seeing her as a compulsion, an infatuation to work out of his system, to an integral part of all he wanted.

A month ago, he needed the headmaster position to help define him. Receiving the appointment would provide a tangible measure of accomplishment and a way to affect more lives than he could in the classroom. He wanted his family to be proud of him. More, he wanted to be proud of himself. And now he could. The tension he'd held inside for years could unfurl. He'd set a lofty goal and attained it.

He should be satisfied. Instead, he wanted more. The position to define his life, and Eve to give it meaning. He didn't *want* to want her. God knows, his desire went against all they'd agreed to when they first got together; his hunger for her endangered everything he'd worked for. When he'd fucked her against her door, a good fucking was all he'd wanted. All she'd said she wanted, too. He had one more night to find out how she felt about him now, and then only a short time to make her change her plans.

He pressed closer, holding her head so he could slide his tongue into her moist heat.

She tasted of the vinaigrette dressing she'd had on her salad at lunch. Citrus and tang, sweet and sour. A banquet of flavor with a bite of sassiness that was all Eve.

He withdrew, but only to nip her bottom lip then he went back to sip, licking her nectar again and again. She quenched a thirst in him, but only while they were together. When they separated, he felt parched until he thought he'd die if he couldn't hold her again and feast on her lips.

Last night, lying beside her had seemed the most natural thing in the world. After making love before the fire, he'd carried her to bed like some character on the cover of one of those horrible romance novels.

They'd snuggled under the comforter. Eve had fallen asleep right away but, unusually, Daniel hadn't been sleepy.

He'd propped himself up on his elbow and watched her. Firelight danced across her face, shifting shadow and light. Her hair tumbled around her face and shoulders, the exertions from sex making the ends stick to her cheeks. Charcoal lashes lay like fans under her eyes. Her lids twitched very slightly. At one point, she'd squinted, and her mouth had puckered as though she'd tasted something salty in a dream. He couldn't get over how beautiful she was, completely unaware and without makeup.

But what had struck Daniel the most was how young she looked, and vulnerable. So unlike the vixen who'd bowled him over with her bedroom expertise. Neither did she resemble the confident business woman who managed a thriving business not known for its calm, mannered environment. Such contrast in a woman ensured there'd be no dull moments in life.

He'd reached out to touch her face, then drawn back his hand. Unfortunately, dull moments are what the headmaster of a staid, reputable school required. The changes Daniel wanted to make would create enough controversy without adding to the mix.

Holding her now on the street, however, the inappropriateness of Eve and him fell to the background like so much noise. He wondered how fast they could make it the couple of hundred yards or so to the B&B. Then how fast they could get undressed. She made an endearing whimper just like the one she'd made the previous night while he watched her sleep. She'd turned to him then—relaxed, trusting, open. He'd wanted her in a way that went far beyond the merely physical—just like he wanted her now.

The intensity scared the crap out of him.

"Daniel?"

"Yes, sweetheart." He stayed lip to lip, the better to continue sampling her sweetness.

"Are you going to keep us out here on the street, or are you going to fulfill my fantasy? Not that I'm not enjoying this, but—"

With a wild whoop, he threw common sense over the bluff and into the ocean. He grabbed her hand and dashed toward the B&B.

***

The chill on Eve's back contrasted with the heat on her breasts, transferred from Daniel's chest. They'd draped the quilt from the bed over the Adirondack chair on their balcony, and now she sat straddling Daniel's lap. As she wished, the expanse of the Atlantic could be seen to her left. The salt tang filled the air and the sound of the high tide surf reached them on the wind. Part of her was freezing but she didn't care.

As she rose over him, Daniel's hands shimmied up her sides, then slid to her hips as she sank down. His thumbs stroked the sides of her breasts at the bottom of her ride, then caressed her inner thighs at the top. Finally, he reached around to her butt and held her in place, so he could suckle, first one nipple then the other, searing one with his hot breath, mouth, tongue, then leaving it to pucker when the cold air hit the lingering moisture.

His hips pushed up, delving deeper inside her with each slow stroke.

"I've got to move," she moaned.

"Stay still. I'll take you where you want to go." He took her nipple again, and she surrendered.

Twice she'd almost tumbled over into the abyss where nothing existed but sensation—Daniel's body in hers, moving with her, moving against her, but *moving*. Each time, he'd slowed, bringing her back to awareness before assaulting her senses again. She felt the surge once more, as his pubic bone nudged her clit.

"Yesss."

She closed her eyes. His hands held her fast, his fingers stretched the cleft between her butt cheeks and stroked. He licked her nipples as though they were ice cream cones, leaving a streak of fire on the icy, pebbled texture of her wind-kissed breasts.

And yet he probed deeper. Instinctively, she spread her legs wider and arched her back, helping him seek his natural depth. He took advantage, burying himself then rocking his hips.

Her moan started deep inside, gaining strength as it welled to the surface. Everything in her urged her to rock back, to meet Daniel, to strive for that brass ring just out of reach. She stretched, her muscles undulating. From the recesses of her mind she heard him groan. His mouth came over her nipple, his tongue laving, tickling, bathing her in flames. Her fingers plowed through his hair and pressed him even closer. He moved his head to the valley between her breasts, seeming to fight for air.

The November wind off the Atlantic dried sweat as soon as it appeared, keeping their bodies from gliding, one over the other. Instead of being damp with perspiration, his hair brushed her skin like the finest silk.

"Now, baby!" His hips twisted hard, digging his hot flesh into her throbbing clit.

The fight was over.

Her surrendering intake of air came as a surprise, but then she couldn't breathe at all. Blackness, punctuated with rushing stars of blinding whiteness, filled the backs of her eyelids. Rigid while her orgasm controlled every muscle and nerve, she smiled inside, celebrating the wave rolling through her. The delicious, tantalizing, totally unique wave of perfection she'd come to associate with Daniel.

Little by little, she became aware of the roar of the ocean. The aftershocks her body gave off, rippling over Daniel's cock, still embedded within her. The salty air commingled with the scent of sex, strong and heady. Daniel's soft, soft hair, and his mouth on the side of her breast. The beating of her heart, slowing from that of a jackhammer to the steady thump of a ball-peen.

She could grow addicted to this.

He raised his head. Heavy-lidded, looking more satisfied than any man she'd ever seen, he lazily took her lips in a soul-wrenching kiss. His fingers kneaded her butt cheeks, and with a slow, easy move, his hips rose, matching the action of his tongue pushing into her mouth. If both parts sought to taste, she'd provide the samples. She wrapped her arms around his neck and pushed back, just a little.

He pulled away, rubbing her nose with his, like an Eskimo kiss. His hips wiggled under her thighs. She contracted her pussy muscles to let him know she was well aware of his presence.

"Ummm. God, that was incredible. *You* are incredible." Finally moving his hands off her butt and up her back, he stroked gently, bringing heat with his touch regardless of the light touch.

"I could say the same. I've never ... it's never been like this before." She kissed the tip of his nose and snuggled closer. "Oh, nice. You're like a furnace."

"We should have brought a blanket out to cover us, not just one to sit on. Are you okay, 'cause I really don't want to go in quite yet."

"I'm fine. And you're"—she contracted her muscles yet again, milking his cock—"remarkable."

"We have a mutual admiration society here. I'm only able to be inside you still because of the way you make me feel."

"And how is that?" She wasn't fishing for compliments, she really wasn't. But her feelings for Daniel were so much more than about sex.

"Henry Miller said, 'Sex is one of the nine reasons for reincarnation. The other eight are unimportant.' He might have been right, but he didn't know *how* right because he hadn't been with you."

Tears stung her throat. She fought them back so she could speak. So what if he hadn't quoted something about love instead of sex? *They* weren't about love—that wasn't the agreement.

"What about, 'The right partner is to great sex what a surgeon is to an operation: necessary.'"

"Who said that?"

She leaned back, smiled, and tossed her head. "Eve Star, Europe's most famous exotic dancer."

"Ah, a worthwhile source, indeed."

"So, if you thought the sex was incredible—and I certainly agree—then it must be because we're—"

"The perfect partners." He grinned, and then let the smile fade. His gaze dropped to her lips then to her breasts, where they turned hungry. He leaned forward to kiss the side of her right breast.

"I bruised you. I'm sorry."

"A passion bite is nothing to apologize for."

"God, Eve…" Raising his head, he kissed her hard, his tongue taking control of her mouth, probing, exploring, branding her. The temperature had to be dipping into the thirties, but she burned.

Unbelievably, he was still inside when he broke contact, his hands everywhere, his breathing ragged.

"Again?" She touched his cheek with her fingertips and rocked against him.

He shook his head. "Would you think me wimpy if I said I've never before been able to this soon?"

She laughed. "No, of course not." Wiggling her butt, she smiled at his moan.

His eyes dropped to where they joined. His thumb rubbed her clit and it was her turn to take a shaky breath. "I have to admit, I never expected a headmaster to be so sexy."

"It's time I changed your mind." His voice was deep, harsh. The sound went straight to her core.

"I don't know, I can't imagine Dr. Adams doing this, making love on a balcony overlooking the ocean."

Oh, he hit the right spots, inside and out, stoking the fire which threatened to consume her yet again.

"Which accounts for the sour look on Mrs. Adams's face all the time. The Goodman administration will be very different. Sex will be encouraged—nay, required—on every balcony overlooking the ocean. We'll take weekend tours of each B&B on the coast of Maine."

We? She pushed the word aside as a slip, wouldn't let herself think it was otherwise.

"Very progressive, Dr. Goodman."

"That's what I thought. Not as progressive as this." Daniel shoved his hips up from the chair, filling her completely. He pressed her clit. She pressed forward, wanting to jump inside Daniel, fill him as he filled her.

Their movements were fast and hard. Hungry kisses, gasps, rough hands on heated skin. They came together like a surge of electricity through her system. Panting, sated beyond belief, Eve collapsed against Daniel's chest. They held each other for long minutes, saying nothing.

A gust of wind came up, striking Eve's back.

"Are you ready to go inside?"

"Yes. Unless you want to see a headmaster's ass freeze off."

"Well, an ass is one thing, but there are other parts of your anatomy I'd worry about."

He chuckled.

"As long as we keep it where it is now"—he squirmed under her—"we're fine."

"Too late," she said. "I'm getting hungry."

"Aha." He helped her stand, then hurried into the room behind her. "I'll start a fire if you want to warm up in a hot bath," he said.

"I won't be long."

"Take your time."

Eve hung in the doorway to the bathroom thinking she might ask if Daniel wanted to join her in the tub, but really hoping he would suggest it first. His concentration was on starting the fire, however, so she bit back her offer and closed the door.

While waiting for the tub to fill, Eve took in the bathroom décor. Whereas the bedroom and sitting area were stuffed with furniture and floral wallpaper, the bathroom was pure shore. White bead board walls trimmed in sea green, and fluffy towels, scented candles, and bath beads, combined to make a room as fresh as the sea breeze blowing a few feet away.

The mirror fogged from the steamy water. She sprinkled in bath beads, which filled the heavy air with the fragrance of a spring rain. Droplets of moisture raced down her arms, over her breasts and across her stomach. Sweeping her hair back, she closed her eyes and luxuriated in the heat.

Eve bent to turn off the tap and then swiped her hand through the water, testing the temperature. Hot enough for a good soak, and—she thought again—the right amount of water for two.

Silently, she opened the door but stopped as she heard Daniel talking to someone. Had that Thomas woman called back? She tried to ignore the stab of jealousy the thought inspired. She was planning to leave. Daniel had no place in his life for her. But this was *their* weekend.

Knowing it was wrong, she put her ear to the opening.

"I'm shocked, even though I thought I had an excellent chance of being appointed. But Mom, I hope you understand, I'm still in a sticky situation. I'm happy for you and Dad, and of course you have to do what you want, but I can't afford to be there for the media blitz."

He stopped, rubbing his hand across his forehead. "That came out wrong."

He listened to the person on the other end—his mother?—then said, "You know I love you and Dad more than I can say. My not attending the wedding has nothing to do with that. In fact,"—he smiled, stood, still gloriously naked, and walked to the bag holding the cream pitcher he'd purchased earlier—"I found the perfect wedding gift. You'll be surprised."

One hand on hip, he strolled back across the room, holding the cell phone to his ear.

"Hey, Dad." His voice took on more of a drawl and he seemed to straighten. "Congratulations! I can't believe you're going to make an honest woman of Mom after all these years."

The "wedding" Daniel didn't plan to attend was for his *parents*? Eve furrowed her brow and leaned her head on the doorframe. All this time she'd had him pegged as a man from a solid family, upper-middle class or higher, and ... well, she hadn't thought he was illegitimate.

Daniel chuckled at something his father said. She saw his reflection in the armoire mirror and he didn't look like a man from a bad family. With amusement, there was also affection in his eyes.

"Yeah, well, Jonah did a number on me ... I know, he can be something of a controlling personality. I have the job here, but it's not a sure thing yet. I'm just really worried about hurting you and Mom. I'd never do that on pur—"

He stopped, listening, then closed his eyes.

"Thanks, Dad. I can't tell you how relieved I am to hear you say that ... Okay. Kiss Mom for me, and I'll talk to you again in a few days."

Softly, Eve closed the bathroom door. Without a second thought, she climbed in the tub and sank up to her neck in the fragrant, steaming water.

Knowing Daniel's situation, knowing she'd made up her mind to leave, knowing—or believing—she and Daniel came from two different worlds, she'd still harbored a glimmer of hope something would change in their relationship. Against all reason, like a child reading a fairy tale, she'd wished for a godmother to wave a magic wand and make Daniel want her. He'd ride up to The Bare Moose in his Volvo station wagon and declare he didn't care about her past or present. He'd say he loved her and wanted to marry her, and he knew she'd make the perfect wife for a headmaster of the country's most prestigious prep school.

Now, however, the truth penetrated her consciousness. Daniel would not forget her past or present. Even if by some miracle he loved her, it would make no difference. He loved his parents, after all, and if he would give up sharing in their wedding in order to protect his position, there was no way he'd take a chance on a woman like her.

No, she was no Cinderella, and Daniel no prince. Her life in Italy wouldn't be harsh—Luigi would see to that because of his son. But neither would it be happily ever after.

Chapter Thirteen

"Mr. Goodman!" Jeffrey Torrington walked toward Daniel at a rapid pace. Faster than sedate, Daniel noted, but not quite to the running stage. "Mr. Goodman, did you hear?"

"Hear what, Mr. Torrington?"

He put his hand on the boy's shoulder and turned him back toward the dormitory. Saturday dinner had ended several minutes ago, but he'd lingered over a second cup of coffee after the boys had dispersed to their various activities.

He and Eve had returned from their weekend in Maine just short of a week ago. She'd been strangely quiet on the trip. After picking up her car at the station, he'd followed her home. But at her door at the rear of The Bare Moose, she'd smiled, brushed his cheek with her fingers, and kissed him gently. Then she'd said, "Bye," and gone inside. Since then she hadn't taken a single one of his calls. Nor had she joined him when he went to the bar and asked Jed to tell her he was there. She hadn't answered his two letters. Daniel had even stooped to visiting Timothy and asking him to ask his mom to call, to no avail.

Confused, frustrated, and—yes, he'd admit it—mad as hell, he'd decided to ignore her as she was ignoring him. At least for a week. If he hadn't heard from her before Thanksgiving, he'd storm the castle, so to speak.

For now, at least, there was no reason to rush back to his room to phone Eve. There was no reason to rush back to his empty rooms at all. Physically, his living space was unchanged from how it had been before Eve. But now the atmosphere was different. Barren and hollow, solitude didn't hold the same appeal it once had.

Torrington caught his breath in the slower pace Daniel set.

"About Timmy, sir. He's leaving after Christmas and moving all the way to Italy." The boy lifted his face. "Is that a very long way?"

Christ! So she was serious. *Very* serious if she'd told Timothy they were leaving.

"It's quite far, Mr. Torrington. All the way across the Atlantic and then halfway across another continent."

Torrington walked a few steps in silence.

"I don't think Timmy wants to go. I looked through the window in his door and he was crying when his mom and that man talked to him."

Daniel snapped to, like a pointer to a covey of quail.

"That *man?*"

Torrington pointed toward the dormitory.

"That man there."

Skipping the reminder that pointing was not polite, Daniel followed the direction of Torrington's finger and caught his first glimpse of Eve in nine days. His breath caught in his throat. His heart rate raced from zero to ninety in a split second. He stopped, his entire focus on her.

As though she felt his presence, she raised her gaze, meeting his. She stepped back. The man beside her stopped any further movement with his hand on her lower back. A burst of jealousy struck so hard that Daniel sucked in a breath. The man—the same one who'd been with Eve in Boston, making him Timothy's father—looked to see what had startled her.

"Mr. Goodman?" Torrington turned a questioning face to him.

Daniel started walking again and Torrington fell into step beside him, talking about something Daniel didn't process. The man with Eve, his hand still firmly at her back, pressed forward to intersect them. She didn't seem to be coming too willingly.

Finally, the group met and stopped, the men metaphorically toe-to-toe.

"How are you, Jeffrey?" Eve spoke to Torrington, her voice weak and low.

"Very well, Mrs. Knowles," he answered, reciting the standard Westover Academy response. "And you?"

"Fine, thank you."

"Mr. Torrington, you'd better go and get ready for homework time." Daniel set his mouth and never took his eyes from the man standing before him.

"But I have free time, Mr. Goodman."

"Then *go* and get ready for your free time."

"Yes, sir."

Daniel felt Torrington's surprised reaction to his sharp tone, but he ignored it. The boy walked off.

Eve took a breath. "Daniel Goodman, I'd like you to meet—"

"Luigi Donatello," the man interrupted, holding out his hand.

Daniel shook his hand and made a quick evaluation. They were the same height. Donatello had white hair, dark eyes, and an olive complexion. He smiled, showing straight, white teeth. Then he quirked his brow, adding to the amusement in his expression.

Women would find him sexy as hell. Men would hate him. Daniel already harbored a strong dislike that could morph into something physical if the bastard didn't take his hand *off of Eve's back.*

"It is very good to meet you at last," Luigi Donatello said. His near perfect English held only the barest of accents. When he retrieved his hand, he shifted his shoulders in a way that showed off his pecs and filled the suit jacket. The bull preening for the cow.

Well, I can be a bull, too, you Italian asshole.

"I've heard a great deal about you," Luigi continued.

Daniel aimed a pointed look at Eve. "Not too much, I hope."

A deep rumbled laugh surfaced from the Italian. "Oh, not from dear Eve. No, from Timoteo. My son."

The words hung between them. No matter how many weekends in Maine or the number of balconies overlooking the ocean, Timothy owned Eve's heart and Luigi was half of Timothy. Daniel's competitive spirit shriveled up. If this move really was for Timothy's good, and good for Eve, he had no right to put up a fight. He loved Eve far too much to wish for her unhappiness, even if it meant she wouldn't stay with him in New Hampshire.

Daniel tilted his head toward Eve. "Does Timothy know?"

She shook her head. "No. Only that Luigi is a friend and that we're moving in a few weeks." Raising her chin in a stubborn gesture, she continued, "He doesn't need to know everything right now."

"It will take me a month or so to find the appropriate home for my son in Florence. Then he will have time with me. He'll get to know and love me then, yes?" He'd directed the last at Eve.

Find a home for his son? Timothy will have time to know him? What about *his* getting to know Timothy? This Luigi jerk sounded like it was all about him. And what about Eve? It didn't sound as though she were anywhere in the equation.

Daniel still addressed Eve. "Are you planning to get married?"

"That is not possible," Luigi answered. He shrugged. "My family would not permit it."

"And besides, you're still married," she murmured.

Looking Daniel in the eyes she said, "I'm going back to Florence so Timmy and his father can get to know each other, and so he can benefit from all Luigi can provide for him."

"That doesn't include a family, evidently," Daniel snapped. "Not a father and mother, or friends, like he has now."

"What would he have here?" she countered, anger in her tone. "Someone very much in the know told me that lies catch up eventually. If Timmy were kicked out of Westover, what then? He'd have none of his friends. And he'd have only a mother."

"A mother with few skills of which a boy would be proud," Luigi added with a sneer.

Eve dipped her head, looking as defeated as Daniel had ever seen her. "He needs more."

"But of course." Luigi swept his hand down his torso and raised his head. "He needs me."

My God. He thinks he's the fucking king of the fucking universe.

"Be assured, my son will have a father and mother, though"—he spread his hands in an offhand, Italian manner—"not in the traditional way. It happens."

He shrugged. "I can provide more for him than anyone here can."

Okay, point taken. Until you consider one little thing. Love. The bastard isn't saying anything about loving Timothy, is he? Or Eve.

"And you, Eve. Will you be happy back in Florence?"

She glanced away. Her fingers laced tightly at her waist. "I was before."

"She will be if she wants to be," Luigi said.

The look Eve gave back to him was cool. Or maybe Daniel simply wanted it to be.

"You make certain *Timmy* is happy, I'll take care of myself."

Luigi shrugged yet again, and his eyes sparked with humor. "As you say, my star."

Ha-ha. Funny guy with his stupid puns.

"So the decision is made."

Weeks ago, Daniel might have thought he'd miss no more than the great sex. After the last week, unable to talk to her, touch her or even see her, he knew he'd miss everything about her. Being cut off after the intimacy of Maine had been torture. He cared for Eve. He cared for Lauren. He cared for whatever the hell this woman called herself. Or whatever the hell she *was*. A sinkhole formed in Daniel's gut. What could he offer her to stay? Nothing.

"I'm afraid so," she said without looking at him.

"But of course, there is always the chance for good friends to visit," Luigi interjected. He skimmed his hand across her shoulder. She crossed her arms, taking each elbow in hand, virtually distancing herself from him. He seemed not to notice. "I shall find an apartment large enough for all of your friends to come to visit, *mia cara.*"

Finally, Eve's eyes met Daniel's again. "That won't take a very large space."

They stared for what felt like forever. Could she read in his eyes what he couldn't say? Was he sure he wanted her to? Given time, they might have found a way to make things work. Daniel couldn't take a chance with his new position. He wouldn't, not without knowing if she wanted him as he did her. Right now, she seemed pretty damn content going off with Mr. Italian GQ.

"I suppose we'll see each other on campus before you leave." He tried to sound cordial though he had the perverse urge to use "fuck" every other word.

"Perhaps not. Thanksgiving is next week, and then you'll be busy preparing for exams and I'll be packing and such." She held out her hand. "I think this is probably goodbye, Daniel. Thank you being such a good friend, to me and especially to Timmy."

Feeling as though his world were tumbling out of control, he took her hand. His fingers engulfed five shards of ice. Frowning, he studied her eyes and rubbed her knuckles with his thumb, trying to infuse some heat.

"It's been my pleasure knowing Timothy, and the greatest of honors being your friend."

Her eyes shimmered. She jutted out her chin once more, but this time with a tiny quiver. God! He wanted to take her in his arms, to kiss her senseless and assure her she'd never have to leave.

"Mr. Goodman!"

Keeping control of Eve's hand, Daniel sighed and faced the voice. Judging from the speed at which the sound approached, Torrington had to be running. The boy would never learn.

"Mr. Goodman," Torrington said, gulping for breath. "Dr. Adams is looking for you. He said to find you and tell you to come to the board room right away, sir."

"Thank you, Torrington. I'll go there shortly."

"He said *right away*, Mr. Goodman."

Shit. "Thank you, Torrington. Back to the dorm with you. And *walk*," he called out to the boy who'd taken off at a tear.

"Well," he said, releasing Eve's hand with reluctance. "It seems I must go. Take care, Mrs. Knowles. I will always treasure our time together. And our friendship."

He only nodded toward the Italian then spun on his heel and walked away, feeling he was leaving a major part of his heart behind.

***

"Good evening, Daniel."

Portly Dr. Adams came forward as Daniel walked through the door to the boardroom. The light from a crystal chandelier reflected off Dr. Adams's pate and white, bushy brows rose in concert with the edges of his lips.

From the other end of the large table, several men turned their way. The eleven or so were all members of the executive board, which meant they had been on the regular board longer than other members and/or they'd donated more money. They acknowledged Daniel but remained where they were, leaving him and Dr. Adams alone. Sydney's father, Creighton Thomas, smiled and nodded, as did a few of the others.

"Come in and join us in a glass of sherry."

Adams handed Daniel a small glass of cut crystal filled with a rich caramel-colored liquid.

Daniel had never enjoyed drinking heavy alcohol, but he liked sherry even less. He'd learned to tolerate it because it was the drink of refinement. Perhaps as headmaster and part of the true inner circle, those who hobnobbed with the very wealthy patrons and benefactors, he'd learn if they served sherry in the meetings of their companies. He'd be surprised if Mr. Thomas, a man who'd built an empire in development and construction, drank sherry when he was away from the Westover Academy boardroom.

This evening, however, after facing Luigi and the fact that Eve would be leaving in a few weeks, anything alcoholic would do. He took the glass and only just stopped himself from knocking it back .

"The board and I wanted to have a little congratulatory meeting with you before we announced your appointment publicly. That will be done with the full board present, at the Thanksgiving break chapel service, before the boys leave with their families for the holiday. So"—Dr. Adams leaned in as though sharing a secret—"you have one more week of anonymity." He chuckled. "And then a few more weeks in the classroom. After Christmas you'll be spending your time in the administrative building, where the wheels turn to keep the academy running and our traditions alive."

"I'm looking forward to working with you, sir."

"Gentlemen," Dr. Adams said to the gathering, "I give you Daniel Goodman, the twenty-fourth man in two hundred forty-nine years to head Westover Academy."

He raised his glass.

"To Daniel."

"Daniel," the men intoned, and downed their drinks.

Daniel wondered if they'd smash the glasses in the fireplace, but then he realized he held fine crystal that probably belonged to the school. New England thriftiness wouldn't allow Adams to go so far.

He was right. The men at the other end of the table set the sherry glasses on a waiting tray.

Weak autumn light filtered through the wavy glass of the upper mullioned windows. The newer, lower panes revealed a swirl of burnt sienna and gold leaves dropping to the ground. A fire crackled in the fireplace and, disliked or not, the sherry fired a path down his throat, adding to the warmth from the ambience. The room took on an otherworldly hue, and Daniel felt himself slipping into his new role, the one he'd dreamed of for years, the one he'd worked for, hoped for. The position which would define him, and place him in *Who's Who* and the annals of great educational leaders of the country.

Westover Academy had been founded before the Revolutionary War. The first headmaster had been a British citizen. Now here he was, one of only twenty-three other men. His parents would be proud seeing him here, among these men. He was sure Mark would appreciate the honor, and even Jonah couldn't help but be proud of having a brother in such a select group.

But, more than the pride and distinction, Daniel was pleased he'd be able to make some of the changes he thought would benefit the boys. And the academy, of course, but mostly the boys. After all, tradition was great, but change was also necessary for an institution to meet the needs of the students who would later meet the needs of the country.

He smiled, fingering the glass, half-absorbed in his thoughts.

"I know that look," Dr. Adams said. "It's quite a responsibility, isn't it?" He stared at Daniel with a knowing expression.

The others kept their distance, as though agreeing to allow the new and old heads their time together during this first, formal transitional moment. Daniel appreciated their consideration. For the first time in all the years he'd taught at the academy, he felt close to Dr. Adams.

"It is, sir, and an honor."

"You'll do well. Just never forget whom you serve."

"The boys are always in the forefront of my mind."

"Not the boys, Daniel. Nor their parents. You are here to ensure the reputation and continuity of the academy. To that end you serve the board, which is also here to protect and secure the welfare of the school. Without that, we have nothing to offer the parents and students, now or in the future. You see?"

Daniel wrinkled his brow. "But the boys—"

"Are important, yes. But you'll no longer be a teacher, you see. The boys are *their* purview. You'll have to find it in yourself to hold them at a distance. The teachers, too. Your decisions—like the board's decisions— must always be first for the academy and then for the student population. No one student can ever come before the good of the institution." Dr. Adams smiled. "That's how we've survived since 1769, how we built and have maintained our reputation as the finest preparatory school in America."

"But…" Daniel was at a loss as to what to say. Suddenly he felt like the child who'd waited all day for an ice cream only to discover the cone he'd received was of a flavor he didn't like.

"I know." Adams placed his hand on his shoulder. "You have dreams. They can all come true, I promise. Perhaps not exactly as you'd planned. The man who loves books must still run a business if he expects his bookstore to survive. We're the ones who ensure the business runs. Teachers have the luxury of loving the books."

Great. Just fucking great. Daniel cast a glance around for more sherry.

"I can see this is coming as a shock, just as it did for me when I was appointed to the post a good twenty-one years ago. Don't worry, you'll find plenty to stimulate you once you learn how to separate yourself from the more personal aspects of the school—"

Like the kids?

"—and you'll find that the board is quite reasonable to work with."

Like the hoops I had to jump through to be appointed?

"You'll make decisions that will affect not only the current student population but those in years to come."

Yes, but are they the non-traditional ones I wanted?

"While the board ultimately must approve any major decisions, you are the man representing the academy. I don't mind telling you that your spotless reputation and steadfast application and support of academy rules earned you the most admirable remarks of any candidate. I feel sure that your wife, when you choose her, will be of your same caliber. All of us, even those members who, shall I say, didn't wholly support your appointment, agreed that we couldn't have found a man with any finer character to lead the school into the next many years."

Thank God no one has followed me around the past few weeks. Eve!

His heart constricted. In no way would she fit the standards Adams just detailed. But then, neither did he, Daniel.

Push it out of your mind! You have your prize, and Eve has hers. You always knew there was no future with her.

Dr. Adams smiled, looking like a grandfather, though Daniel knew he never acted as such to the boys. At last he understood one of the reasons why. The relationship between the headmaster and student population was one of the many things he wanted to change, as well as opening admissions to more scholarship boys, introducing the merger of classes with the girls' school in a neighboring town to enhance class offerings, and relaxing some of the restrictions on student life that had carried forward from previous decades, but which served no purpose other than tradition. Now he saw he'd fight an uphill battle for most of his plans.

"Shall we join the others?" Adams nodded toward the far end of the room where the executive board mingled and chatted. "I asked them to allow us time to talk, but I see you have a great deal to absorb. We can chat again in the next week. Make an appointment with Edith."

Edith Whitelaw matched her employer in warmth and temperament.

Daniel hoped she planned to retire with Adams.

"Of course. Thank you for your advice and insight, Dr. Adams."

They moved down the length of the table to the men who now stood and smiled, ready to greet the new headmaster. Even those who'd fought his appointment—and Daniel knew exactly who they were, thanks to Sydney—looked ready to put the past behind them.

Twilight made silhouettes of the trees against the last vestiges of light in the sky. The evening began to weigh on him as the night did on the waning day.

He first shook hands with the board chairman, Albert Wainwright. The man's pompous attitude had worn off onto his son, but Daniel steeled himself to work with the man. Next, he greeted Creighton Thomas, whose support he enjoyed. For an hour or more, he smiled and laughed, chatted, and shook hands with the men who would have control over whether he succeeded in fulfilling his dreams for the academy. Most were the age of Adams, set in their ways and ideas. A couple were younger, meaning about the age of his father—men of business who understood the bottom line.

One, Creighton Thomas, didn't have a relative or friend attending the academy, and neither was he an alumnus, though he surely endowed the place for a reason. Maybe he supported more than Daniel's becoming headmaster. Perhaps he approved his daughter's ploys in the romance department. Did he hope to send a grandson to a place with the reputation and solid, unchanging traditions of a two-hundred-plus-year-old school?

Everyone he spoke with echoed the same theme—that Daniel had a sterling reputation, and only someone of such pristine character would they entrust with the reputation and traditions of Westover.

Daniel had only two thoughts. First, *what the fuck am I doing here?* And second, *God, I need Eve.*

***

"I think the talk with Timoteo went well, don't you?" Luigi swept off his coat and settled on the sofa in Eve's apartment as though he belonged.

Eve sat in a facing chair and slipped off her shoes. Her feet ached. If men had to wear heels, they wouldn't find them so alluring. She stretched her toes, then rested her right foot on her left knee so she could massage her instep and heel.

"If you call making him cry 'going well', I suppose it did."

He shrugged. "Timoteo will get used to me."

What a difference between Luigi and Daniel, who worked at getting to know the boys, not expecting them to first get to know him. She sighed. Comparisons did no good. In a few weeks, she and Timmy would be in Florence. He'd be surrounded by art and history. She knew he'd pick up the language with little effort, and hoped he'd adjust to the school as easily. If Luigi seriously took him in hand, Timmy would soon be more Italian than American, which filled Eve with sadness. If he adopted his father's gestures, though, she'd scream.

Luigi had only been here a day and already she hated his shrug. It was so uncaring, so dismissive, so … Italian. In the past, that simple undulation of muscles charmed her. It represented the way he let things roll off his shoulders, a carefree life where small things didn't bother him. Now it only reminded her of how he'd considered her and their unborn son "small things."

"Explain again why you came to find us?" She switched feet and continued rubbing.

Luigi's eyes focused on her hands, and a smile lit his lips. "I can give you a massage, *cara.*" He patted the sofa beside where he sat. "Come here and place your adorable feet in my lap."

Eve dropped her foot to the floor.

"We are not going to become lovers again. Don't think it, don't plan on it."

"But that may not be so. It is true that you have lost your appealing dancer's body." He wagged his finger at her. "I think you have also lost your sense of humor." He shrugged. "I am not attracted to you as I once was, but a man such as I has many appetites. One never knows but that you may be invited back to my bed now and then."

Perverse, aggravating man! "I don't make the same mistake twice."

But of course she had, falling in love with Daniel, another man who didn't love her enough.

"Besides, you're still married, and I love—" She snapped her mouth shut.

His brows shot up. "You're in love? But with whom?"

"Concentrate on *your* love life, like with your wife. You're separated, not divorced. You told me years ago that your family would never accept me. How will they feel about Timmy?"

"My mother and father are old-fashioned. But where they would never accept my mistress as my wife, had that happened, they will welcome my son. As for my wife, she does not matter. She has moved back to Rome, and in Rome she shall stay. I see my daughters frequently enough, but they take after their mother, shrill and demanding." He flicked his wrist, dismissing his girls. "I need a son, someone who will take my place in the business, someone who will carry my name into posterity."

"Your brothers have boys to carry on the Donatello name. Why *did* you come to find Timmy?"

For the first time, discomfort crossed his face.

"You told me you were carrying my child. When Sophia left, I remembered. He does resemble me." Waving his hand toward his face, he said, "His eyes are like mine. They are my best feature, you know." He smiled. "The women will love him when he is older."

He shrugged, as though he'd explained everything necessary. Eve slid the bolster pillow from her back and threw it at his head.

"Stop shrugging as though the topic isn't important. You're talking about our son."

His eyes flared. He slammed the pillow on the sofa and leaned forward, elbows on knees. "I hired an investigator to find the child. And if you'd delivered a boy, I wanted to know if he truly was mine. After all, you were not exactly a virtuous woman, *cara*."

"How dare you!"

"You danced in clubs. You bared your body for the pleasure of anyone who could pay the entrance fee, and you taunted and teased."

"I danced, I didn't sleep around."

"Yet, you slept with me, and it took only one dinner and a cheap bouquet of roses."

"I thought you were special. *I* thought so for a long time."

"I thought you were common. And I have thought so for a long time."

Choking on a sob, Eve launched out of the chair. She wouldn't cry in front of this man, she wouldn't. Hugging herself, she paced before the sofa, then fairly ran to the one window, overlooking the parking lot.

Halogen lights illuminated it in large overlapping circles. Happy Hour had just ended, and cars filled more than half the spaces. Suddenly, music blared, then immediately quieted as Jed adjusted the volume of the CD player. Laughter drifted up through the floor.

"You keep insisting we will not be lovers. That remains to be seen, but you should know, I did not come for you. There will always be others waiting to fill my bed, it's a fact of who I am. But I have obligations I can fulfill only with a son. My brother's sons are worthless, uninterested in the business or sacrificing for the good of the family. As the eldest, I shall inherit the bulk of the business when my father dies. I will not see my nephews destroy what I have worked hard to build. I need a son, someone young I can teach and mold. If Timoteo proves to be mine, I shall train him."

"He is yours!"

"So you say."

Turning, she faced him with dry eyes. Fury filled her now.

"Yes, I do say. I thought I loved you. For years—even after you threw me out—I stayed faithful because I loved you. Timmy could be no one else's."

"A blood test will support you or prove you a liar. I will have the results before I give him my name, of course. I would be a fool to do otherwise."

"I will not let you make my baby into a clone of you. I'll fight you any way I can."

Luigi stood. Eve wished she hadn't removed her heels, so she could look him in the eyes.

"You'll fight *me*? You stripped for a living, and then you lived off me. I supplied you with an apartment and everything you had. You forced an end to our arrangement by becoming pregnant and then insisting on keeping the bastard, no doubt to force me into divorcing my wife and marrying you."

Imposing figure or not, she slapped him. His cheek bore the red marks of each finger, but the strike hadn't even knocked him back a step.

"If I had found you married, I might have approached the situation differently. After all, a child in a loving home should stay there, perhaps. But you're single, raising Timoteo over a tavern filled with drunks. My investigator reported how you serve tables and work behind the bar, your breasts half bared. I shouldn't be surprised if you don't dance privately for some of the men, or perhaps do more. After all, once a—"

He gave a mocking shrug.

"I know how you lie to the school and to your friends. Do you lie to Timoteo, too? Do you tell him his father is a wealthy, powerful man, or do you tell him I am dead?"

Guilty. And for the first time she didn't feel bad about it.

Luigi studied her face. "I thought so."

He took a step closer. "Know this. If a blood test proves Timoteo is mine, he will *be* mine. No court in the world would rule against me." He swept his arm to encompass the room. "Look what you have given him, and think what I can provide."

"You can't take him."

Unbidden tears stung her throat. When she'd thought of Luigi over the years, she'd remembered him first as her lover, a generous man who laughed often. Only later had she remembered his meanness in tossing her to the curb. How could she have forgotten how cruel he could be?

"He is too young now to be without his mother, but in a few years he will no longer need you. And neither will I."

Swiping his coat off the end of the sofa, he said, "I will be in touch tomorrow about my flight and when I shall expect your arrival in Florence."

Then he left, closing the door with hardly a sound.

No, no, no! She sank into the chair and buried her face in her hands.

She'd worked hard to make The Bare Moose a place men *and* women could come to relax and feel comfortable and safe. A lounge, not a bar. Now she saw it through Luigi's eyes: a simple beer joint, a mutt cleaned up to look like a show dog. And she and Timmy had lived in worse places when he was younger, as she'd struggled to support them. Luigi's investigator had no doubt compiled that information, too. Only when Timmy had reached school age had she searched for a way to give him the very best. She'd based her decision to return to Florence on the same thing—whatever proved best for Timmy, she would do. In the past week, while struggling with her decision, she'd thought Luigi would give their son what she never could, all the things a boy could want.

But now she knew Luigi would never give Timmy the one thing *she* could—love.

Eve stood and unzipped her skirt to prepare for work. Until Christmas, her life still revolved around the bar, the school, and her son. She wanted to stay. But she ended the thought before it progressed to a wish or a dream. Daniel would never be hers, the life she truly wanted would never be hers, no matter how much she wished for it.

As she was about to step out of her skirt, someone knocked at the door. Perversely, the idea that it might be Daniel kicked her heart into overdrive.

"Yes?"

"Ms. Eve Star?"

Frowning, Eve tried to recognize the voice and came up blank. She rezipped her skirt and stepped to the door.

"Yes?"

"Open up, please. This is the police."

Eve felt the blood drain from her face. Confusion warred with an irrational fear. She hadn't heard any disturbance from the bar. What could they want?

She opened the door.

"Yes, officer?"

"Eve Star, you'll have to come with me. You're under arrest for contributing to the delinquency of a minor."

The officer nudged her back into the room and turned her around. Handcuffs encircled her wrists.

"You have the right to remain silent. Anything you do say can be used in a court…"

The rest of her Miranda rights went by without her comprehension. What had happened? How could she keep this from Timmy? How would Luigi use this latest sin against her? Who could she call?

For that last question, she knew there was only one person.

Chapter Fourteen

The police car pulled out of The Bare Moose parking lot, lights flashing, though without siren, at the same time Daniel swung his Volvo in. "What's that about, I wonder?"

He pulled into the empty spot at the back door, his preoccupation with the meeting he'd just left already overriding his curiosity about bar and police problems.

After leaving the board room, he'd taken just enough time to warn his dorm assistant he'd be gone for an hour or so. He couldn't get over the feeling of dread that crawled through him, the more slaps on the back and congratulations he'd received. *I need a shrink*, he thought now, *because here I am, I've been awarded what I've worked years for, and I'm not sure I want it.*

Correction. He still wanted the position, but only if he could have Eve too, and every word he'd heard that evening said he couldn't. Even having his plans for the students dashed didn't begin to compare with his personal sense of loss. The board members hadn't said anything he hadn't told Eve or himself these last few weeks, but hearing it spelled out so coldly had hit him like a slap in the face.

He had to talk to her, to explain that he loved her and wanted to marry her. She felt the same, he knew it. Or maybe he wanted her to so badly he wished it true.

Think positively. If she loved him as much as he loved her, they'd discuss what to do about it. Either she'd wait until he had a solid hold on the headmaster job before they announced their engagement, or he'd take a chance on losing it to marry her now. That's what had him swallowing his tongue, as his daddy used to say. He didn't want to lose the headmaster position. He hoped he wouldn't. But he'd give it up if had to, to marry Eve.

The outside door was unlocked. Strange, but he didn't give it a thought. He bounded up the steps and knocked on her apartment door.

"Eve! It's Daniel."

No answer, yet a light shone under the door. He knocked again with the same result, then headed down the steps, prepared to walk around to the front of the building. When Eve worked, she kept the door into her office locked.

Daniel stopped, wary. Whether she worked or not, she kept the outside door locked too, but it hadn't been. Just as he was about to go back up to her apartment, the office door opened, and Jed stuck out his head.

"Doc, thank God you're here. The police just left with Eve."

Daniel stood dumbstruck. "Just now? Why? What happened?"

"I don't know. A guy in here saw a cop car go around back. By the time I heard about it and came to investigate, they had her in the car and a cop was closing her door. He said she'd be at the Overbridge station. I was on the phone calling you when I heard you knocking."

Daniel was out the door before he turned. "You okay handling things here?"

"Yeah, fine. Just find out what the hell is going on."

He nodded and ran for the car.

"And, Doc," Jed called after him, "tell her anything she needs we'll get it done for her."

"I'll tell her!" He slammed the door with one hand and turned the key with the other. Gravel flew out from under the wheels when the station wagon burst forward, belying its age and size.

The Volvo had never been pushed to such speeds in the mountains before, but between Daniel's driving skills and the solid build of the car, it handled every curve with a precision Jonah would be proud of. Daniel reached the police station in under eighteen minutes, found a place along the side to park and hurried inside.

"I'm here to see whoever arrested Mrs. Lauren Knowles a few minutes ago," he said to the uniformed officer sitting at a window cutout in the wall. "I mean, Ms. Star, Eve Star."

"Don't have a Knowles, but I'll check with Lieutenant Jackson about Star."

He picked up the receiver and punched in three digits. Daniel drummed his fingers on the counter, trying to be patient and failing.

"Okay," the officer said, "I'll send him back."

He looked up, pointing at a door to the right of the window.

"Through there, down the hall, second door on the right. Lieutenant Jackson."

"Thanks."

Daniel stepped through the door. He supposed the wall on his left indicated a "hall," though the room opened up on his right to a bullpen area. Two boys in ripped jeans and dirty tee shirts were slumped in chairs at one of the desks, their expressions screaming disrespect for the officer sitting with them. Daniel pulled his attention away from them and toward the task of finding Eve.

A man opened the second door on the right at Daniel's sharp rap.

"Lieutenant Jackson?" Daniel evaluated the man. His jacket off, sleeves rolled to his elbows, tie loose and skewed, he could have been Joe Blow settling down to an evening of sitcoms instead of the man detaining the woman Daniel loved. The guy started off in Daniel's bad graces.

"Yes. You're…?"

"Daniel Goodman, a friend of—"

"Daniel, what are you doing here?"

Eve's voice came from behind Jackson. Daniel moved forward, ready to push the policeman aside if he stood in his way. Fortunately, he moved.

Pale, her hair disheveled, and the suit she'd worn earlier that afternoon twisted and rumpled, she gazed up. Her eyes filled with humiliation before they filled with tears. Her hands lay in her lap, and when he sat beside her he saw why. She was handcuffed.

He pulled her into his arms and a sob broke from her.

"I don't want you to see me here, like this. But I-I didn't know who else to call. I had to leave you a message."

"Hush, honey. Hush. You called me? I came from the tavern. Jed told me you were here."

He stroked her back and rocked her. Glancing up at Jackson, who stood, hands on hips, watching them, he asked, "Are these cuffs really necessary?"

Jackson considered for a moment and jerked his head at a uniformed cop standing in the corner. The officer removed the cuffs and then took his position again. Jackson sat across the table from Eve. She sat up, but Daniel kept his arm draped across the back of her chair, his fingers caressing her shoulder. Eve wiped her tears with her fingers, and Daniel handed her a handkerchief from his pocket.

"What has she been arrested for?"

"Contributing to the delinquency of a minor."

"You're kidding. Who's made this charge?"

"Two boys who were stopped tonight for drunk driving. They claim she's supplied them with beer and other alcohol for the past several weeks."

"I've never done anything of the kind," Eve exclaimed, and Daniel felt heartened that she sounded more angry than upset. "Who says I did?"

Daniel remembered the boys he'd seen sitting at the desk right outside the door and knew intuitively they were involved somehow.

"Morris and Pete Whitney."

Eve dabbed the handkerchief at her nose.

"I've never heard of them, who are they?"

"They say they know you. Told us a few things about your apartment only someone who's been there would know, like pictures you've painted, how good your pot roast is, the color of the sweater you're knitting for—"

"Those boys have never been in my apartment, and they don't know me!" Irate, Eve had leaned forward and jabbed her index finger on the table.

"Eve, sit back," Daniel coaxed. "I think I know what's going on here."

He faced Jackson. "Did they say how they knew Eve?"

"Through another boy, Michael Haynes. We have a patrol car going to pick him up right now."

"To his home or to Westover Academy?" Daniel wondered who would respond if the car had gone to Michael's home.

Jackson frowned. "He goes to Westover?" At Daniel's nod, he asked, "What's he doing hanging around with a couple of losers like the Whitneys?"

The phone rang before anyone responded to the question.

"He is?" Jackson sighed. "Okay, send him back." He stood and walked to the door to meet the next arrival. "Mr. Haynes, thank you for coming down, sir."

"He gets a 'sir'," Daniel muttered to Eve. He examined her face, pink from crying. "Are you all right?"

"Yes, but Daniel, you shouldn't have come. I was wrong to call you. It can only cause trouble for you."

"I had to. I lo—"

"Have you given my son alcohol?" The voice boomed from the man standing half in and half out of the room. "Because if you have, I'll make sure you don't see the light of day for years."

Daniel stood so fast his chair flew back and banged against the wall. "No, she didn't, and you'd do better to get all the facts before you start making threats, Mr. Haynes."

"Sit down," Jackson ordered. At the same time Haynes asked, "Who are you?"

Daniel shot Jackson a look of irritation. "I'm Daniel Goodman, Michael's English teacher."

Reluctantly, he held out his hand and Haynes took it for a limp shake.

Jackson pulled out a chair for Haynes, but the man ignored him. Since Haynes didn't sit, neither did Daniel. With a heavy sigh, Jackson pushed his chair back under the table, too.

"What are you doing here?" Haynes asked. "I understood the woman was to blame for this fiasco."

Daniel clenched his hands. "She isn't to blame for anything."

"Daniel," Eve said quietly, "it's all right."

He shifted position, exposing her to Michael's father for the first time.

"I assure you, Mr. Haynes, I have done nothing to harm your son." She looked at Jackson with clear, guileless eyes. "Or those other boys."

"We'll get to the bottom of this when Michael gets here," Haynes pronounced, pulling his coat around him as though to protect himself from the police station atmosphere.

"You should have gone to get him yourself." Daniel all but gaped at the man before turning on Jackson. "Or, all of this could have been settled tomorrow morning in the headmaster's office at the academy, rather than dragging the boy down here."

Jackson, aware of Haynes's position, threw out his hands in capitulation. "That would suit me fine. I can take Ms. Star back to a cell and send everyone else home."

Eve sucked in a breath.

"No!" Daniel moved to cup her shoulder. "I'll vouch for her and will guarantee she'll be available tomorrow."

"No offense," Jackson said, "but I don't even know why you're here."

"As Eve's friend."

Jackson's eyes switched from Daniel to Eve and back. "Uh-huh."

"Frankly," Haynes blustered, "I don't care why he's here, but I intend to settle this tonight. I have to be in Boston tomorrow morning. I don't have time to waste with this mess."

Jackson looked ready to throw all of them out when a knock sounded at the door. An officer ushered in not only Michael Haynes but also Dr. Adams, who took in the scene with one glance. Daniel met his eyes, keeping his expression neutral, even while he felt his new title slipping away.

Adams looked stern. Michael stared at the floor, and Haynes stood stiffly at his son's side, but without touching him. Daniel wondered if maybe Michael wasn't better off with the butler than with a cold fish of a father like this. A thought flashed through his mind of how his own father would act in this situation, and the contrast couldn't have been greater.

"I should have claimed the big conference room," Jackson muttered. He faced Adams. "You are…?"

"Dr. Frederick Adams, Headmaster of Westover Academy. When Michael's dorm master called to say he was being summoned to the police department, I felt I should accompany him." He looked over his glasses at Daniel. "I didn't realize Mr. Goodman would be here, however."

"Never mind," Haynes boomed, like a rocket blasting off in the tiny room. "Let's get this taken care of so I can get home."

He turned a heated gaze on Michael. "Do you know this Eve Star woman?" He flung out a finger at Eve.

"Yes, sir," Michael mumbled.

"Has she ever given you anything alcoholic to drink?"

Michael snapped his head up. "No, sir. Never."

Haynes fixed an eye on Lieutenant Jackson. "I don't know why my son would know her"—he nodded toward Eve—"but I knew he wouldn't have anything to do with drinking, unlike those delinquents you've got sitting out there."

"The Whitneys, sir?" As soon as he spoke, Michael knew he'd made a mistake.

"How do you know them, young man?" Finally, Jackson decided to take control of the room.

Michael looked helplessly from Daniel to Eve. "I'm so sorry, Mrs. Knowles. Mr. Goodman, I never meant to get everyone in trouble."

"Of course you didn't," Eve said.

Daniel smiled. "Just tell the truth, Michael. Everything will be fine."

Dr. Adams narrowed his gaze at Eve. "Mrs. Knowles? But Mr. Haynes called you Eve Star."

"I can explain." Daniel, Eve and Michael spoke at once.

"I wish someone would," Lieutenant Jackson said, and sank into a chair.

***

Eve sat in silence listening to Michael explain how he knew her and why the Whitney brothers thought he knew her much better. She kept her eyes on the boy, smiling encouragement when he faltered and taking comfort herself from Daniel's presence and from the light touch of his fingers on her shoulder.

She'd never been more surprised to see anyone as she had him, when he'd pushed past the lieutenant to get to her. Or happier, though since Dr. Adams had arrived and she'd seen the look he'd shot Daniel, she wished he hadn't come. Almost.

When Michael finished, and the lieutenant asked a few questions to clarify, he excused himself.

"I'm very disappointed in you, Michael," his father said. The boy hung his head.

"He did nothing wrong except make a bad choice," Daniel said. "Nothing more or less than any of us in the room have done as kids. No one was hurt and he's learned a lesson, haven't you, Michael?"

The boy looked up, the need for approval in his eyes so blatant it made Eve's heart ache.

"Yes, sir. I felt bad enough. I'll never do anything like that again."

"We now come to your part in this episode, Mr. Goodman." For the first time in twenty minutes, Dr. Adams spoke up. "You were responsible for upholding the rules of the academy. You should have reported Mr. Haynes."

"And have him expelled?"

"Would have served him right," Haynes groused. "That would have *taught* him."

Eve was shocked. "How would that have taught him anything? I'm glad he came to me, and that I could help him. And Daniel has done much more for your son than—"

She stopped before she said something that would hurt Michael.

"Punishment is the prerogative of the headmaster," said Dr. Adams. "A position you do not officially have." He addressed Daniel.

"He didn't need punishment. He's a good boy who needed someone to care for him. Care *about* him." Daniel sent Haynes a glare. "In the absence of anyone else, Mrs. Knowles and I did that to the best of our abilities."

Haynes pointed at Daniel. "Don't tell me how to raise my son!"

"That was not your decision!" Dr. Adams pointed at Daniel.

Eve had the urge to giggle and tell the men that pointing was impolite. But Daniel didn't look like he was about to giggle, so her response must have been due to the surreal circumstances.

"And you." Now Dr. Adams aimed his gaze at Eve. "Who *are* you? The manager of a tavern, or Lauren Knowles, wealthy widow and patron?"

"I'm … both."

"You left out a few things about her," Daniel said. "She's a wonderful mother who'd do anything for her son, a fine businesswoman, and a good friend." Daniel looked at her. His thumb stroked her shoulder blade. "And the woman I love."

She gasped.

Michael laughed out loud and said something like, "That's cool!"

"Nothing more romantic than being proposed to in a police station," Daniel said to her, and then he grinned.

"This is the influence your school has over our children?" Haynes boomed. "A liar who runs a bar, a teacher who flaunts the rules and hides the fact that the students drink? I'll have my boy out of there in nothing flat. And others will hear about this, too."

"No!" Michael cried out.

Eve saw that in two seconds he'd gone from being happy for her and Daniel to dismay. And she was to blame for much of the trouble. In the guise of Michael's father, she saw Daniel's dreams disintegrate.

"Please, Dr. Adams, don't blame Daniel or Michael for this fiasco. I did lie in order to get my son into the academy. I'm not a widow with lots of money, and I don't live in Manchester. I manage The Bare Moose. I begged Daniel not to expose me because I wanted Timmy to start life with the best education. As it turns out, I am planning to withdraw him at the end of the semester to return to his father's estate in Italy."

At the words *estate* and *Italy*, Dr. Adams's eyes grew round, perhaps thinking they represented money.

Lieutenant Jackson came in at that moment.

"Okay," he said to her, "I just ran a plainclothes policewoman by Morris and Pete and asked them if there was anything they wanted to say to Eve Star. They both made snide remarks to her. The upshot is, they don't know you from Adam. Based on the boy's explanation, I don't see I have anything to hold you on."

He flicked glances at the rest of the room. "You're all free to go." He left.

"Well, *this* has been a night," Haynes said. He looked at Michael. "Your mother and I have to be away for two weeks, but we'll talk when I return, have no doubt about it."

Michael jumped to his feet. "But Father, Thanksgiving is next week. You won't be home?"

For a moment, Haynes looked nonplussed. Then he cleared his throat and stared at the wall. "It can't be helped. I'm sure the school can make some arrangements. And we'll call you, of course."

With a nod at Dr. Adams, he pulled open the door and strode away, leaving his son struggling to hold back tears.

Daniel went to Michael. Placing an arm over his shoulder, he spoke to the boy in low tones.

Eve leaned toward Dr. Adams. "Please don't blame any of this on Daniel. He'll make a wonderful headmaster for Westover, can't you see?"

"This has been a most surprising night." He made a face as though he'd swallowed something distasteful. "And not in a good way."

Standing, he said, "Young Mr. Haynes, let us be going. Mr. Goodman, I shall see you in my office tomorrow morning at precisely nine o'clock. Mrs. Knowles, if you would be so good as to join us?"

"Of course."

"Don't worry," Daniel told Michael, "Everything will be fine." The boy nodded and followed Dr. Adams out the door.

Daniel and Eve faced each other. "*Will* everything be all right?" she asked.

"I hope so." He opened the door and she walked through.

Outdoors, she leaned against the building and stared without seeing. She had no doubt that tomorrow Timmy would be dismissed from school. How could she explain why? He was too young for the truth, but she was tired of all the lies. She'd have to ask Luigi to take them with him when he left, a move she hated to make. But what choice did she have?

"Will you have me?"

Daniel leaned his shoulder against the wall, watching her think, reading her mind, it seemed.

Sad, she still smiled because Daniel always made her want to. She couldn't believe he'd rushed to her defense tonight, and … had he proposed?

"Will I have you for what? A friend? Yes, thanks very much for being my friend tonight. I think I might have screamed if you hadn't been here."

"A friend is good. I like being your friend. But you know I want more. I love you. I want to marry you—didn't you hear me say that earlier? Maybe I wasn't clear. A bad trait for a man who teaches youngsters how to communicate."

He hadn't said the exact words, but she'd caught his meaning, all right. *And* the look of disapproval in Dr. Adams's eyes. The new headmaster's wife couldn't be a bar manager, or a liar, or someone who would be in a police station under arrest for giving minors alcohol. She couldn't ruin Daniel's life.

"Look, Daniel, I appreciate your offer and your help. But Luigi and I had a long talk this evening. He loves me, and I could grow to love him again. We decided that Timmy and I should join him in Florence as soon as possible. So there's no way I could marry you, not when Luigi wants to make a life for us there."

The pain passing through his eyes wrenched her heart. He'd get past it—most of what they had was physical, anyway, and anybody would serve. *Liar! Always lying.*

"As we saw tonight, living with a father isn't always the best answer. In my brief conversation with your—with Donatello—I didn't get a feeling of warmth. Are you sure that's what you want, Eve? A father for Timmy who'll treat him much like Haynes treats Michael?"

She pushed away from the building, tired, though it couldn't be nine o'clock yet. "Timmy will have me."

"Yes, and he's lucky to have you, but what else will he have?" He huffed a breath and stood straight, too. "You can't really want to leave. I love you. I somehow had a feeling that you love me."

She shook her head, trying to keep her heart from showing in her eyes. "You imagined it. I do care for you, but not in the way you want me to." Looking out into the parking lot, she rubbed her temple and asked, "Will you take me home? I have a lot to do."

"Eve—"

"Please, Daniel. I can't handle anything else tonight. Can you take me home or should I call a cab?"

He stared, his eyes questioning, his jaw tight. He waved her out into the parking lot. "Come on. But this isn't finished."

That's what she feared.

Chapter Fifteen

Edith Whitelaw sat behind her desk as though she guarded royalty from the peasant riff-raff. Trying to rein in his impatience, Daniel looked at his watch for the second time. Nine-fifteen. He'd stood outside the building for fifteen minutes or so, hoping to catch Eve before they had to appear, and then cooled his heels in here for fifteen more, under the watchful eye of Edith.

He should have been in class. In order to appear at nine, he'd left his senior English students with an assignment and asked Tony, the teacher in the next room, to keep an ear out for any disturbance. He couldn't leave the boys indefinitely.

And where was Eve? Hadn't she said she'd be here this morning, too? Daniel stood, swept back his robe and suit jacket in order to jam his hands in his pockets and strode back and forth in front of Edith's desk.

"I'm *sure* Dr. Adams will be with you as soon as he can," Edith said.

"Yes, I know." Knowing didn't stop his pacing or curb his edginess.

Eve hadn't given in last night. At her door he'd reiterated that he loved her, but before he could get his arms around her for a kiss that would leave no doubts in her mind, Jed had come through from the bar, along with one of the waitresses and the back-up bartender, all wanting to know what had happened. Daniel had left her with the admonition he'd see her this morning. He'd intended to press the point of his love once more, but so far, she was as late as Dr. Adams.

He stopped at Edith's desk. "You're sure you haven't seen Mrs. Knowles this morning?"

She stopped typing and raised her gaze. Either Dr. Adams's office had suddenly relocated to the Arctic, or she wasn't happy with another interruption.

"As I explained when you first arrived, Mrs. Knowles has not been here this morning. If you will *please*—"

The phone rang, saving Daniel from being told to sit down and be good, as though he were a child.

Edith answered, still frowning at him, listened, said, "Yes, sir," then hung up. "You may go *in* now," she said.

"Thanks." Daniel knocked once on the headmaster's door and then entered.

"Good morning, Dr. Adams. As you requested—"

His voice ended when he saw Adams wasn't alone. Praetorian guards Creighton Thomas and Albert Wainwright flanked the imposing desk behind which the emperor, Frederick Adams, sat. Eve wasn't present. Where was she?

Daniel nodded to the men. "Gentlemen."

Creighton returned the nod. "Sit, please, Daniel." Adams gestured to an empty chair in front of the desk. "Now, regarding last night's events—"

"Excuse me, sir, but shouldn't we wait for Mrs. Knowles?" Daniel frowned at Wainwright, who sneered and coughed into his hand.

"There's no need," responded Adams, waving a sheet of paper. "Lauren Knowles or Eve Star—or whatever her name—is gone."

Panic filled Daniel. She couldn't have packed, withdrawn Timothy and found that Italian all in one night.

"But her son…?"

"She claimed him from the dormitory this morning. This letter explains everything, and exonerates you, by the way."

Adams did all the talking, rendering his companions pillars of silence. They used stares to impart seriousness. Oddly, their rigid, smug postures made Daniel want to laugh.

"I'm happy to hear that, sir. Especially since neither of us did anything wrong." *Not too wrong, anyway.*

"That's not totally true, now, is it?" Adams lost his neutral tone and switched to patronizing.

"I maintain it is. She met Michael accidentally before she became a patron of the academy or knew he attended here and halted seeing him after. Neither of us provided the alcohol to Michael or his companions. In fact, in the absence of his parents or any supervision, we took charge, saving him from who knows what fate at the hands of those other boys."

"You should have reported him. You flaunted the very rules you'll be sworn to uphold as headmaster. Example starts at the top."

"I'm in favor of rules, Dr. Adams, but tempered with common sense. Calling in the school officials would have caused trouble for Mrs. Knowles, when she was working at The Bare Moose only to provide the best for her son. Reporting Michael would have led to his dismissal, when all he needed was a little guidance. Isn't that why we're here? To *best* serve the boys?"

"As I explained yesterday, my position—soon to be yours—is the welfare of the academy, not the protection of one boy. That's why there are rules, to assure an even application of action, regardless of the circumstances."

Adams glanced down at the sheet of paper on his desk.

"Now, to the double identity of Mrs. Knowles"—he looked up over the rim of his glasses—"something else about which you had knowledge that you chose to keep to yourself. No action need be taken since she has already withdrawn the boy and left the area."

"She shouldn't have."

"She lied on her application."

"Not in a material way. She paid her bills, didn't she? She presented herself properly when on campus."

"That is not the point."

"That's precisely the point. Why should she have had to hide where she works? She did nothing to besmirch Westover's reputation."

"She lied to us!" Adams voice rose.

"Would Timothy have been accepted if she hadn't?"

Adams fiddled with his glasses. "*Probably* not, but perhaps as a hardship case."

"Perhaps she didn't want her son to be a 'hardship case'. Perhaps she wanted him to start off on an equal footing." Daniel addressed Albert Wainwright. "With boys like your son."

"Takes more than just paying the bills," he replied. "It takes character and a certain standing in society."

Pompous ass.

"Lauren Knowles is a fine woman, and her son is a smart, funny boy. It's your son's loss if they wouldn't have been friends."

Wainwright scowled. Adams cleared his throat and moved on.

"Last night you expressed a desire to marry the woman. Her letter says she's returning to Italy with the father of her son, and that she will build a home there. In light of that, and after much discussion, we have decided not to withdraw your appointment as headmaster."

Eve had gone, leaving him with memories and a sense of fun and life he never had experienced before. She made him feel that he belonged. With her he had dared to break the rules, to give in to his inner desires.

The carefree style of living Jonah and his parents exhibited continued to elude him, but at least he'd had a glimpse of what true living could be. His time with Eve would make him a better headmaster.

"I am choosing to see this episode as a young man's flight of fancy," Adams continued, "and I presume you've gotten the wildness out of your system."

"Sydney would like you to call when all of this has settled." Creighton Thomas raised a brow and gave a half-smile. "Put this behind you, Son. You have a lot to offer Westover."

Yes, I do.

"Thank you very much for the honor, gentlemen. I appreciate your faith in me and believe I can fulfill all of your desires for Westover Academy." He leaned forward and fixed each man with a determined look. "However, this is what *I* need."

***

In a fast food restaurant and gas station near the Massachusetts line, Luigi sighed for the fourth time, and they'd only just sat down with their meal.

"Eve, is there no way you can control the boy?"

Timmy fussed and whined as he hadn't in years. Now he pushed away his hamburger and begged to be held in Eve's lap.

"He's tired. I woke him up and took him away from the school and his friends and he's confused."

Eve understood how her son felt. Because of the arrest, she'd moved up their departure from the States. In one short night, she'd arranged for Jed to take over as manager of The Bare Moose, called Luigi and pressed him into arranging their travel, and packed their things. Last night was the first time she'd been grateful they didn't have too many personal items.

The last thing she'd done before fetching Timmy was write the letter to the headmaster, and one to Daniel. Like a good friend, Jed had stayed through the night helping. He held the letter for Daniel and would hand deliver it after her flight left.

Daniel's proposal had surprised her in a good way, like Luigi's rejection when she confided she was pregnant had surprised her in a bad way. Both had felt like her heart was being ripped apart. Luigi's because she had so badly miscalculated the man he was, and Daniel's because accepting would destroy his dreams. Strange that in rejecting Daniel she'd had to seek help from Luigi.

She pulled Timmy onto her lap and hugged him.

"It's okay, sweetie. Luigi's taking us on a big airplane and we'll fly all the way across the ocean. Won't that be fun?"

"No!" He rubbed his eyes. Despite the early hour she'd roused him, he hadn't slept on the two-hour trip south.

"Eat your lunch," Luigi said in his I'll-brook-no-argument voice.

"Not hungry!" Timmy spat back.

She kissed his head and snuggled him. "I know you're tired. Mommy's tired, too."

"You coddle him. No wonder he behaves so poorly." Luigi had passed on the assembly line hamburgers and decided on coffee alone. He doctored it and took a small sip.

"He doesn't behave poorly. He's a sweetie, normally."

She hugged Timmy again and rocked him like she had when he was a toddler. Since starting school, he hadn't let her hold him on her lap, claiming he was a big boy. She'd hated giving up their closeness, and relished the softness and the clean smell of him now.

"He's too old to be held on your lap."

Luigi cast a stern look at Timmy. "Sit down and eat. We shall leave in a few minutes whether you are finished or not."

Timmy shrunk against her and clung to her arm. She cradled him closer. "Luigi, let me handle this, okay?" Lord, she was too tired to deal with Timmy *and* his father.

Luigi looked thoughtful. "I think before we find your apartment, I shall hire a nanny. The boy needs time away from you, that is obvious. I'll also check into the school my brothers and I attended. When he is older, then I shall begin his business training."

Suddenly wary, Eve asked, "What school? I thought we would be living in Florence, so you can get to know Timmy."

"Well, yes. But I had not thought him quite so … young. He acted differently when we saw him before. He needs to grow up, to toughen."

Her baby? He was already growing up far too fast. Despite the morning's upheaval and his hunger, Timmy had fallen asleep in her lap. His body hung heavy in her arms, but she didn't care. From the start, from when Timmy had been in her womb, she'd handled her own affairs. Things hadn't always been easy, taking care of the two of them alone, but she'd always relied on herself. She'd done better than survived, she'd *prevailed*, even getting Timmy into Westover, the premier school for boys in the States. As soon as she began relying on others—on Daniel for emotional and physical relief, and Luigi for financial support and escape from her problems—her life had turned upside down.

She should have stayed on her own. Loneliness was better than what she felt now—uprooted and just as alone as before, but with Luigi to deal with. Why had she agreed to go to Florence?

Why? So Timmy can know his father, so he can benefit from all Luigi has. Eve knew before he'd spelled it out so clearly that Luigi's family would not welcome her into the fold. But if Luigi recognized him, Timmy would enjoy being part of a family. She could put up with a lot of crap in order for her son to flourish.

Luigi placed his empty coffee cup on the table. Pointing to Timmy's lunch remains, he said, "Toss that out and let's go. I want to get to the airport and check in."

Great. Hours on the road followed by more hours at the airport. Their flight didn't leave until eleven that night, meaning they'd have nine or ten hours of waiting. She was glad she'd put several of Timmy's books in his carry-on backpack.

Gently, she shook him awake. "Have a little milk, honey, and wait here with Luigi while Mama goes to the bathroom, okay?"

"Okay," came the grudging reply.

She shifted him off her lap and stood.

"He'll be fine," she said to Luigi. "I'll be right back. Okay?"

He gave that annoying shrug. "Do not worry."

Easy for you to say. She stroked Timmy's head, his short hair like silk under her fingers, and prayed she'd made the right decision in going back to Florence.

Not more than ten minutes later, she came out of the bathroom to find strangers sitting at the table. She looked around, confused then panicky.

"Did you see where the man and little boy who were sitting here went?"

The woman shook her head. Eve rushed into the store area where she saw Luigi examining the selection of bottled water in the cold case. Breathing a sigh of relief, she hurried to him.

"Here you are. I was worried when I saw—" She stopped. "Where's Timmy?"

"Right over there. I told him he could choose one piece of candy, as long as it would not make a mess in the car."

"Where?" Panic rose in her again, ringing in her voice.

"There by the—" Luigi frowned. "I left him by those candy bars and *told* him to stay. You have not trained him very well."

"Go to hell, Luigi."

Rushing up the aisle, she strained to look over the racks. He wasn't there. He wasn't standing at the counter, either. She ran back into the restaurant, searching every table. No Timmy. He wasn't in the ladies' bathroom. Uncaring of who she might embarrass, she charged into the men's room.

"Timmy, are you in here?"

"Damn, lady!" A man standing at a urinal hastily turned his back as much as he could.

"Sorry, but have you seen a little boy, six years old, about this high?" She held her palm at her waist. "Dark hair, wearing blue jeans and a denim jacket?"

"No, now get outta here."

In full blown panic mode, she headed back to the store, turning her head to study everyone as she walked. Luigi stood at the counter. Hadn't he even looked? Didn't he realize the importance of finding Timmy *right now?*

She *had* made a mistake. Luigi was no more interested in being a father than the man in the moon.

"Please," she said to the woman behind the counter. "My little boy is missing. Call the police."

"Police!" Astounded, Luigi stared. "Surely the child is only hiding somewhere. You can't want to involve us with the police *again.*"

She'd told him about her arrest—she'd had to, to explain why she and Timmy were going back to Italy with him earlier than planned. He hadn't been happy until she'd told him his name hadn't entered into the story, and then he'd given that dismissive shrug that made her want to slap him. Now she wondered what he would have done if she'd called *him* for help. Thank God Daniel had been there.

Daniel. Her heart ached just thinking about him. He never would have let go of Timmy. He knew about children, whereas Luigi didn't have a clue.

"The police," she said to the woman behind the counter.

"Is that him?" Another woman at the other end pointed out the window.

Eve looked, and her heart swelled. Walking into the building, Timmy had a firm grip on Daniel's hand.

In three strides, she crossed the floor and swept Timmy up. His little arms went around her neck and she crushed him to her. Tears of relief and fatigue ran down her cheeks.

"Are you all right?"

"Yes, but I can't breathe, Mommy."

She started laughing, loosening her hold. Finally, she set him down and crouched in front of him.

"You should never, *ever* walk away when you're told to stay with someone."

The look of abject fear on Timmy's face when he saw his mother crying sobered him.

"But I saw Mr. Goodman putting gas in his car. I knew you wouldn't mind if I was with *him*."

He cast a sneaking glance over Eve's shoulder. She knew Luigi stood there.

For the first time, Eve looked up at Daniel. "Thank you so much."

He ruffled Timmy's hair. "I thought you might be looking for him."

Eve's mind reeled with might have happened to her son. She stood, pulled Timmy to her side and hugged his shoulders.

"What are you doing here?"

"Looking for you."

"What?" Startled, her eyes widened.

"I was on my way to the airport, which is where I assumed you were going. It was sheer luck I needed gas and decided to stop here."

"Why?" Her heart began hammering. She shook her head. "I mean, why were you going to the airport?"

Daniel also looked over Eve's shoulder. "To stop you from going with him."

"This impossible situation can surely be discussed somewhere more private," Luigi said.

They were blocking the door, Eve noticed now. Where could they go? Daniel put out his arm and nudged her into the aisle and out of the traffic path.

Again, he looked at Luigi.

"Last night I asked Eve to marry me." He shifted his gaze back to her. "I didn't do a very good job, and I want to rectify that. I love you, Eve. I miss being with you, talking to you, holding you. I love you no matter what's happened in the past, no matter where you work or how you dress. I love you, and I want you to stay here and be my wife. If you insist on going to Italy, well, I'll have to go, too. And the only Italian word I know is *ciao*."

Her tears flowed freely once more. Timmy tugged on her hand and she looked down. His eyes had grown to the size of saucers, but he didn't seem upset by Daniel's proposal.

"Mommy, Mr. Goodman would be my father?"

Daniel squatted to look into Timmy's eyes. "Timothy, you already have a father. But if your mother marries me like I hope she will, then I'd love to be your daddy. How does that sound?"

Luigi spoke up. "Do I not have a say in this?"

Daniel stood and looked at Eve. "Of course you do," she said.

Daniel stepped closer to Luigi. "I know you have rights," he said in a low voice. "But I love Eve, and I think she loves me. I can provide for both her and Timothy. Maybe not with a mansion and lots of fancy cars, but well enough and with lots of love."

"I am his—"

"Don't!" Eve broke in. "Daniel would you mind watching Timmy for a minute while I talk to Luigi?"

Daniel and Luigi eyed each other for a few more seconds, then Daniel relaxed and took Timmy's hand. "Let's pay for my gas and move the car, okay?"

Timmy's eyes suddenly gleamed and a smile creased his face. "Then can we get a hamburger? I'm hungry."

Daniel started walking toward the sales counter. "Sure. And some milk?"

"Thanks, Mr. Goodman."

"Why don't you call me...?" They moved out of earshot.

"Shall we step outside?" Luigi pulled his coat around him. "I believe these people have heard enough of our business."

Without a word, Eve pushed open the glass door and walked to the other side of the ice machine.

"So," Luigi began, "this is the man with whom you have fallen in love."

"Yes. But I didn't know he loved me until last night."

"When he rode to your rescue like a knight in armor," Luigi said dryly.

"Yes."

"Timoteo is my son."

"Yes, but you've seemed to have your doubts."

"For business, yes, but in my heart I know you don't lie about something this important."

Eve struggled to find the right words to tell Luigi that she and Timmy wouldn't be going to Italy. How could she prevent him from knowing his own child?

"I think it's best if you stay in America," Luigi said.

What?

"It is obvious this man will not let go of what he wants. It will not look good if he follows you to Florence."

Anger flooded her. Fatigue and recent events were all taking their toll on her emotions. "Because of your family and business and how things would look? That's why you want us to stay?"

His features softened. "I think you should stay because your heart is here, *cara*. And Timoteo's, too." He jerked his head in Daniel's direction as he and Timmy walked to his station wagon to move it from the pumps. "For him the boy is hungry. For me, he cries." He shrugged, then smiled at her cringe. "I fear I am not so expert with children. Sophia took care of the girls and kept them out of my way, which suited me.

Eve's eyes followed the Volvo until it turned the corner. She could see Daniel talking to Timmy and the animation in Timmy's face when he answered. When she looked back at Luigi, the smile had faded and his face sobered.

"However, he is my son. When do you plan to tell him?"

"When he can understand."

"I will want updates of his progress. When he is old enough, I will want him to spend time with my family."

She hesitated. "If Daniel and I marry, and if he's willing to adopt Timmy, I'd like him to." Luigi's face darkened with anger. She rushed on, "It will be easier for Timmy."

He turned his back to her, but she kept speaking.

"Luigi, he's six years old, and you've never shown a shred of fatherly interest. We don't owe you a thing, and, quite frankly, you don't owe us, either. That train left the station years ago. But when you gave us up back then, you relinquished certain rights now, too. If you want to acknowledge him to your family, fine. If not, that's fine, too. Someday, Timmy will ask me about his father and I'll be truthful. What you and he do at that time is up to the two of you. Until then, he's *my* son, and I'll do what's best for him."

"I shall cancel your airline tickets." His shoulders rose with a deep breath. "I shall look for your reports."

"I promise to let you know how he's doing."

He faced her. "Then this is goodbye."

"Don't you want to say goodbye to Timmy?"

"What would that serve? He is a child. A baby, the way you treat him. He wouldn't understand." He nodded once, turned on his heel and walked away.

Eve watched until Luigi was out of sight. Then, she pulled open the door and went in search of Daniel and her son.

***

Looking up from where Timmy was sipping orange juice through a straw stuck in a carton and devouring a cheeseburger, Daniel saw Eve walk toward them. Alone. Their eyes met. He saw love in hers and hoped his reflected the same. He hadn't lied. If she'd insisted on boarding that overseas flight, he would have found a way to be right behind her. He might not be a free spirit like his parents or Jonah, or a genius that Italy would have welcomed like Mark, but he fought for what he wanted.

"Hi," she said, her hand on Timmy's head.

"Hi."

"Look what Daniel bought me, Mom." Timmy held up the cheeseburger.

"That's very nice. Did you thank him?"

He took a big breath, letting his shoulders rise and fall with the effort. "Of *course.*"

Smiling, she looked at Daniel. "He had one just like that earlier that he refused to eat."

"Kids have a comfort level, just like adults."

"Do you have a comfort level, Daniel?"

"I'm looking right at her."

"Back at you."

She took a seat next to Timothy and Daniel couldn't take his eyes off her. So beautiful, inside and out.

"So, have you considered my offer?"

"I'll have to know a few things, first. Like can you provide a good place to live? You know my current situation, and I had hoped to move up."

"I think we can work that out. Anything else?"

Silently, she stared.

"Mom?"

"Yes, darling."

"I think you and Daniel should get married."

"I think we should, too," Daniel tossed out.

"What about your job? I couldn't marry you if it meant giving up your dream."

"I can have both dreams—you and a headmaster position. But you are what I want most. Take a chance on us, Eve."

"I think I might."

Tension flowed from his body. He hadn't felt this good in ... forever. She didn't act like she caught his reference to "a" headmaster position. He wouldn't be going back to Westover except to finish the term and pack his belongings, but, surprisingly, he didn't mind.

"Uh, about those living conditions," he said. "Do you think Jed's taken over your old apartment, yet? We might need it for a few weeks."

He chose to ignore her look of dismay and tried to capitalize on his success with Timothy instead.

"Do you know what next week is?"

Timothy thought hard.

"Thanksgiving!"

"Right. And do you know where we're going for Thanksgiving?"

Timothy shook his head.

"To a wedding."

"Wow," Timothy breathed the word, his eyes big and excited.

"Whose wedding?" Eve ventured.

He saw awareness in her eyes and wondered how she knew what he was about to say.

Daniel grinned.

"My parents'." He adopted his Southern accent. "It's time you knew the whole truth about me, darlin'."

Epilogue

"Wow, Jeff, is this really your airplane?" Timothy walked the aisle for the third time since they'd boarded the Cessna.

"Nah, it's my uncle's." Torrington sat on the edge of his seat and swung his legs to kick the seat in front of him.

"Are you going to do that all the way to North Carolina, Jeff?" Michael Haynes leaned around the armrest and gave a mock glare to Torrington who burst into giggles.

"Sorry, Mike. No more kicking." He swung his legs and knocked Michael's seat once more. "Well, maybe once more."

Torrington burst into giggles again and then screamed and raced down the aisle as Michael jumped up and chased him.

"How long before we land in Ashville?" Daniel moaned.

Eve chuckled. "They'll settle down once we take off."

"Sorry for the delay, folks." Neil Torrington, Jeffrey's uncle, sat down on the arm of the seat in front of them. "The pilot has just finished the preflight checks and says we should be wheels up in about fifteen minutes. I'll make sure the boys are all strapped in and settled down. You two just relax. Y'all are newlyweds, after all."

Daniel shot a grin at Eve. He'd never been so happy. He prayed he'd be able to make her and Timothy just as happy.

Eve squeezed his hand as if she knew his thoughts.

"Mr. Torrington," she said, "I can't tell you how much we appreciate this. The few days we have off wouldn't have been long enough to drive to North Carolina and get back to New Hampshire in time for classes next week."

"And the trip would have been hell."

"I think the boys would have been fine," she chided Daniel.

"I meant for *us*."

"Call me Neil, please." Neil Torrington said. "As soon as Jeff told me about your marriage and then your parents' wedding, I knew I wanted to help out if I could. Living all the way in Oklahoma, I don't get to see Jeff very often, and with his folks gone I like to make him happy if I can. And you're about all he talks about, Daniel. Can I call you Daniel?"

"Sure. Of course."

"Now he tells me that you're leaving the academy. And, Mrs. Goodman, now your son is gone from the school, well, he seems to be drooping a bit, if you know what I mean. I wanted to talk about what your plans might be. Plus, he says your brother works with some NASCAR teams. Jeff and I, we like NASCAR. Will we get to meet him this weekend?"

"Jonah. Yes, he'll be there. He's bringing NASCAR caps for the boys."

"Once he told me all that, *I* actually wanted to come to the wedding of the century. That's what they called it on one of the morning shows, you know? It sounds like fun."

"Oh, I'm sure it'll be fun all right." Eve laughed and, after a short cringe, Daniel joined in.

Neil looked to the front of the plane and stood.

"Boys, come on and get seated. We're ready to get this show on the road." He strapped the young boys in and chatted briefly with Michael before turning back to them.

"I usually sit up with the pilot, but I'll check back in a few minutes to make sure you're okay. And let's make sure to talk sometime over the weekend, okay?"

"Absolutely. And thank you again."

Neil waved off Daniel's comment.

"I was coming to get Jeff anyway. We didn't have anything particular in mind to do. He'll be happier with his friends."

Neil turned and left them.

"Is everyone all set?" Daniel asked the three boys.

"Yes!" Jeffrey and Timothy shouted.

Michael turned toward Daniel and Eve and smiled. The difference in the boy since his father had decided to allow him to join Eve and Daniel in Carolina was palpable. He smiled often, and relaxation had softened his features.

"How did you get Mr. Haynes to allow Michael to come with us?" Daniel looked sheepish.

"I'm not proud of myself. I went to see him and suggested he let Michael come with us for Thanksgiving. He said no. I said that he should allow it for his son's wellbeing and happiness. He said no. I told him that Michael didn't say it but that I had it on good authority that he left his liquor out and available and that that's where Michael first tasted alcohol. I told him I would make a case to the police, the board of directors at Westover, and anywhere else I could, including some of his clients. He reconsidered."

"Daniel, you are devious."

"I am."

"I like it," she purred in his ear. She sighed. "Too bad these kids won't sleep and the trip is so short. I'd like to become a member of the Mile High Club."

"And I'd like to *make* you a member." Daniel leaned over to kiss her. Unfortunately, considering the audience right across the aisle, the kiss had a PG rating. But they had all weekend.

Holding Eve's hand tightly in his, he thought about the upcoming visit. It had been years since he'd seen his parents, and even longer since he'd seen Mark. Jonah had tried to act nonchalant when Daniel had called to say first that he was married and second that they were coming to the wedding with three kids in tow, but incredulity came through loud and clear. Then he'd surprised Daniel by saying that Kelly Shepherd would be at the wedding, and that she taught at a small private school outside Asheville. Daniel had touched base with her and she'd arranged for him to talk to her principal on that Friday. He was just putting out feelers, but he wouldn't mind moving closer to home. He thought it would work out for his family, too.

His *family*. God, he was the happiest man in the world. If everything worked out as planned, Timothy would be starting his new school with the name Goodman. If only Jonah could be half as happy as Daniel was now, he'd be set for life. Jonah could use an evening star of his own to guide him. Maybe, with Jonah and Kelly back in the same place ... But, no. They were grown and different people now.

Still, it wouldn't be all bad, would it?

The End

About the author

A few years ago, Dee S. Knight began writing, making getting up in the morning fun. During the day, her characters killed people, fell in love, became drunk with power, or sober with responsibility. And they had sex, lots of sex. Writing was so much fun Dee decided to keep at it. That's how she spends her days. Her nights? Well, she's lucky that her dream man, childhood sweetheart, and long-time hubby are all the same guy, and nights are their secret. Dee loves writing erotic romance and sharing her stories with you. She hopes you enjoy!

Coming soon from Dee S. Knight

One Woman Only

As one in a set of triplets, Jonah never felt as identical in personality as in looks. Where his brother Daniel was serious and completely focused, Jonah shunned commitment. Where his genius brother Mark was hailed in the world of mathematics, Jonah hid beneath a car, tinkering. Thing is, Jonah was finally admitting that being different wasn't all it was cracked up to be. It took a woman to make him see that focused and recognized in his field could turn a "good man" into a better man.

Chapter One

"Where the hell are you?"

His brother Daniel's voice could have carried all the way from their parents' home in North Carolina to his home in Darlington, South Carolina without benefit of telephone.

"What do you mean where the hell am I? I'm at home."

"Well, I'm here in Lucky Strike, with my wife and new son. This is where you've been begging and nagging me to be for weeks now, isn't it? So why aren't you here, too?"

"Keep your shorts on. I'm leaving in a bit. It's only a four hour or so drive."

"Well, Mom was getting worried. Tomorrow *is* Thanksgiving, and the wedding is coming right up."

Yeah, right, *Mom* was getting worried.

"Are you nervous for me to meet your bride? Think she'll realize her mistake in marrying a prig like you and run off with me?"

"I'm nervous she'll take one look at you and worry about the gene pool. Mark is okay. Having a genius as a triplet brother is a good thing. But a lazy, good for nothing mechanic? Not so much."

"Go fuck yourself. I'm the best of the three of us and you know it."

"Right. Sure." Daniel hesitated before speaking again and Jonah just *knew* what the topic would be. "You know Kelly is going to be here for the wedding, right?"

Did he know Kelly Shepherd would be attending his parents' wedding? Hell, yeah, he knew. *He* had told *Daniel*, if he remembered correctly. And that was why, despite virtually kicking Daniel's ass to get him home for the event, he, Jonah, was dragging his feet in South Carolina. He couldn't skip the wedding, and now he had four hours or more of driving to figure out how to avoid coming face to face with Kelly.

"Just tell Mom and Dad that I'm on my way, okay? And get off my ass. I'll be there in plenty of time. Set a place for me at the Thanksgiving table."

"No need to get your briefs in a twist. I was just checking on you. Mark's already here. I've talked him into going out for a beer tonight before all the festivities, and it would be nice for you to go with us. The three Goodman brothers, you know?"

Yes, he knew.

"I'm hanging up now. Maybe I'll get there in time to meet up with the two of you."

"Drive carefully."

Jonah disconnected the call. It might be his imagination, but Daniel sounded better since leaving that fancy private school up in New England. More relaxed. More like he used to be before he had dreams set on getting out of their small town and creating shock and awe with his brilliance in the academic world. Maybe that new wife was good for him. He looked forward to meeting her.

"But no one will meet anyone if I don't get my ass in gear."

Grumbling, he jammed another pair of jeans in his duffle and went to the bathroom to gather toiletries into his leather ditty bag. He found a place for that in his duffle too and zipped the army green bag closed. Jonah slung it over his shoulder and slapped his pockets. Keys, check. Phone, check. Knife? Yup. He never left home without his knife. Without having to check he knew he had duct tape and hose clamps in the trunk. A man never knew when he might need a sharp blade to cut a hose and the means to repair it again.

"Okay, I guess that's it."

No more excuses. He locked the front door and then headed out to his car, Ginger. She was as sleek and beautiful as her namesake on *Gilligan's Island*.

Jonah loved his classic GTO. He'd worked NASCAR crews long enough to pay for the restoration and she was a true beauty, right down to the high gloss red paint job. Having stored his bags in the back seat, Jonah settled in behind the wheel. He spent a moment, as he usually did, stroking the steering wheel, admiring the car's lines, and anticipating the feel of power when he turned the key.

"Goin' for a ride, Ginger. Open you up a bit."

As though the vehicle understood his words, her engine virtually jumped in excitement and then purred like a satisfied cat. A big cat, not a wimpy kitten curled up in a someone's lap.

And that slammed the image of Kelly Shepherd right back into his mind. She loved cats, and the last time he'd seen her she'd been sitting on her front porch holding a tabby in her lap. He'd slipped behind a large rhododendron and eavesdropped while Kelly explained to her best friend what an asshole Jonah Goodman was.

***

"Oh good, you're home." Nancy Shepherd patted her short auburn hair into place in front of the hall mirror. "I have to go out right now, but I'll be back in a few hours. We'll expect you for dinner, of course."

She picked up a clutch that matched her rust colored suit and gave her daughter an air kiss for each cheek before gliding out the door.

"It's nice to see you, too, Mother," Kelly muttered. For the tenth time at least, she mentally debated whether the decision to stay the weekend at her parents' house was a wise one. Too late now.

"Is that you, missy?"

Mama Rio bustled into the hallway, wiping her hands on her apron. Kelly broke out into a smile.

"You never change. You're still the gorgeous woman I remember from childhood right through college. How do you do it?"

"Go on with you, girl," Mama Rio said before wrapping her arms around Kelly for a big hug. *Now* Kelly felt she was home. The housekeeper stepped back for an appraisal.

"You are just so beautiful," she said, and hugged Kelly again. "Let me get your bag."

Kelly snatched her rolling suitcase away.

"Oh no. You don't wait on me. I should wait on *you*. Let me put this upstairs and clean up a bit then I'll come down and you can fill me in on all that's been going on over a cup of coffee."

Mama Rio smiled and cradled Kelly's cheek with her hand.

"I have missed you, angel."

"And I have missed you." She took a moment to enjoy feeling cherished and then said, "Be right back."

Dashing up the central staircase, Kelly took a right at the landing and continued to the second floor. Three doors on the left, she opened the door to her childhood bedroom. The room she'd left the summer after graduation and had barely seen these last seventeen years. When she'd visited Lucky Strike in years past, she had made blitz visits—quick attacks that might or might not include dinner, and rarely ever involved an overnight stay. The first time she'd come home, at Thanksgiving in her freshman year at UNC Chapel Hill, her parents had already turned her room into a guest room. Her posters and photos, yearbooks and stuffed animals had all been boxed for storage in the attic, the walls had been changed from a cheerful floral wallpaper to a bland taupe textured paint treatment. Nothing felt like her. No trace of Kelly remained in "her" room.

No matter. Regardless of the décor, she didn't belong in the house, much less in this room. In four days she'd be on her way back to her own home in Asheville, fifty miles as the crow flies, seventy miles by road, and a world away in contentment.

Kelly deposited her suitcase on the bed and removed the dress she planned to wear to the Goodman wedding. The style was simple—an A-line with cap sleeves—but the fabric was a rich autumn-green silk. It had cost her nearly a month's salary but was worth it for the way she felt in it—royal and pampered. She hung the dress in the closet along with the cashmere pashmina in just a shade darker that she would wear with it. She wasn't one of those redheads who only stuck to a few muted shades of green and blue, but this dress had spoken to her when she'd spied it in an Atlanta boutique.

After throwing a handful of cold water on her face and brushing out her shoulder length hair, she took the back stairs directly into the kitchen. Just as she'd suspected, a plate of cookies rested on the island between two cups of coffee.

"You still trying to fatten me up?"

"You could stand a little weight on those bones, girl."

Mama Rio basted a roast, sending aromas of beef and vegetables wafting through the kitchen.

"Oh my gosh! Will you please come home with me? That smells so darn good."

Closing the oven door, Mama Rio said, "We had to have a special meal for our girl. And tomorrow we'll have all the fixings for a traditional Thanksgiving."

Kelly stopped the cookie headed for her mouth.

"You mean you are going to be here fixing our meal? What about your own family?"

Mama Rio came and sat on the counter stool next to Kelly.

"There's hardly anyone left at home, now, sweet girl. My boy Jeffrey is going to Knoxville to spend the day with his girlfriend. Susanna is married and they're headed down to Charlotte to be with her in-laws."

Kelly started to protest but Mama Rio raised her hand to stop her.

"I don't like traveling over holidays, and I'd just as soon stay home. And if I'm staying home I'd prefer to be busy."

"Well you aren't going to do all the work by yourself. I'll be here to help."

Kelly knew that her mother wouldn't lift a finger in preparing the holiday meal. To her parents, Mama Rio was just their housekeeper. A familiar one, and someone they had employed for more than thirty years, but still an employee. To Kelly, Mama Rio had been "Mama"—the woman to whom she'd run with her scraped knees, teen woes, and college discussions. The woman had a forever place in her heart.

"Cooking dinner together will be fun," Mama Rio said, nibbling on a ginger snap.

"Are you going to the Goodman wedding?"

"No. Your parents were invited but not me."

"Well, I'm inviting you. I need someone to sit with, and I'm not sitting with Mother and Dad. They'll take all the fun out of the day."

She sipped her coffee, but almost spilled it when Mama Rio said, "I thought you might be sitting with that handsome devil, Jonah."

"You have the devil part right, but I not only will *not* be sitting with him, I don't plan to waste a single moment speaking to him."

The bastard!

See more of our titles on

Their Lady Gloriana by Starla Kaye
Cowboys in Charge by Starla Kaye
Her Cowboy's Way by Starla Kaye
Punished by Richard Savage, Nadia Nautalia & Starla Kaye
Accidental Affair by Leslie McKelvey
Right Place, Right Time by Leslie McKelvey
Her Sister's Keeper by Leslie McKelvey
Playing for Keeps by Glenda Horsfall
Playing By His Rules by Glenda Horsfall
The Stir of Echo by Susan Gabriel
Rally Fever by Crea Jones
Behind The Clouds by Jan Selbourne
Trusting Love Again by Starla Kaye
Runaway Heart by Leslie McKelvey
The Otherling by Heather M. Walker
First Submission - Anthology
These Eyes So Green by Deborah Kelsey
Dark Awakening by Karlene Cameron
The Reclaiming of Charlotte Moss by Heather M. Walker
Ryann's Revenge by Rai Karr & Breanna Hayse
The Postman's Daughter by Sally Anne Palmer
Final Kill by Leslie McKelvey

Our back catalog is being released on Kindle Unlimited
You can find us on
Twitter: BVSBooks
Facebook: Black Velvet Seductions
See our bookshelf on Amazon now!
Search
"BVS Black Velvet Seductions Publishing Company"

www.blackvelvetseductions.com